M. Lee Musgrave

Black Rose Writing | Texas

ISBN: 978-1-68513-215-6
PUBLISHED BY BLACK ROSE WRITING
www.blackrosewriting.com

Printed in the United States of America
Suggested Retail Price (SRP) $21.95

Off Kilter is printed in Minion Pro

*As a planet-friendly publisher, Black Rose Writing does its best to eliminate unnecessary waste to reduce paper usage and energy costs, while never compromising the reading experience. As a result, the final word count vs. page count may not meet common expectations.

As an artist and author, during my many decades within the international art community I have met and worked with a vast array of engaging individuals. I am especially thankful to those who enthusiastically encouraged and championed my creative efforts. Among those helping with this project are long-time ally and mate Doug Walsh and new friend Wagstaff Distinguished Professor of Law John W. Head, of whom, despite their extremely full schedules, took time to suggest ideas and changes thereby helping to make the story unique and a joy to write. I honor and value their friendship.

Off
KILTER

CHAPTER 1

It was a lazy spring day with only a few clouds loafing around the distant horizon. The warm, calm air had only a smidgen of stickiness and the sea was in repose with barely any white caps sliding across its placid surface. Even the quietly dissolving waves seemed lethargic and at peace with the soft, yielding shore.

Such tranquility has been going-on for eons in this crescent bay, I mused as I took another sip of refreshing orange juice letting it caress my papillae, but as soon as I swallowed a silent echo of doubt reminded me in the City of Angels serenity can be deceptive, even fraudulent.

Still, I was happily enjoying the morning and smiled as a gull, perched on the nearby streetlamp, flashed a wink. That benign gesture and the tranquil sea are evocative of a passage in the oft-told tale about a behemoth who rose from the silent depths of its dark aquatic dominion, rolled a defiant eye at everything men had stationed in its path and without hesitation obliterated every plank of it.

Had it been a real monster or was it just another creation of a writer's id? I mulled the thought for a quiet moment as the gull tilted its head with a twitchy nod and what looked like a smirk then swopped down to retrieve an object floating near a fluffy, she Poodle parading at the water's edge. The fluff ignored the gull and nosed a small crab attempting to hurriedly bury itself in the soppy sand.

"Appearances can be mendacious," I said to Duie who angled his head to eye the fluff scrutinizing the crustacean as it sank from sight. Turning to sniff surf a gentle breeze, the fluff ventured across the undulating sand to languidly saunter past us carrying an enticing fragrance of lavender permeated air with her as she drew near. Duie's eyes and mouth glistened as he anxiously stood to attention. I sensed him about to attempt a mount.

"Stay," I ordered in a hardened tone.

Duie flinched, but didn't move and his blatant curiosity about this aloof distant cousin, wrenched at him as she began to sashay back and forth. He was probably wondering why its coat was puffed up, cut to look like a macho lion and sported a pink ribbon atop its narrow head. If he wasn't, I sure was. The creature looked like some sort of a four legged he-she.

As we both pondered the oddity an unexpected gust invited the Times off my lap causing Duie to turn his attention toward the tousled newspaper and me to splash my drink all over it. The resulting stain made an odd abstract blotch across the story I had been reading and melded it to the article on the reverse side of the now translucent newsprint.

Glaring at the uninvited guest, frustration swept over me for reading my chosen article was now tricky as I could see the text on both sides of the page at the same time whether I wanted it that way or not. The befuddling image led me to carefully place the paper in direct sunlight hoping all laden moisture within it would evaporate quickly. It didn't, the air was not impregnated with enough heat though the sun was shining brightly. A common occurrence this time of year in L.A..

I rose to my feet and laid the paper down on the towel I'd been sitting on. That helped some for the warm cloth drew much of the dampness from it. Now stooped, I endeavored to continue reading the thought-provoking article when I was rammed from behind and sent flying off the deck. Landing with my face immersed in clammy sand. I rolled over clearing grit from my eyes, mouth and nostrils to see missy fluff and Duie both smiling at me and romping about ready to frolic.

With clenched teeth I scanned the beach searching for the owner of the coiffed wonder, but there was no one within chewing-out distance. My first instinct was to chase after both of them, to feel my bare feet grip the moist sand and my leg muscles propel my body in a full-on charge that would fill my lungs to capacity, causing my heart to throb and maybe scare the hell out of them both. But my somber-self thought better of that hair-brain idea so I just sat and smiled. Missy Fluff's mane of tresses and curls made me recall how I wasn't able to discern the contrast between surface beauty and what lies beneath until I was eleven or so and caressed my first girlfriend.

"Where do you belong little lady?" I said as I picked myself up still spitting and snorting granules of sun-bleached salty sand.

She strutted about in a willy-nilly manner as Duie snuffled every inch of her and I fumbled for her collar sparkling in the sunlight beneath her elaborate ringlets. After a moment or so of her boogie-in about I managed to read the contact information engraved on her I.D. tag.

"Son of a bitch, you're local." I said as her wet tongue stroked my ear.

"Right on both counts," a soft, yet resonant voice behind me said in a seductive whisper.

I turned to see a scorching tangerine bikini filled with a red head standing at about 5 foot 9 with her hands on her curvaceous hips. Hips that were in wonderful proportion to her waist and breast.

Her deep verdant eyes, enchanting smile, and perfectly symmetrical face were radiant and her diminutive bikini left little to my imagination. I was appreciative of that and not having to fill in any blanks was enticing, especially since her loveliness was completely in sync with the natural harmony of the superlative day.

All I could do was to look pleasantly surprised and prepare for her next move.

"Hi neighbor. I'm Merra Dawne and this is Ms. Shotola," she said with ease. "I guess the way you both were eyeballing her conveyed you wanted to cavort. I hope the tumble she gave you wasn't too low a blow."

"Uh no, ah I'm fine," I said as I brushed another layer of irksome granules from my arms and legs striving to stand as tall as I could while sinking further into the sand. "I didn't realize anyone was living next door."

My mind kept rerunning her mouth pronouncing 'eyeballing' over and over until she spoke again.

"Oh, it's a duplex. I live upstairs. There isn't anyone living in the downstairs unit at present. And I've been out of town for a few months. Are you a guest or do you live here?" she purred.

"Yes, I live here. I moved in with Nicole back in November."

"Ah, but you're not her husband. He is a much older man. Is he not?"

"Yes, that's right. They got divorced and I'm the new man in her life. I'm James Terra."

"Wow, she is an eager-beaver."

"Oh, well we've known each other for more than a year."

"I see, well that explains the divorce," she said with a mischievous grin that revealed her glistening, perfectly formed teeth.

"Not necessarily, but it's too nice a day to go into all that," I said as I gathered up the Times and sat back down on the lounge-chair fully expecting her to take charge of Ms. Shotola and walk away. In fact, I found myself looking forward to watching her walk which caused me to hide my increasingly flushed face behind the Times.

"Hey, I was just about to make lunch. Why don't you and Nicole join me? Since we're neighbors and all it would give us a chance to get to know each other," she said as she reached down to pet Duie and give me a full view of her more than amply breast. "You can even bring him along. I'm sure Shotola won't complain. Will you girl? What's his name?"

"Duchamp, but he answers to Duie," I said as I forced my eyes up to meet hers. "Ah, well something to nibble on would be nice, but Nicole is not at home right now. Perhaps another time?"

She smiled sweetly before responding. "Oh, come on. I'm sure she won't mind if it's just the two of us and I hate lunching alone," she said with an even more tempting smile. "Besides Duchamp, ah, Duie can chaperon. OK?" Her unusually throaty voice had a husky quality, but was oddly pleasant to listen to. I found myself wanting to hear more from her.

The whole picture was looking too good to be true. The clear blue sky, the gentle waves, and the warm sun radiating off of a beautiful woman offering me nourishment. What could go wrong I thought as I watched the tangerine-tinged sunlight sparkle on the hills and valleys within the hidden regions of her alluring form?

As I rose again from the comfort and security of the deck chair, Merra turned and started walking toward the stairs on the opposite side of her deck which caused Shotola to circle Duie and take off in the same direction, as did I.

"I assume, James, since you're here at lunchtime at mid-week you have no need to be anywhere at a certain time, is this correct?" she said over her shoulder.

"I'm an artist and to me time and place are all relative," I said with a grin as I considered how ascending the stairs had activated her hips.

"Oh, how wonderful. What kind of artwork do you create?" she asked as she turned and bent down to face me. Which brought me face to face again with her rounded, full bosom. I replied through an even fuller grin "Landscapes, uh, I paint abstract celestial landscapes."

"So, you don't do any figure studies? What a shame, it would have been fun posing for you," she said with an alluring laugh and bouncy jiggle that caused my head to bobble uncontrollably.

My mind flashed on Marilyn Monroe and how she always seemed filled with the joy of life, but before I could regain my composure, Duie, who was at the front of our little group, did a 180 and quickly scampered through all of us heading down the stairs in a full dash which caused Merra to slip toward me.

In the commotion my unshaven chin brushed against the satin smooth nipple area on the left side of her bikini top.

"There are times when I think I should reconsider what I'm doing with my life," I ventured hesitantly as I regained my footing and composure.

"Remember darling, the stakes can be high when thinking too wildly," a voice I recognized said from behind me.

"Oh, hi Nicole. How nice you made a timely return. I just invited James up for lunch," Merra said with a polite gesture. "Now we can all partake together."

"Hi babe, I thought you weren't coming back until around 5. What's up?" I said with a stumble as I gripped the handrail to steady my retreat back down the stairs.

"We have some things to discuss James," she replied with no fun in her eyes or the timbre of her voice.

"Right. OK. I'm coming," I said as I shrugged my shoulders at Merra and double stepped the stairs down.

"Are you back for long?" Nicole asked Merra. "Or will you be leaving again soon?" she continued with dyspeptic clinched teeth, squinted eyes and a skewed brow.

Merra adjusted her bikini top, winked at me, headed up the stairs and parted with "Not sure just yet. I'll let you know."

Nicole also gave me a sharp eye and headed straight into our place. I scooped up the Times and trailed her. Once inside she went directly to the kitchen where she had set out some Bay City Deli fare.

"Yum, you picked up my favorites. Did I do something right for a change?"

"Not from what I just observed. What the hell were you playing at?" she said with razor precision. "In fact, Duie deserves these delicacies more than you."

"I was just feeling a bit peck-ish, that's all."

"Looked more like prick-ish to me."

"OK, I made a mistake. It won't happen again," I said as I took her in my arms and kissed her pouting lips while fondling her hips.

"Just stay away from Merra. She's far more trouble than she looks and very dangerous," she said as she placed her hands on mine. "You have more than enough of this kind of action available to you right here."

"That sounds like you know her way beyond being neighborly," I said with relief that I was no longer the only target in her sights. "How long have you known her?"

"Years, we met at uni. Now eat your lunch before I change my mind and really give it to Duie," she said as she flipped the lids off of each container. "You know James, I don't want to be worried about leaving you alone here every time I have to go out. You better stay away from her."

"I will, you don't have to worry, but I'd like to understand what the problem is between you two. I mean, OK, you met at uni and then what? Obviously, you've kept in contact with each other through the years, but what else?"

"We used to work together that's all. It's not important, now eat your lunch."

"Well, that's surprising to hear too. What kind of work did the two of you do?"

"I thought you were starving or are we going to play twenty questions instead of filling your supposed empty stomach?"

"I'll eat and you talk. How's that for a compromise?" I said with a smile and twinkle.

"OK, look, you know how you kept your illness a secret from me?"

"Yes, but only until we made a serious commitment to each other."

"Right, but your illness is a big thing it's not just a former girlfriend like Stephanie or one of your others. Would you agree?"

"Yes, you are right it is a big thing to live with and I love your generosity in accepting it as part of our life as a couple."

"Good, now keep that thought in mind," she said as she walked to the glass wall and appeared to be looking out at the open sea, but was obviously contemplating something far deeper and maybe even darker.

"Merra and I were ambiance escorts for international businessmen," she carefully enunciated while she checked her reflection in the glass then turned to face me and gave a nippy chew to the right side of her lower lip.

"Ambiance escorts that's a new one. What did it entail?" My mind was reeling with all sorts of suppositions, some of which were not very appealing, but I quickly concluded Nicole deserved the best open mind I could offer while I filled my mouth with some pasta-verde salad.

"We were hostesses at businessman dinners and project proposal gatherings. We made sure everyone felt good about being there. We…"

"Stop, I think I have the general idea. You don't have to go into details. Just explain why the two of you are at odds now," I said as I interrupted her revelation.

"Let's just say we both went after the gold ring on the carousel and I got it while she's still twirling in circles."

"I see, but you're still friends, right?"

"In a way, yes. It's just that we don't hang with the same crowd anymore. She's still flying high and I'm definitely more grounded," she said as she snuggled up against me and we kissed.

"I understand, now can I eat some more of this wonderful lunch?"

"Same old James. Look, I've got to get back to Nellie's. I promised her I'd help her organize the Spring Fling Garden Art Tour and as you know, it starts tomorrow so why don't you finish that yellow scalene painting you've been working on all week then you won't need to sit out on the deck. OK?"

"You're right, I should finish it."

After Nicole left and I wolfed lunch, Duie and I went into the studio, but rather than paint I succumbed to my new lazy boy and continued reading the Times article which had dried out and was only slightly smeared. The story was about an extensive database of major loan agreements secured by pledges of artwork as collateral in the United States and in some European as well as Asian capitals.

As I read, I recalled art collector Norten Peterson mentioning he needed to come up with some serious cash to cover the loss of artworks he had pledged as collateral in a similar loan agreement. He'd gotten the loan for his new start-up web venture, but the paintings had been destroyed in an unfortunate fire at his home last fall.

To me, the whole subject of art as collateral for loans was intriguing and I was sure it would be of interest to Liz Weinstein, producer of the California Arts Log (CAsLog) program I host for public television. The article talked about the more than 500 active art loans in a new database involving over 100 individual lenders and borrowers. I wondered how many of those individuals were located in California and especially in L.A.. The article stated the database provided not only the names of everyone involved, but also details on the pledged artworks. This was the part I felt would be of most interest to CAsLog viewers. However, the database was available only by expensive subscription which I was sure my producers would not pay for.

The article also stated the system used a very sophisticated interface fully integrated with another holding details about the world's most valuable artworks allowing for instant comparison and appraisal of new works pledged as collateral for loans. The story also included some snippets of the business side of the art world I found surprising to be in the Times for the art community has never been forthcoming about disclosing its vibrant commerce side. Its finance activities have always been very discreet because major collectors prefer it that way, even if the government doesn't.

To make a CAsLog on this subject would require more than interviewing just one artist or collector, it would mean talking with art appraisers and advisors as well as bankers, financial gurus and especially authenticity experts.

The timing for the project was perfect because I had three new CAsLog programs completed and the next shoot was scheduled for several days off. That provided me with enough time to pull together a strong synopsis to present to Liz for her thumbs up and to get it on the schedule … perhaps as a special summer edition.

The first step was to come up with a working title. I was thinking Money Mirage. Next was to establish a linear trajectory and like all the best CAsLog's made to date it meant I had to start with selecting the right artist. An artist whose works are in high demand by collectors and museums, who garners accolades from critics and peers, and who commands high prices for everything he or she creates, because loans are not given for cut-rate, bargain basement, tawdry decorator stuff.

The first name to come to mind was Snookz Jefferies. His work met all of those standards and I had never made a CAsLog about him for he refused every invitation I had extended to him over the years.

"Mmm, how to get past that barrier?" I said with full volume so I could feel its vibration on my skin and within the inner hair follicles of my ear drums, which led directly to my brain.

Duie jumped to his feet jerking his head back and forth between the front door and the sliding glass back door. He was convinced I was shouting at someone somewhere and he was right. That someone was me. I was the one who needed shouting at.

Without a word of warning once again the blues walked in and sat down beside me.

Ever since I was shot twice last November, I've had an insatiable need to have my senses roused, to experience life through every receptor of my being in a constant uncontrollable rush. However, to do so could exasperate the twisted artery at the confluence of my spine and brain and cause it to collapse and if it did, I would no longer have any needs of any kind.

I felt like I was always on a high wire with no net and only my wits to keep me from falling headfirst into an abyss of forever darkness. I really did need to listen to some real good foot shuffling blues to keep the feeling of life within me moving forward.

I'm not sure when I walked out of the studio or how much time elapsed before I realized I was tired of staring at my own reflection in the living room glass wall overlooking Ocean Park beach. Perhaps it was only a minute or two or maybe an hour, I'm not sure. Either way Duie needed out and I needed to feel the sea air so we headed toward the pier.

Even though it was early in the season, people were everywhere including kids which meant it must have been late afternoon. All of them were enjoying the day and none seemed to care about what time it was. The important things were all in place - warm sun, fresh air, clean sand, inviting waves, friends and family. That's all that really matters.

Duie fit right in for he was running around chasing gulls while I sat to watch some kids bury themselves in the sand. As the middle child covered the last bit of her arms, a gull landed at about where I supposed her knees to be. It was a funny kind of image of rolling hill like forms with a bird at one end and a human head at the other. It made me think of Henry Moore.

Duie approached it and looked perplexed, but made a choice. He charged the gull who let out with a shriek while the kid squealed with joy causing my mind to flip flop and alight on Landchilde.

Terratan Landchilde is an Art Advisor who counsels well-heeled art collectors on who's hot and who's not and more importantly, on which paintings have the greatest potential to become financially profitable to have in one's collection.

He knows Snookz Jefferies well and I know him well. So, there it was, my way to advance on target. I will go around the barrier labeled Snookz and go directly to the one labeled Landchilde. He will surely know where there is a Jefferies painting being offered as collateral for a loan and probably has access to the new database mentioned in the Times as well.

Originally based in New York, where he was a top expert for one of the major international auction houses, Landchilde jolted the art world by leaving his powerful position and turned to private art advising based in L.A. la-la-land. From here he counsels art museum acquisition committees, curators, and prominent collectors world-wide. He was most likely drawn here by the more than 300 beautiful days like this one which occur in SoCal annually.

For decades, art advisers were a small clique who used their scholarship and connoisseurship to guide private clients in their drive to shape important collections.

They rarely were involved with making financial deals, but today the rapidly expanding art market has made the art of the deal one of their primary functions. As prices for the most desirable artworks have soared so have advisor's fees prompting scores of newbies to enter the field. Landchilde, however, is of the older generation and thus has an abundance of expertise and connections, much like my so-called acclaimed CAsLog resources file.

Now that I had a way to proceed, I gestured for Duie to follow me as I headed back toward the studio, but it took a moment or so to get his attention away from the kids and the gulls.

When we got back, I went directly to my computer and sent Landchilde an e-mail inviting him to Fromins restaurant for lunch the following day. His response was quick and surprising. He questioned why I wanted or even needed his help. I assured him it was because of his professionalism and a host of other accolades. I also pointed out by appearing on CAsLog he would be introduced to a vast new cachet of potential clients. It took a while, but he finally replied he would meet me at noon.

It was late when Nicole arrived home. I knew she would be too tired to think about fixing dinner so I made Trout Almondine with roasted red potatoes and had it ready when she drove up. It's one of the few things I know how to cook. After dinner it was too cold to sit out on the deck or terrace so we curled up in each-other's arms on the sofa in the living room, turned off all the lights to stare at the opaque ocean and sparkling night skyscape above.

It's wonderful to have a large, open space with no lights visible other than the distant stars, right in view from your living room. Plus, there is an appealing simplicity to sitting in the dark, especially during the first thirty minutes or so, your eyes see fading afterimages followed by almost nothing but a deep black and your sense of depth perception doesn't work so your brain has no need to use contour and form in identify objects. However, one's hearing fine-tunes in order to catch even the most-faint of sounds. The condition was perfect for us both to concentrate on each another and considering how our lunch time meeting went, I knew she would want to know how I spent my afternoon, but I felt a strong desire to hear about how her day went with Nell Meyerhoff and I also wanted to know more about her past relationship with our red-headed bomb shell neighbor.

Nell is L.A.'s leading social art guru and her husband, Paul, is an extremely successful real estate developer. Together they have amassed one of the largest and most significant contemporary art collections in the state and perhaps the entire country. Nicole strives to learn all she can from Nell with hopes of someday filling her shoes so she is always volunteering to assist her with any of her many social/art event fundraisers for charity.

"Did you finish your painting," she questioned as she stirred restlessly and walked her fingers about my chest.

"No, when I finished reading the paper, Duie and I went for a walk on the beach and when we returned, I worked on a new idea for my summer CAsLog."

"Oh, so you spent most of the day inside alone?"

"No, Duie kept me company," I said with a smirk in my voice since she couldn't see my face in the dark. "So how are things shaping up for the Spring Fling social?"

"Pretty good. Besides Nelly's garden, we supervised the installation of sculptures in the other two as well," she said with a hint of pride.

"Great. Are the other gardens as big as Nell's?"

"Yes, in fact, we were able to site 100 works so this will be the largest Spring Fling ever and the Brentwood site I'm in charge of looks great."

"What about the parking problem?" I queried.

"I stayed out of that discussion," she said while finger-walking down to my belly button.

"Why? What happened?"

"I'm not sure. All I know is Nellie wasn't happy about what the city wants her to do this year and the last thing I overheard she was phoning her lawyer."

"Yep, you're right. I'd stay far away from the whole thing," I said as I pondered how to get the conversation around to Ms. Dawne.

"Why don't we go up to bed? It's still a little too chilly down here after dark," I said as I fiddled around for the light switch remote.

"Ok, but bring the glasses and what's left of the wine with you. That'll warm us up," she said as we both blinked our eyes trying to readjust to the flood of artificial light.

After finishing off the wine and enjoying some heavy petting there just wasn't any opportunity to bring Merra into the conversation so I let the thought go for the evening. "Probably just as well," I thought as I rolled over feeling completely exhausted yet sated.

CHAPTER 2

It was 11:30 am when I left for Fromin's and just a few minutes before noon when I slid into my favorite booth. I ordered a glass of blueberry-pomegranate juice and tried to gather my thoughts as to what to say to Landchilde. To my surprise I almost didn't recognize him when he walked up to the hostess desk right at the stroke of twelve. His usual casualness of rumbled suit, loosened tie, unpolished shoes, and shaggy hair had been completely replaced with a bright, up-to-date metrosexual look complete with a spiffy men's hair-stylus-do. I wondered what was going on considering he is in his late 50s. It crossed my mind, perhaps he was having a mid-life crisis.

"James, good to see you looking so well after your ordeal last fall."

"Thanks, Terratan. It's good to see you too and I must say you are looking especially impressive today." Terratan has always had a well-crafted jovial manner about him that made everyone enjoy his company.

The waitress approached quickly and he ordered a straight up black coffee and we both selected Tuscan salads for lunch. As we dined, we discussed how the CAsLog program has grown over the years and how I hoped the special summer edition would be particularly meaningful.

"Judging from your new look, I would venture that advising has moved even further upscale," I suggested.

"Well, the profession is changing rapidly that's for sure. There are so many new advisers, all aggressively pursuing trophy art, that one has to be on top of everything including how one presents oneself," he said with a level of dismay. "These new walking and talking dogs work in packs and move fast. Their gyrations in the financial arena are an especially annoying challenge to keep up with."

"Mmm, you've always struck me as one of the very best advisors around Terratan. You've shown that you wield great authority in contract negotiations far more than any of the high-minded fledgling consultants I've dealt with in recent months."

"That's kind of you James, but it's not yet clear what effect these new two-legged Hyenas are having on the art market in the short term or down the long-twisted road. In the good times of old I could count on one big sale garnering a half-a-mill for myself and I was very happy with that, but today I view what's happening with real concern. This new wonder breed isn't satisfied with a million here or there they want every morsel for themselves."

His whole demeanor was out of sync with his bright new look. In fact, he looked downright bewildered. His shoulders were drooping and his chin was almost on the table. I hesitated to speak too loudly so I softened my tone.

"What aspect of the business are you specifically worried about?"

His eyes fixed while his jaw clinched. "These new practitioners are so inexperienced at providing sound or even trustworthy counsel their tactics threaten to sully the profession."

"In what way exactly?"

"They have no hesitation to dealing behind their clients back or demanding outrageous broker's fees from both their clients and the galleries," he voiced in a louder volume as his right hand slapped the table alarming everyone nearby.

"I see, well maybe we could address some of those issues when we shoot the CAsLog. Perhaps you could even get the artist or a client to speak about them?" I suggested as I leaned forward and nodded my head.

He looked up through the top of his grey eyes and sneered a little. "Which artist are you thinking of for the program?"

I saw my smiling reflection in his new ultra-modern glasses as I replied, "Snookz Jefferies."

His eyebrows raised as his head concurred approval. "Good choice, but I seem to recall he's refused past invitations you gave him to be on CAsLog."

"Yes, he did, but when he knows you are participating and what the theme is I think he will most likely acquiesce."

"Well, I suppose it's worth a try, but I strongly suggest you have a second choice in mind just in case he's not interested," he said as he finished the last of his lunch. "I'll stop by Snookz's studio on the way back to my office or do you want to invite him personally?"

"No, I tried that approach twice and it didn't work. I trust he'll be more amenable to you. All we need at this point is to know what aspect of the art-for-collateral process he would be willing to talk about on camera."

"Well, I can tell you now, in the past he has always been keenly involved in the market evaluation part of the process. He's very concerned about how his work is converted into monetary value beyond what he or his gallery rep sell it for."

"Yep, understandable. Most artists would like to get some compensation when their work goes up in value after it's left their hands and resells over and over again at higher and higher prices," I said as I handed the waitress my credit card.

"How do you plan to address the issue of what these collectors are doing with the funds they get when they put paintings up as collateral for a loan?"

"I'm not at all sure yet. No doubt some of them turn around and use it to acquire more art. It will be more interesting to find out what the others are using the money for."

"Yes, I came to that same conclusion several years ago myself. I even started making notes about it with each transaction I logged into my business journal. I found it fascinating how these very smart, plush individuals would get themselves trapped in a financial squeeze and their only way out was to borrow money by putting the art they love up for collateral. Crazy," he grumbled as he walked toward the exit.

"Yeah, it's rather unnerving when you watch how a friend's rational thoughts can be overpowered by their irrational desires," I added.

"Uh-huh."

We agreed we would talk again tomorrow and then went our separate ways. He headed toward his car in the parking lot and I was thinking I would walk up Wilshire to the used car lot on the opposite side of the street. My old car was getting a bit costly to keep repairing and I just felt a need to experience something different. After all I couldn't keep asking Nicole for her Mercedes 550s. We actually needed two reliable cars.

When I reached the lot, right in the front row was a sweet metallic blue BMW 230i. I liked its personal size and it appeared it could hold a painting in the back fold down seat-trunk area. I barely had time to walk around it when a young woman approached and started giving me her well-rehearsed sales patter. The bottom line was the car had everything I wanted, seemed to be reasonably priced and had only been driven by some little old lady from Pasadena...uh huh. All I really needed to do was to test drive it.

As the sales rep went to get the key, a Luther Allison refrain blistered out of my cell. "Hi babe, how's everything going with the Spring Fling?"

"Great, it's been a good turn out so far. What are you doing? Not sitting on the deck, I hope?"

"Not at all, I had a productive meeting with Terratan and now I'm just about to test drive a used BMW. A metallic blue one that looks real-good," I said as the sales rep reappeared.

"Oh no, don't do that please," Nicole said in a quick soft whisper.

"What's the problem?"

"Just don't do that right now and we'll talk about it when I get home. OK?"

The sales rep was definitely disappointed, but seemed to understand when I explained who it was on the phone, but I was baffled.

"Before you leave take a look at this BMW E36/7 Roadster that just came in," she suggested. "I'm sure your lady friend would be impressed if you drove up in it."

The Roadster looked fantastic. It was a metallic gun metal gray with natural leather seats. A combination I especially like and it was stick shift too.

"It blends sportiness and elegance into an expression of pure driving pleasure," said the sales rep. "You know we have a 24-hour test drive policy. If you don't like it, you can bring it back. No questions asked."

I was definitely tempted, but decided to walk back to my old wheels which I had left in the parking lot at Fromin's.

By the time I arrived home, Duie was very nervous about wanting out, so we headed for his favorite spot near a small group of palm trees just down the beach. When we got there, I quickly discovered why he had run all the way. Shotola was secured to one of the trees and Merra was playing in the volley ball game just beyond.

Watching her romp around in a bright yellow poke-a-dotted bikini was more than I could take especially when she bumped up against her female team mate then gave me the eye while diving low to return a spiked ball.

Duie was disappointed when I insisted, he follow me back inside the studio and Shotola even whimpered at our leaving.

Two anticlimaxes in a row were a lot to endure in one afternoon. I was beginning to feel like Nicole needed to come home soon. At that moment, my computer signaled I had e-mail waiting. It was from Terratan and stated everything was a go with Snookz Jefferies. It was a small triumph, but it felt good to have step one on my agenda list completed.

Terratan even found in the new data base a group of older paintings by Snookz currently being offered as collateral for a loan by a collector in Malibu so completion of step two was looking like a real possibility as well.

As I sat staring at my computer screen a knock on the sliding glass door brought me back to reality. It was Merra holding Shotola with one hand while striving to fix her disheveled hair with her other.

She was covered with sweat and sand, but still managed to look like she was ready for sex if I were to invite her in.

"Oh, hi. You look like you had fun," I said as I slid the door open just a foot or so. The look on her face was of complete dejection. "I'm sorry I can't invite you in. I'm just on my way out. I've got to go see a car before it gets sold."

"Right, you could use a new one," she said as she gave me a warm smile, brushed sand off the top of her breast and snuggled Shotola. "Is your shoulder all right?"

"What do you mean?"

"Oh, one of the guys in the game told me you got shot last year and I was just hoping the knock Shotola gave you yesterday didn't aggravate anything."

"No, no, I'm fine. Well, got to go," I said as I smiled, closed the door and gestured for Duie to follow me. I managed to get all the way through the living room without looking back even once.

I don't remember the drive to the used car lot, but I know I got there in record time, signed the 24-hour test drive forms and drove off in the Roadster knowing exactly which road I wanted to put the little beauty through her paces on. I was ready to be taken for a real ride.

Pacific Coast Highway (PCH) hadn't started backing up yet so I made a rapid run to Chautauqua then onto Sunset toward Brentwood. Traffic was light in that direction so I was able to burn a lot of penned-up juice and it was fun. The Beamer fit me like a glove and handled perfectly for the challenging road. I especially enjoyed driving with the top down.

Duie was even able to stand on the passenger seat, with his front paws on the dash in a position reminiscent of a hood ornament from the 30s. He even held his footing while I downshifted and accelerated through every curve with sweet ease.

At Kenter Avenue I spotted the first sign giving directions to the west-side Spring Fling Sculpture Garden Tour, I knew it was decision making time. Should I explain my rash behavior to Nicole now or save it for later? There seemed to be little reason to delay the inevitable. Besides I was the invited guest speaker for this event so I followed the signs quickly and reached the house just as the last docent led tour was about to begin. However, I decided to roam around on my own so I could cool down and ponder what I was going to say to the group in my talk and what I might say to Nicole about the Roadster. Plus, I wanted to watch how the parking attendant handled the car especially since I didn't own it yet and had stationed Duie on guard duty in the front seat.

The variety of sculptures strategically placed throughout the elaborate grounds of the ultra-modern house was endless, but engaging. There was even an early ceramic Jon Doh comprised of three-foot tall dancing tea pots. It brought a smile to my face and a salvaged memory from the deep recesses of my mind of him together with our mutual friend Camille.

As I walked along a winding dirt path toward the next sculpture, I was fascinated by the thoughtful use of drought resistant plants and how different they made this event look compared to the green jungle like atmosphere of past Spring Flings. There was more color, but instead of it being deep and lush, it was muted and pale which gave a vaporous, soft, pastel appearance to everything.

I could see a small, lovely niche area at the far end of the garden. It was dominated by a large, whimsical, looking, stainless steel kinetic sculpture. The form moved gracefully and quietly with the slight early evening breeze coming up from the beach. At over ten foot tall, it had at least a dozen or so moving parts that glistened in the dappled sunlight coming through the surrounding trees and looked like an enlargement of something originally designed as a child's toy. It was enchanting, almost spellbinding and I wondered who the artist was so I bent down to read the rather small type on the label which was on a short stake nearby. The name was new to me and as I studied the accompanying artist's statement a shadow swept across it causing me to glance over my shoulder. As I turned, my eye caught a glimpse of a shiny long appendage streaking right for my head as the entire sculpture began to plunge toward me. Dodging, I jumped backward to evade the whirl and gyration of forms and tentacles that were colliding with one another while ripping up and slicing through all the plants in their path. A jarring racket barraged my senses forcing my blood to boil and my hair to stand on end as the main body of the towering contraption smashed to the ground with tremendous force showering metal shards and diced plants everywhere. I felt trapped inside an ear-piercing junk yard squall.

As the gale and screeching settled, I realized I was on my back in a bed of cactus and sharp stones while all manner of commotion, shouting and hullabaloo was swelling up about me. By the time Nicole appeared I was completely surrounded by a crowd of dumbfounded onlookers who weren't sure if this was a misfortunate calamity or a performance art piece staged just for their enjoyment. When Nicole emerged from the throng the first words out of my mouth were "can it be fixed or is it a goner?"

"What the hell are you talking about? We'll just change the label and leave the pile of junk right there," she said in a voice of authority. "And I'm going to have a hard talk with the dimwitted installer who screwed this up royally. Are you alright, do you need medical help?"

"I'll be ok, just get me to the bar," I said bluntly. "What the hell is that buzzing noise?"

"After all that metal clanging it's probably in your head. Who knows, who cares? Come on," she said as I hobbled while leaning on to her.

As we approached the refreshment tent and the lights came on throughout the entire garden, I discreetly started picking thorns out of my back side while wondering if I would be able to borrow a pair of pants from the man of the house.

It took an hour for everyone to regain their composure and to settle down enough so I could say a couple of jokes about how lively the contemporary art scene in L.A. is and at least one about the tradition of the leaning tower of Pisa. After the laughter relaxed everybody, I discussed how important it was for society to have events such as the Spring Fling Art Garden Tour and how appreciative all the participating artists were for the great audience turn-out. I had spoken for close to 90 minutes before Nicole gave me the high sign to wrap things up. So, I did.

After shaking a few hands, talking briefly with friends and politely declining a couple of dinner invitations I walked toward Nicole as she stepped out from behind a table to reveal Duie by her side. I didn't have to wonder if he had found her on his own or if she found him, the answer was written on Nicole's face and definitely in her body language. There was an interval of silence and at that point the only thing worth doing was to hand the Roadster keys to her.

We decided Duie and I would go home in her Mercedes and she would drive the Roadster after making sure everything at the event had been taken care for the evening including roping-off the wayward whirligig and reassuring the homeowners I would not file a lawsuit.

As she scurried off to deal with lingering guests and confused parking attendants, I went to check out the dervish that almost decapitated me. I approached it in the now shadowy garden and it looked totally destroyed, which seemed odd for there hadn't been much of a breeze that afternoon yet it looked as though a strong wind had uprooted it. When I managed to maneuver through the debris and reach the base of the structure, I could see why it fell.

As I approached the homeowner stepped out from the shadows and sighed deeply, "it looks to me as though it was unbolted from its substantial concrete base."

"Or it had never been secured to it in the first place," I added. He nodded sadly and his eyes moved with difficulty as he walked back through the shadows toward his house.

"Either way the crash was not an accident. It was a deliberate act of violence for considerable strength was required to topple this heavy mother over," I said through my teeth to Duie who kept well back from the disaster zone. "I'm sure glad you weren't with me boy."

The real mystery was, who the intended victim was meant to be? An art collector, the homeowners, the tour organizers Nell and Nicole, an innocent bystander, me or the Spring Fling itself? The answer to that troublesome question was in the timing." Duie had already turned his back and started for the parking lot. As did I.

Lots of visitors had viewed the sculpture before I arrived on the scene and surely the homeowners plus Nell and Nicole had all looked at it several times, so the perpetrator had lots of opportunities to select a victim. But he had waited until I got there. So why me?

Rather than standing around in the shadowy parking area, Duie and I took off in the 550 and headed home. The 550 is a comfortable car to drive, but isn't a roadster so I drove straight to Ocean Park. Besides I still had a number of thorns in my butt that were starting to irritate me. Plus, I wanted to see what I could find out about artist Luc Blondin, the creator of the giant whirly gig come scrap heap.

When we arrived at the beach house, Duie wanted out quickly. I can't say I blame him for he hadn't been allowed to wander around the garden party so he'd held it in for some time. I let him out the sliding glass door and walked onto the deck myself to get some much-needed fresh air and solitude.

As I stood there in the dark gazing out at the deep thalo sea with its subtle white caps a whiff of cinnamon found its way to me. I suspected it emanated from Merra. I turned to see if I was right... I was. She was wearing a red bikini bottom and a very shear multi-colored poncho style cape that cast a rainbow effect over her bare breast. As she walked toward me the visual effect was magnetic so instead of standing face-to-face I suggested we sit in the deck chairs. Which I thought was a good idea until I actually did it and a thorn pierced my left cheek.

"Ouch, damn it," I yelped.

"What is it?" Merra said as she rushed to my side. "Is your shoulder bothering you?"

"Uh, no it's not that," I said as I shifted my weight to relieve the sharp pain. "Damn it," I yelped again as I rolled completely onto my stomach and reached back to locate the spikes.

"What the hell is it," Merra said as she bent down to see what I was reaching for. "I see it," she said as she pulled a couple of barbs out and began rubbing the spot.

I turned to look at her and couldn't help but notice the deck light made the poncho look completely transparent. A truly beautiful sight. As I forced my attention away from her rosy, pink nipples to focus on her blazing emerald eyes a resolute voice interrupted my searing thought process.

"I'll take care of it Merra. You better get back inside, the way you're dressed you're likely to catch a cold or something worse," said Nicole as she scowled at both of us. "And Duie get off of Shotola… Now!"

I sat up quickly, Duie dismounted Shotola and Merra started toward her place.

"Come on girl, we need to go," Merra said as she smiled at me and then to Nicole while reaching over to pet Duie. "It's OK Duie, you're a good boy, I understand." I wasn't sure if the message was meant for him or me. Either way, I'm sure Nicole didn't like it.

Merra and Shotola left. I got up gingerly to stand and face Nicole, but she was already inside and heading upstairs. Her candor in these awkward situations often leaves me feeling vulnerable, embarrassed and uncertain as to how to respond. After closing up downstairs I headed up too even though my growling stomach was still craving dinner.

When I got upstairs Nicole was completely undressed and waiting for me in the bathroom with the hot shower running.

"Come in here," she said. "Get out of those cloths and I'll find those pesky thorns although I should leave them there and let you suffer, but then again if I do someone else will volunteer to remove them. Won't they?" she said in snorty huff.

After she removed about a dozen or so thorns, I was more than ready to stick something into her and really felt great when I did. When we finally got into bed, she proceeded to tell me she wanted the Roadster and I could have the 550 ... and in her opinion the Roadster was more in keeping with her personality than mine. I was feeling so good I just agreed to everything she wanted, rolled over and went to sleep with my stomach still grousing.

I woke up around 3 and couldn't sleep any longer. I was preoccupied with figuring out why someone wanted to dump a load of metal on my head. I went into the studio office and checked google to see what I could find out about artist Luc Blondin.

There wasn't much on the web about him other than his name listed as an invited artist for the Spring Fling and his own website. His website listed merely the usual artist stuff about where he came from and a general statement about his approach to creating kinetic sculpture. The only thing giving any insight was a photo of him installing his sculpture at the Spring Fling. I found nothing providing any connection between us other than perhaps the fact I'm the host of CAsLog and he's an emerging artist in search of attention. Maybe he thought I'd interview him or at least there would be something in the evening news if he pushed the thing over near me. I decided to go back to bed and sleep on the whole incident.

***

It was Saturday morning, the second day of the Spring Fling, and since it was going to be a long day for Nicole, I got up early and made her breakfast. It was the least I could do after she had been so nice to me in the shower, besides I had questions I needed answers for while she was still home. To say nothing about the fact I was ravenous.

"You know, you're probably going to be required to file an insurance claim for the collapse of the leaning tower of Brentwood. Does anybody beside Luc Blondin own it?" I said as casually as I could.

"His is the only name on the forms we gave him to fill out when we invited him to exhibit the piece. Why do you ask?"

"Oh, just trying to figure out who benefits from its destruction. Cause you know its demise was no accident. Someone deliberately unbolted it from the concrete support base and shoved it over."

"How do you know?" She insisted.

"By the photo on Nell's Spring Fling blog. It shows Luc standing next to the piece after he finished installing it and all of the bolts are visible and secured in place. He's even leaning against it and it isn't falling or even tilting."

"Couldn't the nuts just have slipped?" she said with a chuckle.

"No, I checked them last night before we left. The nuts and bolts are not broken or bent and aren't even scratched or scuffed. In fact, everything still looks brand new. Someone simply dismantled the bolts and left everything laying there. Then pushed the thing over."

I suddenly realized that must be the message. There was no purposeful attempt to make the event look like an accident. But was the message really for me?

"Do you know if there is any connection between Luc and the owners of the garden?"

"Oh, they definitely didn't know Luc. I introduced them to him. You know we even took the time to make sure his piece wasn't visible to any of the neighbors just in case they were the kind of people who hate contemporary art."

"OK, well perhaps someone wanted to give the Spring Fling a black eye. Was there any artist who wanted to be in the exhibit and was refused?"

"Not that I know of, but I'll check with Nellie to make sure. You know she prides herself on having curated the entire exhibit so artists can't apply to be included. And before you ask, Luc wasn't there when the piece fell, he had to leave early to get to his job. He's some kind of orderly at the VA hospital. Now if you have no other questions, I've got to get going," she said as she grabbed her purse and headed for the garage.

"OK, take care of the Roadster because the test drive insurance is only good for 24 hours which will be up around 3pm," I said quickly which brought her to a complete standstill. "Are you certain you want that particular car?"

She turned and walked back into the kitchen. "Are you saying you don't?"

"No, I'm just pointing out the test drive expires at 3 and so the car has to be returned by then or the purchase agreement as to be signed."

"Right, sign the purchase agreement," she said with a big smile. "Oh, and please keep Duie away from Shotola," she said scowling with apprehension and a sharp focus in her eyes.

"I will, I promise."

"And what are your plans for your old clunker?"

"I think I'll donate it to the homeless charity. You know they have a program where they fix up cars and sell them. It's not in real bad shape, so they'll be able to make a little money off of it."

"Good idea. Will you take it to them today?"

"Yep, will do. I just have to figure out how to get it there. Oh, by-the-way, were those people yesterday wearing masks, having hay-fever problems?"

"I don't know. They might be afraid of that Asian flu or virus thing or whatever it is."

"What are you talking about?"

"It's in the Times. Some new kind of virus. I've got to get going. See you later. Love you, bye."

After I shaved and dressed, I phoned the charity and was told I should drive the car to them, sign the ownership transfer papers and they would drive me home or wherever I needed to go.

Considering I had left my old car at the used car dealership on Wilshire Boulevard I would have to drive the 550 there, then take the old car to the charity's office in Studio City and have them drive me back to the dealership. I wasn't looking forward to that scenario, but there it was and it had to be done.

Traffic was fairly heavy for 9 am on a Saturday, but I managed to get to the dealership in only 20 minutes. However, completing the purchase agreement for the Roadster was a very slow process. The only person happy through the entire ordeal was the sales rep. She was thrilled when I signed the last form. I was ecstatic when I finally got to drive away even though I was in the old car.

By then traffic was even heavier, so I decided to head up Wilshire Boulevard to Beverly Glen Drive which turns into Coldwater Canyon Drive and take it through the hills toward Ventura Boulevard instead of getting on the congested freeways.

It had been some time since I'd last driven through the canyon and it felt right to be doing so in the old car. I rolled down all the windows just to smell sage and all the spring blossoms. If I weren't ever able to live at the beach, I'd find a place in one of LA's canyons. I really enjoy being in a place where you can look out at nature and not see a house or building of any kind right next to you. Although Coldwater Canyon was about as over-built as it could get.

The old car didn't take the curves anywhere near as well as the 550 and especially not as well as the Roadster. Its tires and shock absorbers were soft and should have been replaced long ago. The engine even struggled a bit as I got close to the top of the ridge and could see the San Fernando Valley in the distance, but heading downhill was almost effortless. In fact, I found myself going over the speed limit so I slowed down and got a real surprise. The guy driving the truck behind me decided to pass on a curve, but the oncoming traffic was so heavy it forced him to pull back in behind me. As he did, he clipped the left rear of my car and sent it flying off the road onto the soft gravel shoulder where I lost control and careened into a massive concrete culvert.

The sound of the car smashing into the hard wall was horrifying. Glass shattered and metal screeched as it bent and twisted around me in tortured distress. I was feeling like a dozen whirly-gigs were careening all-about me when everything came to a sudden halt except the airbags smothering over me. I was surprised and grateful they still worked, but the front of the car was so damaged I was pinned into the seat. With the seat belt and the airbag pressing against my lungs and the car filling up with gas fumes I was finding it hard to breathe plus I could feel my heart hammering in my chest and temples as my blood pressure escalated. I'm not sure how long it took for the fireman to arrive or to use the jaws-of-life to cut me out, but when they did, I took the deepest breath of air ever plus I was bruised in several places and my left knee felt especially bad. The car was totaled. It looked like a giant metal accordion rather than a classic. There was no longer a need to get it to the charity folks, it was destined for the newest junk yard.

The few eyewitnesses who stopped to help had told the police the truck didn't even slow down after it hit me. It had kept going and no one got the license plate number or a description of the driver. There wasn't, much the officers could do except take statements from everybody so I told the paramedics I was fine and would not accept their offer of a ride to the hospital. Instead, I used my cell to take a few photos of the car, e-mailed them to my insurance company and called Uber.

As I watched the tow truck pull my old heap out of the culvert, I was surprised I had survived the crash for the car was far more destroyed than I had realized.

"Two accidents in two days is just too much for me," I told the Uber driver, but I wasn't sure he understood me. I needed a drink and wanted to hear some down-home blues. I told him to head for the Indigo Club on 4th Street in Santa Monica. Again, he looked puzzled.

I don't remember much of the drive back through Coldwater Canyon and when I woke-up I knew for sure we weren't at the Club.

"Mister you not look good," the driver was saying in broken English as I shook my head trying to clear the fog in front of my face even inside the car. "This St. John's Hospital you should have yourself checked."

I didn't argue, my head was throbbing. I thanked him for his concern and handed him a fifty as I sat down in a wheel chair somebody provided when I got out of the car. Two hours later I was being told I had a slight concussion, a compressed left knee joint, two cracked lower left ribs, several deep bruises, and a dozen unexplained small punctures to my back side.

"Mr. Terra, I assume you are aware of the Covid-19 virus that is spreading quickly?" said the Doctor. "I advise, if you have to go out, be sure to wear a mask. This thing could turn out to be deadly and a man with your health challenges doesn't need anymore."

The only good news was I could go home, but should stay in bed for at least a week. That thought made me laugh out loud, which scarred everyone around me because the pain was excruciating and I let them know it.

I took the mandatory wheelchair ride to the front lobby of the hospital, shuffled to the sidewalk, got into a taxi and had it take me to the Club. By then it was dinner time, so I hobbled to my favorite booth, ordered a veggie burger and beer. I had only been there for a few minutes when Club co-owner, Spider Washington brought over another beer and sat opposite me.

"You feelin' poorly Sketchy? Been in a rumble or som'in, huh?" he said as he gave me a concerned grin and looked at my tattered clothes. Spider and I have known each other since we were kids together in New York's lower east side. He's great on the harp and has a fine voice for the blues.

"No just a car wreck that's all," I said as a sharp pain nipped at my left side. "Some asshole in a truck bounced me into a culvert up in Coldwater Canyon. Totally destroyed my chariot."

"Yeah, well you don't look too good yourself. Maybe you should go home?"

Before I could think of a retort in walked Cisco. Homicide Detective Francisco Javier Rivas to be exact whom I have known since moving to LA and we were young dudes in Santa Monica's Pico barrio.

"Hey Cis, good to see you man," I said as I finished off my beer. "Spider was just saying we should all get together for some good vibes."

"James, this is foolish. You've got an concussion, broken ribs and you're not thinking clearly. Now come with me I'm driving you home," he said in his official policeman's voice.

"How the hell did you know I was here?" I said as the fog thickened around my head again.

"The security guard at St. Johns is a retired officer and an old friend. He thought I ought to know you were there. Now come on," he said as he searched my face for signs of fatigue and anything else that would suggest he should return me to the hospital. I struggled to give nothing away.

"Ok, ok, just let me eat my burger. I haven't eaten much in the past 24 hours," I said as I felt myself slumping.

"Right. By the way, is Nicole at home? I'll call her to come and pick you up if you would prefer her company?" His warm sienna eyes were filled with concern and totally disarming as if they could see straight to my soul.

"No, don't. She's busy with the Spring Fling tonight. Let's go, I'll take the burger with me and eat it on the way," I said as I inched my way carefully out of the booth.

Cisco had parked his official detective's car right in front of the Club with all of its special lights flashing and blinking. Everyone we walked past to get to it surely thought I was being arrested. But what the hell, I was only concerned a mug shot of me wouldn't appear on the evening news, in the newspaper or social media in the morning. Thank goodness I didn't see any paparazzi or camera hounds about.

"So, you going to tell me about the accident or do I have to beat it out of you," said Cisco with a grin.

I chuckled painfully. "Which one?"

"Well, I guess I mean the one that put you in the hospital. What else are you referring to?"

"The leaning tower of Brentwood. It almost fell on me," I said with a deeper cackle that hurt even more.

"What the hell are you going on about?" His voice sounded muffled and exhausted, but after I explained both so called accidents he was stirred and concerned, but didn't seem to believe I had no idea why someone was targeting me. He asked for a description of the truck and when I explained I didn't have a reliable one he said he'd check with

L.A. Traffic Control to see if any cameras were located in Coldwater Canyon.

His other thought was a little more sinister. He wondered if perhaps Nicole's former husband, Patterson, hadn't decided to get some retribution. I had to admit such a possibility never occurred to me, although, even in my foggy condition I couldn't conceive of Patterson being so blatant. After all there wouldn't be much upside in it for him. His primary interest in life is money. He didn't really care about Nicole. She was just a trophy to him and if I remember correctly, he is on a business trip somewhere in Asia.

When we arrived back at the studio, I insisted I only wanted to recline on the living room sofa rather than have Cisco help me to the bedroom upstairs. From the sofa, I would be able to let Duie outside and get to the frig both of which seemed like top priorities at moment.

Duie is a remarkable dog. He always seems to instinctively know when I am not feeling well. I let him out, hoping Shotola wasn't hiding in the darkness somewhere. I was very happy when he went directly to the edge of the deck, took care of his business, and came right back in.

I refilled his water and food bowls and got a glass of water for myself then worked my way into the studio and sat down carefully in my lazy boy. Duie followed me and laid next to the chair. The unfinished yellow scalene painting on the easel seemed more or less ok, but maybe I was just too spent to really know.

I'm not sure how long I slept, but when Duie jumped against my left leg I woke up quickly and realized instantly I was in pain. As I sat there squirming and rubbing my knee, I heard the clicky-dee-clack of high heeled shoes walking toward the front door. If the door opened it would be Nicole, if the doorbell rang it was most likely Merra. Happily, the front door opened and the high heels stepped inside, but I heard no further noise. Duie, however, scampered out of the studio and from his wagging tail I surmised Nicole had taken off her shoes and was quietly making her way up stairs to the bedroom.

"What the hell is going on Duie? Where is he?" I heard her say as she came back down the stairs and into the studio.

"What are you doing in here and where is the 550? She said with an audible shudder as she stood in front of me looking totally bushed.

It took some time to explain how my day went and even more time to convince her I would be alright in the lazy boy. All I needed was a blanket.

CHAPTER 3

It was well past 10 am when I finally woke and by just walking to the sliding glass door to let Duie out, I could tell I was feeling better. Sunday was the last day of the Spring Fling and it was only going to be open from noon to 6pm with a party for the staff and VIP's at Nell's starting at 7pm.

Nicole wanted us both to stay home, but I insisted she fulfill her remaining hosting duties and I would join her at Nell's party. She could tell from the expression on my face arguing would be fruitless even though she wasn't convinced I should go anywhere. She left the house with tears welling up in her eyes which made me feel remorseful for having been so harsh with her.

The taxing, down-right grueling part of my day was getting up-stairs, getting undressed, getting in the shower, getting dry, getting dressed, and getting back down-stairs. Everything in between went ok and I was especially surprised that at no time throughout the entire day did I see Merra or Shotola. At 6pm I phoned for Uber to take me to the used car dealer on Wilshire to get the 550 and then I drove to Nell's. To my delight my head stayed clear all the way there.

Once at Nell's I quickly discovered walking was more challenging than doing anything else. It was not only smarting with every move I made, but the anguish caused my eyes to blur and my brain to slip into stupefied slow motion.

As I wondered, down the coca plumosa lined driveway and into the house, looking for a comfortable chair in a quiet corner, from out of nowhere Nicole found me and walked me to a perfect retreat spot in the study. She also insisted I take a couple of aspirin and drink only fruit juice. I didn't argue. I didn't really want to think about anything, but I knew my mind wouldn't shut down.

"James you're turning out to be a tough old bird, aren't you?" said Nell as she sat next to me. "And I'm damn glad you are. We wouldn't want to lose you."

"Thanks Nell. I've had better weekends for sure, but if this is the worst of it, I'll be ok," I said with a stiff upper lip, but with some real doubt in my mind.

"Good. By the way, there's a fellow here who's been looking for you," she said as she stood up. "He's some kind of authenticity expert and says Terratan Landchilde told him to talk to you. Is that correct, if it isn't, I'll have security escort him out." She turned her head to one side and threw her words away as if she was in a hurry to get back to her guests.

"No, don't. I'll talk to him. Show him in here."

"OK, but don't let him wear you out or anything." She crossed the room and disappeared into a dark corridor. Nell is in her late 70s, stocky, with a full head of gray hair and radiates an aura of authoritative clout in every situation I've ever seen her in. Nicole admires her immensely.

It seemed odd someone Terratan talked to would seek me out at this event. I mean after all, no one other than Nicole and maybe Nell, even knew I would be here. Or maybe my mind was so muddled I'd forgot I told somebody. I wasn't sure.

There was a rustle and creak in the corridor again. "Hello Mr. Terra. I'm Cornish Tweed, our mutual friend Mr. Landchilde suggested you might like to talk with me," he said wearing a big smile followed by an extended elbow which I wasn't sure why.

"Forgive me Cornish if I don't get up. I've had a rather straining weekend," I responded as I reached up to shake his hand, but he stepped back.

"Yes, so I heard when I saw the infamous sculpture at the Brentwood house. You're lucky you were able to get out of its way. That must have been a really close call."

"Well, good timing is everything as they say," I quipped.

"Don't tell anybody, but while I was there, I stepped passed the sawhorse barriers and took a look at the base of the sculpture and I must say Mr. Terra the whole thing didn't look like an accident to me. If it was, the installer is brainless, the thing wasn't even bolted down. But, hey, the new title sure said it all. Did you write it?"

"Title, what title?" I asked.

"Oh, I thought you probably scratched out *Untitled* and wrote *In Coming*, he said.

"No, I didn't, but it's intriguing," I mumbled.

Cornish Tweed was anything but traditional looking, but did appear somewhat like an accident himself. He had dark brown hair, a sort of dented forehead with deep set eyes covered by large rimmed glasses and was wearing a shiny polyester suit of an undefined garish color. Plus, his general body structure was that of a defensive end with skinny legs. He was not at all what I was expecting in an authenticity expert, but then again, perhaps he was the kind of individual Terratan had tried to descript to me as a new breed of art aficionado.

"It's interesting you took the time to check it out and I appreciate you mentioning your findings," I said as I could feel my somnolent brain cells awakening.

"Good, well how else can I help you Mr. Terra? Oh, and by the way I really enjoy your CAsLog program. It's a real service to the community," Tweed exclaimed as he pulled the footstool over to sit in front of me. The stool was so low his knees were at his eye level which made him look somewhat like a toad about to leap. "Will this virus thing shut down your filming schedule?"

"It's too early to tell. I'm doing some research on the trend of putting art up as collateral for a loan. So, I'm talking with individuals, like yourself, who weave in and out of this aspect of the art world," I said as the murkiness had almost completely cleared from my brain.

"Are you planning to apply for a loan?"

"Nah, I'm working on a script for one of our summer CAsLog programs," I said as I sat up a little straighter just to see if my ribs would pinch me.

"Oh, I see. Does that mean I could possibly be on the program?" he voiced fervently.

"Maybe, let's take it one step at a time. Have you ever known any art experts who have passed fakes off as authentic?"

His jaw dropped noticeably and he turned his head away from me, but shifted his eyes back in my direction before responding. "Well maybe, but that's not something I'm in a hurry to talk about on camera," he said with another roll to his eyes which seemed magnified in his oversized glasses.

"OK, well as you know Cornish, dubious data and selective use of evidence has often led to forgeries being declared as originals which have ended up being appraised at greatly inflated values."

The look on his face was like a child who was caught stealing cookies, but I decided to push on. "You must know about the fake Chagall painting the court recently ordered burned and the gallery in ah, Instanbul forced to close when it was determined several Miro's they promoted were all forgeries," I said as I leaned forward a bit and was relieved to not get spiked with pain.

"Yes, of course, but I would have thought you would be more interested in the ones who dealt with manipulated evidence," he said as he also inclined forward a bit.

"Of course, I am. Which kind of evidence are you referring to? Historical, scientific or visual?"

"All of the above," he whispered. "However, it would really depend on which works of art you're talking about," he suggested with raised eye brows. "Plus, sometimes corroborative evidence is only used to enhance someone's academic or business reputation."

"True," I responded.

I was beginning to like this young man and wondered if he had a young woman to share is life path with. On the other hand, most likely, based on his choice of suit, I was thinking he probably didn't.

"There's a lot of stuff going on in this field Mr. Terra," he said. "Judgement by eye is most often used only to suit a particular advocate and can be very incompetent. If you're looking for someone to contradict an eyes-only judgement, I'm not interested in that kind of show business spoil."

"Good, neither am I," I assured him. "I want someone who has an acute sense of using evidence in a logical and efficient manner."

"Well, Mr. Terra, I have a Masters in Art History and another in Science, so my approach to a project is anything but chaotic. Documentation, analysis and judgment is how I proceed. I have no undeclared interests and advocate no preconceived conclusions other than getting paid for my work," he said with a smile. "I thought I'd find a position as a conservation scientist preventing damage to priceless museum treasures. You know, focusing on the environment of a whole museum, but those jobs are few and far between. The lucky individuals who have them are holding onto them. So, I work at the intersection of art and science—literally. A conservation scientist who uses analytical chemistry to help preserve priceless artwork. Concentrating on specific paintings and sculptures one at a time," he said with a noticeable degree of pride.

"And you chose LA for your home base, why?"

"Yes, that is the right question to ask," he said. "Basically, because whereas most museums in the east have a conservation scientist on staff, many museums out here do not. They tend to rely on independent contractors."

"I see. What about in the mid-west?"

"Oh, the weather and politics is just too much for me to take there," he said with a faint stutter and a small smile that didn't reach his eyes. "Have you ever considered doing a CAsLog about how everything in a museum contains chemicals that could be damaging to the art?" he said as he moved to stare right at me.

"Mmm, well no we always put the emphasis on the artists," I said. "However, I can see how such a segment could be of interest to our viewers. I'll keep it in mind."

"The typical museum does about a dozen changing exhibits annually. Right?" he said.

"I believe so."

"Well, each of those exhibits floods the entire museum with potentially harmful fumes and airborne chemicals," he said. "Plus, museums are constantly changing things around in their permanent displays. Putting in new pedestals, display cases, backdrops, lights, all kinds of stuff that is hazardous to everything else. For example, acetic acid in a display case liner might be safe for a textile exhibit, but will corrode metallic art."

"Yes, you're right. I get it," I said. "And you want the Cornish Tweed Lab to be at the forefront of preventive conservation, an admirable ambition."

We sat there for a moment just staring at one another in the quiet, when the door to the patio opened and an attractive young woman entered gesturing for us to follow her. "Please join us in the garden. The auction is about to begin," she said with an inviting smile. "Would either of you like a free mask?"

Cornish handed me his business card and helped me to stand. I thanked him for his time and assured him he would hear from me soon. The young woman distanced herself from us as she ushered us out to the garden area.

Cornish seemed a bit hesitant to join the upper crust crowd. Perhaps it was the way a couple of the ladies looked at his suit.

"Art auctions held to raise funds for charities like this one provide an easy way for new art collectors to enter the art community. Bidding is always open to everyone and Nell, ah Mrs. Meyerhoff makes sure each person is given a bidding paddle," I slurred through inhaling a deep breath.

"I won't really need this," Cornish said as he handed his paddle back to the young woman, but paused to study her despite her clear plastic face shield. She gave him a tight smile, but her eyes frowned.

"Not interested in acquiring art or helping emerging artists grow," I said to him as I gestured to the young woman, I would keep my paddle which returned a genuine smile to her face and eyes.

"I'm sure it's a wonderful charity to support, but I have very limited funds," he whispered as he turned away from the woman, shrugged his shoulders, cleared his throat and adjusted his mask.

"Buying at an auction house or gallery provides you with a wealth of information about the provenance, condition and history of each art work, but here little of that gets in your way," I said with vigor so others could hear. "What happens instead is you see something you like and everyone encourages you to go after it, so you bid. It's easy you just raise your paddle in the air… and the price is often less than you'd pay in a gallery."

"Yeah, I understand, you buy with your heart instead of your head," he said as his eyes stayed fixed on the young woman moving through the crowd handing out paddles.

"Mmm, possessing something beautiful is definitely emotional and your response to living with it when you own it becomes very visceral," I said with a smile and gesture as I too watched the paddle girl disappear into the crowd.

"Where does this art come from?" Cornish asked as he turned back toward me.

"It was selected by Mrs. Meyerhoff, the organizer and our host. She gets it directly from the artists and from local collectors. All of whom have agreed to donate anywhere from 50 to 100 percent of the selling price to her foundation which provides free art supplies to a vast network of elementary schools throughout LA," I said with probably too much authority.

"Commendable," he surmised as he continued to scan the crowd, I assumed for the paddle girl.

"You know, my friend Nicole, is one of the volunteers here. Perhaps you would be interested in helping out with the next event? I'd be happy to introduce you to her," I said as I reached for a folded lawn chair. "She knows all of the volunteers."

He took the chair from me, unfolded it, and held my arm to help me sit as he appeared to be pondering my suggestion.

"You know, that's a good idea. I think I would enjoy being a volunteer with this group."

"Smart decision. There are a number of young professionals, both men and women, who work with Nell and Nicole on several different kinds of art events throughout the year. All for charity."

"So, most of it is secondary market art?" Cornish said.

"Yes, that's correct, but as you know often history can add value to a painting, particularly if the previous owner was a prominent collector or major institution," I offered as the volunteers started bringing paintings toward the stage.

"Yea, there was a painting recently, which hailed from the legendary Mellon collection and was estimated at $500,000 then ended up selling at auction for over $3 million just because their name was attached to it."

"Mmm, I think it's reassuring to know others share your enthusiasm and desire for a painting," I said as I caught a glimpse of the painting, I had donated to the auction being carried forward. "It also means it has its own personal history."

"Does anyone research and vet the secondary market stuff before Meyerhoff accepts it?"

"That's a good question and I don't know the answer," I said as I smarted a bit at his use of the term stuff.

"Well does anyone even inspect them to see if they've incurred any damage while they've been in a private collection," he said with renewed interest. "You know there's lots of potential harm that could have been done which won't likely be visible by just a quick visual scan or by studying a photograph."

"I think Nell requires each owner to complete a condition report—but it's probably up to the buyer to read it," I said as I flashed back on how my own donated painting had been mistreated by an intruder in my studio last fall.

The large crowd gathered to listen to the professional art auctioneer were enthusiastic and impatient when he hit his gavel and introduced Nell. There were probably well over 300 people in the massive patio and lawn area. All striving to practice social distancing and yet eager to be wined and entertained while playfully bidding against one another for coveted paintings and sculptures. Nell, a seasoned veteran at running these-kind of events, made me really pleased when she invited Nicole to the small stage and thanked her for co-hosting. Nicole looked wonderful in her new ensemble chosen specifically for the evening. She removed her elegant black mask as she approached the mic.

"Is that your Nicole?" asked Cornish with a somewhat surprised look on his face.

"Yes, it is," I said with pride. "There is nothing more captivating than a radiantly beautiful woman with a deep, perceptive understanding of art." A warm rush swelled my chest and manhood.

"Absolutely. You really are a lucky man Mr. Terra," he said. "Take care of yourself. I look forward to hearing from you and it would be an honor to work on your project."

I watched him work his way through the social distanced crowd and head toward the far side of the stage where Nicole had also gone after her brief words of thanks to Nell and the volunteers. No doubt he was hoping to spot the paddle girl.

While my head seemed clear, my body was telling me it was time to go home. A young couple were just entering the garden so I handed my bidding paddle to them and headed toward the parking area. When I got there the attendant was not in sight, but there was an unused golf cart parked nearby. I drove it down the driveway to my 550. My 550, how odd, yet satisfying that thought felt.

I took Sunset Boulevard to Beverly Drive then headed west on Santa Monica Boulevard and was home in about 30 minutes. Duie was happy to see me and eager to go outside so I slid the door open for him and sat in my favorite deck chair to enjoy the beauty of the moon kissing the Pacific. It was quiet except for the occasional sound of a crashing wave and the usual distant drone emanating from the fun pier which had lessened considerably since the onset of the pandemic. The sky was a deep electric blue with stars that sparkled even more than diamonds and the air was warmer than usual for April.

I was just about to drift into deep slumber-when the next-door stairwell light came on and footsteps approached. It was Shotola followed by Merra, but there was no way I could jump up without my ribs complaining, I remained seated.

The two dogs instantly started romping with one another and Merra approached slowly while surveying everything she could see through the glass walls of the house. No doubt she was searching for any signs of Nicole. Finding none, she walked onto the deck and stood in front of me.

"I hope this means you're feeling better," she said with an uncertain look. "It's good to see you up."

"Uh, well yes, I guess I'm doing a bit better," I said slowly as I fixated on her exposed body. She was wearing only high heels and a short, deep cherry red, terry cloth bath robe opened in the front. At my eye level the sight of her every nook and cranny was enthralling and uplifting... which made me realize she is a natural red head and I hadn't eaten dinner.

I follow no organized religion, in fact, the nearest I get to one is admiring a long list of historic artists who specialized in religious paintings and listening occasionally to Elvis, sing gospels. Rather than focusing on a formal creed, I prefer to practice principles of tolerance, compassion, and generosity to everyone in hope I receive the same respect in return. Merra was certainly generous, but I wasn't sure how understanding or compassionate she was. Before I could make up my mind about that, Duie abruptly abandoned Shotola and ran into the living room straight for the door that leads into the garage, then stood there listening and wagging his tail. That meant only one thing, Nicole had pulled the Roadster into the garage.

When I turned back to tell Merra, she and Shotola had vanished making me wonder whether the image I'd seen was a mirage, a dream, a well-planned hoax or just a fig newton of my imagination. That query was answered by the lingering hint of cinnamon in the air confirming the image had been real and not a vision I'd conjectured in my mind.

Nicole petted Duie and followed him through the house toward the deck. When she saw me waving, she shed her shoes and dress and walked out to join me wearing only her bra and panties.

"Wow, that's a big smile you're wearing," she said as she stood right where Merra had just been. "You must be feeling better."

"It's been a stimulating day," I said as I stared straight ahead again straining this time to see through the intricate patterns of black lace.

"I know your ribs are probably still a bit touchy so why don't we go inside, turn off all the lights, I'll lay back on the dining room table, and you can have your way with me. You can move fast or slow, whatever feels good to you. Will that provide for an appropriate ending to your day?"

"Can we leave one small light on?" I said as I stood and took her hand.

"Ever the artist, have to see everything," she whispered in my ear.

"Yes, in-de-dee, but don't underestimate me. I'm feeling strong enough for a double header."

CHAPTER 4

It was Monday morning and I had slept like a rock, hard and unable to move so I was out of bed by 7. After a quick shower and breakfast of strawberries, walnuts, almonds and yogurt plus a glass of blueberry juice, Duie and I headed for our usual fast walk. We always take the broad-walk to the pier then left to the water's edge, then south to Marine Street and back via the broad-walk. I was determined to stick to my usual routine, thinking perhaps everything would begin to feel normal again.

Duie really enjoys splashing in the surf and chasing gulls. I'm usually satisfied when my middle-aged bones and muscles make the loop with ease, but today once again they were still telling me to slow down. So, I did and it was well past 8:00 by the time we got home. Nicole was soaking in the tub, I went into the studio and checked my e-mail. There were several needing response. I did so according to their level of importance.

First, was a short to the point message from Cisco. He found a couple of Traffic Control photos of the errant truck that ran me off the road in Coldwater Canyon and was able to get the license number. It turned out both the truck and the plate were stolen. The truck came from an import furniture whole seller in Vernon and the plate from an old Dodge van that had gone to the junk yard years ago, unfortunately, neither photograph showed a clear view of the driver and the truck hadn't been located yet.

My reply informed him about what Cornish Tweed and I had concluded concerning the sabotage of the giant whirly-gig sculpture.

Next up was a message from Terratan stating he had set up a meeting for 10am at the Malibu estate of the collector of the early Snookz Jefferies paintings. It also included an inventory list of the paintings and directions on how to get to the guy's house. I replied I would see him there which meant I needed to change my cloths and leave within 45 minutes.

The last e-mail of any real importance was from my CAsLog assistant Tilly Tamzlin reminding me we had a shoot date set for Wednesday morning at artist Alexis Chacon's studio in Eagle Rock. The segment is going to be part of a Log featuring three emerging artists, something we haven't done on the program before. Alexis is the second in the trio. The first was artist Jenny Fields who creates enchanting pen and ink drawings in a contemporary manner reminiscent of Hieronymus Bosch's *Garden of Earthly Delights*.

At that point I had an urge to go upstairs and talk with Nicole or maybe it was just that I wanted to exercise my privilege of being allowed to view her wet nude body. As I started up the stairs, Duie darted ahead of me in an excited rush which reminded me he and I hadn't had a serious cardiovascular workout, besides fast walking, in some time so I tried taking the steps two at a time, but with the first leap, my ribs let me know the idea should be set aside. I stopped on the third step and looked up to see what Duie was panting about.

It was Nicole, standing at the top of the stairs dressed in only her pink fuzzy slippers and a towel wrapped around her wet hair.

"You look like Botticelli's Venus emerging from the sea," I said with a big smile.

"Doesn't she have red hair? Uh?" she said in a husky voice with her hands on her hips and legs spread apart.

"Oh, I wasn't thinking about that. I just meant you look like a beautiful work of art, a goddess of love and beauty."

"Mmm, that's sweet. How about if I come with you today? You can relax and I will drive you where-ever you need to go," she said as she rose up on her toes and shivered a bit.

"Looks wonderful, I mean, that sounds great and of course we'll take the Roadster. Right?"

"Well, if you insist," she giggled while every enticing inch of her wiggled playfully. "Do we have time to play or should I get dressed now?"

"We'll be going to the Malibu estate of Maytor Kirill, which gives you about 20 minutes," I said as I watched her turn and run toward the bedroom with Duie at her heels. I am sure he believes the fuzzy slippers are some-kind of play toy for him.

It took her only 18 minutes to dress and back the Roadster out of the garage. To Duie's delight, she decided we should take him with us and maybe have a picnic on the beach. Her plan was to drop me off at Kirill's so I could meet with him and Terratan while she would go to the nearest market and get a deli lunch for the three of us. She wasted no time in gunning the Roadster north on PCH. It was good we were heading in that direction, because the Monday morning rush hour traffic was still slow in the south bound lanes even though the pandemic had thinned it a bit.

"It's been over four months since we last drove this way," I said as I gripped my sore left knee and rubbed my ribs. "And I distinctly remember you telling me this stretch of highway has the highest accident rate in the county. Let's not add to that number. OK?"

"You're right. I'll slow down, but some-day soon we need to go out to the desert so I can let this beauty loose."

I couldn't help but feel if it were me driving, I'd want to do the same thing especially since it was a gorgeous day along the coast. The chaparral covered hills were a deep green with blooming poppies and yucca. The ocean and the sky were both cerulean and the air was intoxicatingly good. It's amazing such natural perfection is so close to one of the world's major cities.

It was disappointing how quickly we turned off the highway and headed up Malibu Cove Colony Drive to Kirill's beach side estate. At the gate the house appeared to be in a mid-century modern wave roof style accept the front door landing had obviously been remodeled recently and looked a little out of sync with the rest of the house which was aging badly. Everywhere I looked corrosion and deterioration was setting in. No doubt caused by the salty sea air.

As I reached for the doorbell buzzer, a small screen above it lit up and a woman's face appeared.

"Welcome Mr. Terra. You are expected. Please to come in," said the talking picture as the door magically opened.

I turned and walked back to the car, bent down, petted Duie and said firmly. "You take care of our lady. Don't let her do any crazy driving or anything."

"I like you too," Nicole said as she handed me a mask and hit the gas to zoom away.

I stood there for a moment thinking about how much my personal life had changed for the better in the past few months and wondering if anyone else would be wearing a mask.

"Problem Mr. Terra," a voice behind me said.

"No, no, everything is fine," I said as I stood face to face with a young Asian woman dressed in a black and white maid's uniform. "Has Mr. Landchilde arrived yet?"

"Yes sir, he on patio with Mr. Kirill," she said with a noticeable accent then proceeded to lead me through the foyer to a large living room and on toward what appeared to be a brand-new expansive folding glass wall on the far side of the space.

I was about to assist her in pushing the wall open when she reached behind me and pressed a concealed button instantly causing it to fold back. I walked on through and spotted Terratan sitting with a large man I assumed was Kirill at a table on the surf side of the patio. As I approached, I could see more and more of the crashing waves below.

"Maytor this is my friend and colleague James Terra," said Landchilde to my surprise for I had never really thought of myself as an associate of his, but given the circumstances I suppose he was correct. Maytor Kirill looked to be in his early 60s with gray coarse hair, firm square jaw and ruddy complexion from what I could tell considering his mask covered most of his face.

"Good morning Mr. Kirill and thank you for inviting me to your wonderful home," I said in my best CAsLog host voice.

We bumped elbows, but he did not rise from his seat. The maid positioned a chair so I could sit between the two men.

"Would you like something to drink Mr. Terra?" said my host in a noticeably smoothed over yet coarse manner that suggested he was feeling somewhat socially awkward.

"Some fruit juice would be nice," I said with a hidden smile. "And please call me James."

With a rough textured opened hand Kirill gestured to the maid who then hurried back into the house. From his weathered looking forehead, scruffy hair and general bulldog in a suit appearance he seemed out-of-place in Malibu, but somehow not belligerent.

"James, I've explained to Maytor about the theme of the program we're working on for CAsLog and he has expressed his interest in helping us," Landchilde said in a very gentle manner.

"Wonderful. I understand you have a number of early Snookz Jefferies paintings you are having appraised."

He didn't respond immediately. Perhaps because the maid returned carrying a tray with a tall glass of indeterminate purple liquid. She sat it in front of me and he watched her as she went back into the house. His attention to her implied he didn't want to answer my question within her hearing, but I was only guessing.

"Yes, I have five paintings from his very first solo exhibit," Kirill said with delight.

"Have you selected an authenticity expert yet?" I inquired.

"No. However, the loan officer at the bank told my wife of one they use often."

"Mmm, that's unusual," said Landchilde. "Do you recall the name of the individual?"

"Pasquale Ravanello. His office is in San Pedro somewhere. Do you know him?"

Landchilde and I both shook our heads in a negative gesture. "Do you feel obligated to use him?" I wondered.

"Well, yes, in a way I do. I wouldn't want anything to cause the bank to have second thoughts about approving the loan," Kirill said as he gave us both a hard stare. "Or we could just flip a coin."

To my surprise, he took what appeared to be a silver dollar from his pocket, flipped it about three feet in the air and said loudly, "Heads." He caught it between both his hands then slammed it on the table with one hand still covering it. He then leaned toward me and said with a glint in his eyes, "If its tails, you can select which expert to use."

The full girth of his body leaning forward dwarfed the table, caused his chair to moan and me to lean back.

"I'm not much of a gambler," I replied.

He lifted his hand off the coin to reveal it was indeed Heads before he settled back down in the creaking chair.

"I never gamble unless it's a sure thing," he said as his eyes sharpened their focus on me and he turned the coin over to show the other side was also Heads.

We all laughed, but not very deeply and I found myself a little more intrigued by this mountain of a man.

"Well, two heads can often be better than one," I said as I took a sample sip of the mauve hued stuff in front of me. It turned out to be a really terrible grape juice or at least that's what I thought it was.

"What if after Pasquale finishes his report, we take the paintings to an independent expert and get a second opinion? The comparison will be interesting to the CAsLog audience and you'll have double assurance of the value of the collection."

Kirill flashed a severe focus at me and rubbed the back of his muscled neck for a moment before turning to Landchilde and said, "Who's paying for the second report?"

Landchilde raised his eye brows and nodded to me before speaking, "James is famous for his resources. I'm sure he'll find one to take care of it." He then looked at my glass and continued, "How do you like those grape's James?"

"A little too sweet for my taste, but I believe I do have a resource that will cover the cost just fine."

"Well then, we're all set. Would you like to see the paintings Mr. Terra?" said mountain man as he stood and directed us to walk back into the house.

Before following his lead, I paused to study the spectacular view of the coast line in both directions. It was far more impressive than the house which made me think about how SoCal's coast has been disfigured by over development. Our so-called Coastal Commission seems to have lost its directive and sense of self.

He led us through the living room which was filled with mid-century furniture none of which looked original. Most likely it was all replicas and knock-offs. There were several beach scene paintings and small figure sculptures as well, but Kirill earnestly passed by them and went directly into a wood-paneled study. We continued on beyond a large faux wood office style desk on which were several framed photographs of an attractive Asian woman. She had a healthy figure and appeared to be in her mid-40s. I assumed she was Mrs. Kirill although the poses were a little more provocative than one would expect for family portraits. Everything else in the room looked somewhat shabby, tattered and worn-out.

He then went into a small anti-chamber which had a set of heavy looking metal doors on the opposite wall. From his coat pocket he removed his cell, thumb typed a code into it and within seconds the sound of air pressure escaping overwhelmed the space as the doors opened revealing stairs descending into darkness. He punched in another code and lights came on. We followed him down into a concrete like bunker which had to be at sea level or below.

"How did you manage to make this place waterproof?" I questioned.

"It was tunneled right into solid rock… like King Tut's tomb," he replied as he walked past rows of shelves filled with paintings and sculptures. "Plus, it has a welded stainless-steel liner."

Landchilde chuckled and said, "Impressive, makes me think of James Bond movies. It must be worth more than the house."

"Well, you're right. I bought the house decades ago and only had this vault constructed a few years back."

"Was that when you started your collection?" I asked.

"Yes, my second wife got me hooked on art and insisted I buy the best."

The way he had said 'second wife' implied she was no longer in the picture, but I ignored that and continued with my first thought, "So if you only had this constructed a few years ago, when did you purchase the Jefferies paintings?"

"At that time. I bought them from a collector in Jersey City, my second wife's home town."

"Mmm, did you get documentation with each painting?" Landchilde asked.

"Yes, and I'll have my secretary make copies for you both."

"Are you from Jersey City too?" I couldn't resist asking. "I detect a slight accent."

"No, I'm from South Dakota."

"Ah, mmm, if you don't mind me asking, what business were you in there?"

"Wheat," he said with a sad snigger under his breath. "I still own the land, but the money is all above and below it now."

"Uh, I assume that means wind and oil?" I said with a sideways glimpse at Landchilde.

"Right, you are and here are my beauties," he said as he pulled the coverings off of five Jefferies paintings sitting on the floor and leaning against the back wall.

Three of the paintings were the same size, about 4 ft. x 6 ft. and the other two were both smaller, about 40" x 30".

Landchilde immediately bent down to get a closer look at each painting. I, however, was taken with how familiar the three large ones seemed. Alarms were going off in my head for I had definitely seen them before, but I couldn't recall where or when.

The subjects were typical of Jefferies early work, men and women at the beach in suggestive positions and giving each other sexual gestures and glances. All rendered in lush expressionistic brush strokes of thick paint.

"These will work well for the program. What do you think James?" said Landchilde. "I've never seen Jefferies do images like these two smaller paintings before. Have you?"

"No, I haven't," I said as I turned to Kirill. "Do you have digital images of all five?"

"Yes, my insurance company insisted on it when I purchased them. I'll have my secretary put them on a flash drive for you. Will that do?" He began thumb typing on his phone.

"Perfect. How did you come to acquire these directly from a private collection?" I asked.

"The guy owned a small group of hardware stores in the northeast and the national big box chains plus on-line stores were pushing him to the edge of bankruptcy so he was selling everything he had trying to hold on to his business," he replied.

"So, you were inspired and made good use of a rare opportunity to acquire work by an iconic-artists? You jumped at the chance to get them before they were sent to Sotheby's or one of the other leading auction houses?"

"Right and my second wife had found only a few months earlier, Sotheby's had auctioned off four of Snookz's paintings for $132 million, nearly twice the combined asking price I paid and well above the artist's prior auction record," he said with a noticeable level of satisfaction.

"All of the paintings in the living room are also of this same subject," I said as I studied the two smaller paintings. "Was that your choice or your second wife's?"

"Mine. When you grow up surrounded by miles and miles of wheat fields waving in the dry wind and then endure, years of isolating winter it's natural to dream about sun and surf," he responded thoughtfully.

"I see and the figures are just a bonus?"

"I like people and in bathing suits they appear even friendlier," he concluded. "Beside people at the beach set aside their inhibitions in order to experience the primal self and the best of these paintings explore that side of humanity."

"Well said," noted Landchilde with an affirmative nod. "But it's not a theme which appeals to most women especially feminists. They feel paintings of female nudes by male painters, objectifies them."

"Stark paintings of nudes do, to some extent, but they usually have accessories, like hats, sunglasses, blankets and so on that convey a sense of status and power. At the very least you have to admit this collection is not in any way voyeuristic," Kirill said.

"True, besides the beach is a place where it's ok to freely stare at people. Are you planning to use the loan funds to purchase more art?" I was interrupted by the buzz of a small intercom speaker, mounted on the wall near the stairwell.

Kirill quickly walked to it, pressed a button and said, "What is it?"

The answering voice sounded like the maid and stated Nicole was waiting outside for me so I thanked Kirill and Landchilde, said I looked forward to reading Pasquale Ravanello's report, then excused myself and headed up the stairs. As I emerged, the maid was waiting to show me to the front door.

"Have you worked for Mr. Kirill long?" I asked.

"I work for Mrs. Kirill before she marry him," she said softly.

"I see and where is Mrs. Kirill from?"

"Our families are from Korea," she said with a smile. "We very happy here."

"Are the photos on the office desk of her?"

She blushed faintly and replied "Yes".

"Did Mr. Kirill meet her here in Koreatown?"

"Yes, at the club," she said blushing even brighter. "And at her families dry cleaning business."

Nightlife in LA's Koreatown can be very addictive for a man out on the town. It includes a lot more than late-night dinners and karaoke bars. For-hire party girls, better known as Doumi girls, move in and out of the clubs easily, offering ersatz affections for a couple hundred bucks an hour.

What used to be known as the 'karaoke hostess business' in South Korea has now crossed over to the K-Towns of America, and in LA its particularly strong. The girls originally were hostesses and helpers for corporate clients attending pseudo-business meetings, but now they also offer private one-on-one parties and probably sexual services.

The agencies suppling the girls have even begun accepting immigrant workers who don't carry visas and non-Korean women as well. Its easy cash for the women and according to Cisco there's no shortage of men attracted to the submissive approach they offer. I guess every man needs to feel he is the boss in at least some aspect of his life.

Cisco also told me the more than two dozen hostess agencies in LA's K-town have caught the attention of the FBI. Each agency manages about 50 women, which means there are over a thousand Doumi girls working here and no doubt Mrs. Kirill and her maid are happy to be out of that sub-culture.

I recalled Cisco saying "What started as small-scale mom and pop-type operations has grown large enough to attract organized crime which easily leads to big problems for a city like LA." I wondered which club Mrs. Kirill and the maid had been associated with.

When the maid opened the front door the glare of the morning sunlight blinded me so much the sun behind Nicole's head gave her, Duie and the Roadster a large golden hallow. Walking toward them made me feel as though I was entering another dimension.

"Where are we headed?" I said as I stepped down into the low-slung car and took a deep breath in hopes holding it would prevent my ribs from nipping me.

"Let's go to Dan Blocker State Beach," she replied. "It's nearby, has a new overlook and picnic tables close to the parking lot so you won't have to walk too much."

"Well, that's oddly appropriate," I said.

"How so?"

I explained about the maid and Mrs. Kirill's background and that Dan Blocker had been a Korean War veteran who became a television actor best remembered for his role as one of the stars in a western series called Bonanza. Nicole wasn't familiar with him or the program and her declaration along with my achy ribs reminded me of my age.

"I'm well aware of Dan Blocker Beach. It is a long and narrow beach below the bluff between Latigo Shores and some homes along Malibu Road. It's a prime stretch of coastline that was in County hands for decades, but only recently officially opened to the public," I said with a grin. "It's a south-facing beach so it gets lots of sun. It was donated to the State way back in the late 70s by two of the actors who starred with Blocker."

"Is that right, I'm impressed. You know all that and even better yet you remember it."

I wasn't sure whether to laugh or cry, so I decided to move forward.

"The State donated it and a couple of adjoining lots to the County over 20 years ago, but officials discouraged visitors from using it out of safety concerns. They even posted stern warning signs and a put up a big ugly fence to keep people away from the place."

"And why is it you know all this," Nicole said showing the tip of her tongue between white teeth.

"Well, long before there was ever a parking lot, restrooms, lifeguard stations or picnic tables Cisco and I ignored the signs and scaled or sometimes managed to squeeze through the chain link and scramble down the bluff to the surf. In those days, besides access, parking was also challenging. In fact, we used to park illegally at the Malibu Beach RV Park across the highway.

Nicole's eye widened and her brows arched even higher.

"After sitting unused for years, it now has a scenic viewpoint, named in honor of Blocker. I'm sure he would have been amazed by the tribute. It's a good choice," I said. "It's probably too early in the season for a lifeguard to be on duty, so we'll be able to let Duie run free."

"Mmm, I'm not sure that really explains why you're so familiar with this beach? Nicole stated as she gunned the Roadster into the now fast moving south bound lanes of PCH.

"Cisco and I used to bring our girlfriends there," I said grinning even wider.

"I see and why this particular beach?"

"Well since it wasn't open to the public, we'd have the entire beach to ourselves," I said fondly.

"I'm sure the girls appreciated that," she said swerving quickly through the traffic.

"We didn't get any complaints."

"How nice for you," she said with a little too much sweetness.

"Yes, it was and I would like to live long enough to enjoy your appreciation as well. Perhaps you should slow down a bit."

"Damn it, James, I'm trying to do just that, but the brakes aren't working," she shouted.

"Watch out," I yelled as I pulled on the parking brake which had no effect on our speed. "Put it in neutral and head toward that sand dune."

With lightning haste, Nicole shifted out of gear and turned off the engine as the Roadster flew off the highway barely missing a telephone pole and crashing through several large Sage bushes as it soared up and over the sand dune before slamming down hard across a bed of large bowling ball sized rocks and careening to a stop just short of the surf. The front air bags inflated immediately on impact and all three of us were engulfed by their ever-expanding form which shoved us backwards in an uncontrollable whiplash as the car came to rest about 10' below PCH.

Pinned in our seats, dust and plant debris engulfed us, the car rocked up and down in sync with Duie's jumping about in the back seat as the car slid even further on the rocks. We both struggled to find something to puncture the airbags with when I heard Nicole's slowly deflate. She then began hitting mine with her earring and it too fizzled and collapsed. Duie even took a bite out of it. However, the excessive level of pressure still pushing against my lungs had made it hard to breathe until I was able to reach the seat control button and recline backwards. As the shrinking bag retreated, I took a full gulp of air knowing full well it would cause my ribs to bite me again, but what I wasn't prepared for was a new pain, this time, in my right knee. It was déjà vu all over again.

Nicole appeared to be ok, but her left-hand grip on the steering wheel was so tight her knuckles were turning blue and she seemed in a trance. "What the hell happened?" she said through a growl while throwing containers of deli food in every direction.

I hesitated to say what was on my mind, but I was compelled to.

"Are you sure you were hitting the brake and not the clutch?"

"Shit James, I know the difference between the brake and clutch. This thing has some serious problems and I'm not one of them."

She was fuming, but within minutes we were out of the car and surrounded by a small crowd of people who had stopped to help. Everyone was amazed we were not hurt and the car looked remarkably undamaged at least on the outside. I, however, was certain everything underneath including the frame, axles, gear box, suspension, struts, shocks and much more were all destroyed.

Nicole and I stayed embraced in each other's arms until the tow truck crew and Highway Patrol officers arrived. Both were doubtful of our description of what caused the accident, but one of the officers said he'd heard about some models of BMW roadsters illegally smuggled into the States from Canada equipped with very efficient two-piece floating front disc brakes which fail if not properly serviced and maintained.

That was a neat explanation for the failed brakes, but did not explain why the steering also seized up.

The towing service guys were insisting if the car wasn't lifted off the rocks by a crane, it would suffer even more damage by being dragged back over them and up to the highway.

Nicole's reply was, "I don't give a damn, just get the thing out of my sight."

I told them to take the car back to the dealership on Wilshire and with that we got into a taxi and left the scene. As we headed toward Santa Monica, Nicole cradled Duie in her arms and snuggled up in mine. I was grateful we were all safe and able to comfort one another.

Nicole began speaking softly "I'm not sure why this is important to me right now, but it is. Have you ever wondered why I made my home here in SoCal rather than returning to Philly?"

"Mmm, well I guess I assumed it was because you like it here," I said in an easy whisper.

"It has to do with the way life here rewards you for doing nothing."

"Uh, I'm not sure I understand."

"In many ways, I'm a workaholic and you're a workaholic too James. We both obsess over projects. Why? Maybe it's because we came from the east. We came out of a place cast in a mind-set of hustle and bustle."

"Ok and…"

"We live a life of perpetual interaction. We're always within groups of people; always answering pings or jingles instantly informing us of text, tweets and voice mail. We've lost sight of the importance of being alone together."

"Mmm, our lives do seem to be one big open floor plan," I said.

She snuggled deeper into my sore side and spoke directly against my chest. I could feel each subtle vibration. "I know we're constantly being told connectivity is a good thing and being around other people is necessary for a fulfilled life, but I think we've reached the point of having too much of a good thing."

"All men's misfortunes spring from their hatred of being alone," I said.

Her head sprung back to look directly into my eyes as she snapped "Where did you get that?"

"It's an old saying I remember from college or somewhere."

"You're not really ever alone. Not even in your studio. It's also your office. You answer e-mail and phone calls all day long," she said. "Let's make a pact to ditch this ultra-hip life at least once a week and spend time alone together. No interruptions."

"Ok and?"

"And those that grew up here have perfected the art of doing nothing and they do it well. I mean look at all those folks out there lying on the beach, in April no less. Just feeling the sun and letting themselves drift. They're not working out or typing on a lap top and probably not even meditating."

"It's the siesta culture without the eating and napping," I said shaking my head. "People just want to zone out for a while especially now with all the pandemic protocols closing in on us."

"Well, I think its life giving and I promise I'm going to slow down. I want you to promise you will slow down with me."

"If this pandemic thing turns out to be real, we may have no choice in the matter."

CHAPTER 5

Alexis Chacon's studio is actually the garage of her parent's 1920s era home in Eagle Rock, a neighborhood in northeast LA nestled in the San Rafael Hills named after a massive local rock outcropping resembling that regal bird and didn't become incorporated into LA until the mid-1920s. Richly ethnically diverse the area has always been known for its counterculture artists, writers, and filmmakers. Alexis is considered one of its newest raising stars.

While driving to her studio I re-discovered the area's wonderful array of historic buildings and classical homes. There are Craftsman, Georgian, Moderne, and Art Deco styles galore. Alexis' place is an impressive classic Mission Revival home and when I arrived, I found my crew's official CAsLog van already parked in the driveway.

The garage sat to the left side of the house and was just wide enough for today's average car which made me wonder how it would have ever contained a car from the 20s or 30s when the house was constructed. Those metal beast back then were enormous compared to today's wheels.

"No doubt the chauffer was the only one who had to squeeze in and out, everyone else got out at the front door before he pulled the car into the garage," I said to myself.

The garage door was down and was secured by a heavy pad lock so I followed a small red brick path to the opened pedestrian door on the side wall. As I approached, I could hear Tilly and Alexis talking so I slipped in quietly.

"He always sits to the left facing the camera so this seat is yours," said Tilly as she gestured for Alexis to be seated.

"What if I sit to the left just to be different?" Alexis replied.

I moved into view without saying anything and went directly toward a painting hanging on the wall near the work bench. "This looks like maybe you started it just yesterday, is that correct?"

"Ah, yes, but"

"Wonderful, we'll start here," I said as I signaled for everyone to reposition themselves.

With her usual precision, Tilly swiftly moved the chairs to the new location and positioned them 10' apart. The camera and sound men had no difficulty shifting also. Alexis, however, was still standing in the center of the other space and seemed a little miffed. I took my regular seat, signaled for the camera to start and began speaking.

"There is a fringe area between a lie and the truth. It is often poetic and fugitive, but always present in Alexis Chacon's studio work," I said in full host mode. "With each painting she longs to reveal a particular reality about living in this city at this time. You and I are honored to see the budding of one of those soul filled truths and to hear the artist herself illuminate why she started this painting in that manner."

***

Tilly looked dumbfounded, the camera and sound guys stayed professionally at their post, while Alexis wiped tears from her eyes and walked quickly to the chair opposite me. She was dressed in low cut tight fitting blue jeans and what is often referred to as a white peasant blouse she had pulled down to reveal her bare shoulders and which was short enough to show her lower ribs. She had long wavy black hair, dark brown eyes and stood at about 5.5' in her 4" midnight blue heels. As she approached, I noticed her dangling silver and ruby navel jewelry sparkling. Drawing attention to the inch or so of neatly trimmed pubic hair just above the top of her jeans. Between the two was a small tattoo of what I think was a hummingbird. The image generated a smile on my face and a grimace of concern on Tilly's. However, I wasn't worried for I knew the camera man would zoom in enough to only show our upper torso's.

I've often felt one's clothing tells stories of our selves. It might say something about our bravery or rebelliousness or even acquiescence with the dominant culture. It can create tension within a gathering or signal how we feel or what we believe, want or need. For Alexis, especially here within the confines of her own studio, it is probably a tenacious desire for self-expression or artistic ambition for it obviously goes beyond just striving to be fashionable.

I welcomed Alexis to the show and asked her to talk about the painting between us. She did so beautifully, but with little completeness. Which was ok considering the painting had just been started. We moved to another question.

"Lots of Hispanic-themed murals have been whitewashed throughout LA in recent years. You seem intent on bringing them back, tell us why your studio work looks so different from the murals you restore."

"The early culture of California recorded in most of those aged murals is slowly, disappearing. The elements and the lack of conservation of them are their most obvious enemy, but apathy and indifference are the primary cause for their demise. We need to keep that history visible to the larger public because so many people have no access to art galleries and museums," she said with genuine sadness in her voice. "And their legacy is not taught in schools."

"And I suppose few people care about giving donations to preserve the more aggressive Chicano murals you seem to prefer. Do you agree?"

"Yes, that is true. However, as more and more of those Chicano's have matured and become productive members of the larger community more funds are slowly becoming available."

"Your studio work doesn't have the divisive aura that the Chicano murals you repair have. In fact, the wealthy landlords who decry those murals are among those who purchase your studio paintings. Do you ever talk to them about making donations to help preserve the murals?"

"Yes, I point out to them they have no hesitation to fund the conservation of murals about saving whales, surrealistic street art, children's pastorals, and portrayals of celebrities, even though Chicano murals are more a part of LA's history than those subjects are. They document and illuminate a time and place which is fast disappearing. All of us should help to preserve that visual record."

"Restoration projects were under taken in the early 90s usually by the original artists. Have you spoken with those who are still around?" I asked.

"A little, but those still standing are not physically up to doing that kind of work anymore. And many of the walls themselves will surely collapse in the next big quake. I'm trying to raise awareness about finding a high-tech solution to preserve just the images, life size, but without the walls," she said with her head thrown back and her hands on her hips.

"I see, what about those community leaders who claim many of the Chicano murals promote gangs and include their hate symbols?"

"Well did you ever consider they may be rebelling against an oppressive government and police department?" she said with a retort in her torso. "Those government folks even go out of their way to have bushes and trees planted in front of the murals that raise questions they don't like. Chicano art resonates with a large segment of L.A. especially since the Marin collection established itself in Riverside. When you consider it stems from a long political movement concerned with social justice and issues of equity it's easy to see why it has deep roots in the art community too."

"It's unfortunate so much of its development was shamefully criminalized. Artists such as yourself understand the role art plays in changing those perceptions and the Visual Artists Rights Act has helped to some extent, but I suppose we all need to be more vigilant. Desecration can come from nature and rich vandals alike. The best protection is for us all to get out and view the murals in person so they become part of everyone's history. Perhaps if that were to happen someone would be inspired to come up with a high-tech solution to preserving them."

I knew the moment I said those words my producer, Liz Weinstein, would insist I cut them from the final tape. CAsLog is not meant to be a rant stage or bully pulpit so I took a few more minutes with Alexis to talk about a couple of her most recently completed studio paintings and then ended the segment with this positive note.

"When visiting an artists' studio, CAsLog looks for the details that illuminate the artists' personality, processes and creative inspiration for as fascinating as a well-done work or art is, a deeper understanding can often be discovered within the atmosphere in which it was created. And as every artist's is unique, so too are their work spaces," I said as I smiled at Alexis.

"Each artist we've spent time with in their studio is deeply committed to their work and their modos-operandi. Letting visitors into that realm is a remarkably vulnerable act for them to do. As a result, with each visit, we are giving you, our audience, a chance to see the hard work that goes into making art, to gain insights into what inspires it and to discover how the magic happens in the hands of a creative soul. Thank you, Alexis for your generosity in allowing our viewers and the CAsLog crew into your studio and heart."

Alexis' eyes glistened and Tilly looked delighted.

This particular show was scheduled to be about three artists rather than just one so the filming session was noticeably shorter than normal, but the crew didn't seem to be in a hurry to leave. In fact, they were dilly-dallying around with their gear when Alexis walked over to me and tried to convince me to film an entire program just about her studio work. She spoke softly and stood with her fingers in her front pockets while using her thumbs to stroke her exposed pubic hair and play with her belly-button sparkler. The motion made the hummingbird tattoo appear to quiver. It was a mesmerizing sight and fun to watch until the sound man broke the spell by stumbling against the door on his way out. It even generated a seductive smile from Tilly.

I told Alexis I couldn't make a decision about her proposal until after the trio segment aired in a month or so.

"Visiting an artist's studio brings one to a place where you're usually not allowed … to the womb where art is imagined and created. There is something sacred about it. It feels blessed and set apart from urgency."

She smiled and put her hand on my arm as a gesture of thanks, turned then walked over to speak with Tilly who immediately took off her mask. I took the opportunity to leave.

I drove the 550 onto the Ventura Freeway and headed west to the 405 south through the Sepulveda Pass and then took the 10 toward Santa Monica. My destination was the car dealership on Wilshire. My insurance company had told me they would have a lawyer there to represent me in reaching a settlement with the dealer.

Traffic was light, no doubt because of the pandemic caution to stay home. I exited the freeway onto Lincoln and there was plenty of curb side parking available on Wilshire so I arrived a little ahead of schedule and walked directly into the dealership's sales office hoping to find the young woman who sold me the Roadster, but there was no one about. I walked back outside hoping to spot a salesman in the car lot.

Finding no one, I wandered around the lot looking at cars that caught my eye. As I stopped to get a closer look at a red Ferrari a young woman approached from behind me, but she wasn't the sales person I was seeking. This woman was more mature looking in a smart tailored business suit with a captivating array of delicate scarves draped around her graceful neck and lower face. She carried an expensive looking briefcase.

"Lawyer," I said out loud while staring at her reflection in the highly polished Italian masterpiece.

"Yes, Mr. Terra. I'm your lawyer for the day. Ariella Blieler," she said as she offered her graceful hand, but quickly drew it back and offered an elbow instead.

I bumped it and said, "Please call me James. Should we find somewhere to talk before going in?"

"No that won't be necessary. Just let me deal with them before you say anything. OK?"

"No problem. In fact, if you don't mind, I'll just find a chair. My rips are still biting at me."

"Understood and that will be a direct way for me to introduce your demands," she said smiling pleasantly.

"I have demands?"

"Oh, yes, Mr. Terra. You have lots of demands."

I returned her smile and did not argue as we both put on our mask.

We entered the main office building and the receptionist showed us directly through a door labeled Manager. The big man at the desk wore a pin-striped, dark blue suit and looked as though he could be of middle-eastern origin while the fellow standing to the right of him wore some kind of marooned colored blazer with gray slacks and displayed a face that looked as though it had been smiling since he was three years old.

Ariella placed her business card at the center of the desk and said, "Good morning gentlemen. Please forgive my client, Mr. Terra, his ribs and knees are still painful and prevent him from standing."

"Really. That's surprising the Roadster doesn't look that damaged," said the Maroon blazer with his mouth twisted in a complex smile and his small mustache rising.

"You can go back onto the floor Willard. I'll handle this," said the big man.

Willard's expression didn't change, but his posture slumped as he left the room.

"Pardon my associate. He's a good manager, but lacks the thoughtful perspective needed for this situation," he said as he shrugged his shoulders. "I'm the owner of the dealership."

"Good," said Ariella. "I assume you've reviewed the CHP's report of the accident and are aware of your staff's lack of professionalism in making sure the Roadster was road worthy before allowing my client to drive it."

"Yes," he said without smiling.

"Good. Then I further assume you are fully prepared to give my client a complete financial refund and cover any future medical expenses he or his companion may incur as a result of the accident."

Ariella was a force of beauty. She spoke with the authority of a judge and had the physical demeanor of a referee. I liked her tenacity.

The big man pressed his oversized hands and swollen fingers down hard on the desk as his eyes became blood shot, but he remained seated and calm with his face screwed up. He smoothed it with his hand and repeated the gesture several times striving to confer distinction on himself.

"Do you have any questions?" Ariella said with complete resolve and no sign of retreat.

"Just one," he answered.

"What?" she said as her hands moved to her hips.

"Is your client the James Terra who host the art programs on television?"

"Yes, he is and as such he has a great deal of influence in this city."

I never thought of myself that way and wasn't sure if I liked the notion.

He lowered his head in embarrassed thought, cupping his double chins in his hand. "Are you at all open to a suggested comprise?" he said looking at me instead of at Ariella.

Ariella turned her back to the big man and faced me then winked. I nodded very subtly and she turned to face him again.

"What did you have in mind," she said in a quick clip.

"Instead of a full refund, will your client accept another car and a partial refund?"

She turned again and this time raised her eye brows with an accompanying double wink. I did likewise in return.

"Maybe, depends on the car."

The big man's eyes winced, but otherwise he gave no sign of surprise.

Comparing intelligence and gender doesn't typically yield much in the way of productive banter and I certainly didn't want to open a can of worms, but I had some concerns which weren't being addressed in the very civilized jousting going on before me. Before stepping into the fray, I reminded myself men and women are equal in general intelligence, but not in emotional intelligence and my concerns were probably going to touch that hot button.

Usually, women are pegged as overly emotional and men aloof or explosive, but from what I'd seen so far, I'd say none of those platitudes were true for Ariella or the big man. If they were, I was betting Ariella would have the upper hand because women have greater skill in using emotions to their benefit especially if they have a high level of self-awareness in the heat of the moment.

Of course, men have a tendency to feign no awareness or understanding of their emotions—in the hope of avoiding any accountability for their wrong-headed actions.

The best solution would be if they both channeled their emotions into producing the results I wanted. It was time to find out.

"I have a few questions before we make any further agreements," I said to the surprise of them both.

Ariella turned and faced me in a manner which deliberately made it impossible for the big man to see my face. Her lips tightened and her eyes dilated. I stared back at her and nodded my head to the left in hopes she would sit down in the chair next to me. She did so reluctantly.

"Are you feeling all right?" she said softly as she put her hand on my left knee. "Would you like a drink of water or something?"

"I'm fine and I have no problem with everything resolved thus far. However, there are key issues if not addressed to my satisfaction will disperse this meeting here and now."

The big man's bulbous eyes enlarged even further and his snout began to flare while Ariella slid to the very edge of her chair and swallowed hard.

"Why yes, of course James. Please tell us what is bothering you," she said with perfect elocution.

In my years of dealing, with a vast-array situations, I've learned this is where the difference between individuals, regardless of gender, will reveal how they were socialized while growing up. Some will remain strong and in complete control of their emotions while others lose it.

"First, what did your mechanics determine caused the brakes to fail and the steering to freeze up?"

The big man ran a knotted forefinger across his brow and pushed hard against his temple while picking up a manila folder from the right side of his desk.

"The CHP Officer was correct. The car came in from Canada and maintenance on the brakes had not been done correctly or maybe not at all. We're still trying to contact the previous owner for clarification."

"And the steering?"

"Something went wrong with the computer assisted steering system. We sent the chip to an independent tech firm for review. Their report will take a few days to complete," he said as he opened the top drawer of his desk and threw the manila folder in impulsively. That action made Ariella sit up straight and cross her legs tightly.

"So, what you are saying is your staff and mechanics didn't do any safety checks on the car before putting it out on the lot. Is that correct?" I said as I felt my lips compress and my jaw muscles harden neither of which he could have seen because of my mask.

He did not respond verbally, but did pucker a pout. Ariella grabbed both arms of her chair and stiffened her composure.

"Were they trying to get out of doing their job or trying to save you money or perhaps just following orders?" I said.

His pout changed to an unpleasant scowl.

"Was there anything else James?" Ariella questioned cautiously.

"What about the young sales woman? Does she still get her commission?"

The big man took a deep breath, sharpened his eyes on me and said, "Yes".

"Did she know the car had not been safety checked?" I said.

"No. She assumed it was in good running order."

"Did you sack her?"

"She is my daughter," he said with a degree of shrouded humbleness.

"Are we done James?" Ariella said as she leaned in front of me so the big man could not see her facial expression of guarded exasperation.

"Just two more things," I said with a double-double wink. "I want this entire agreement in writing and signed by you. I want a copy of everything you receive from the previous owner of the car and from the tech company looking at the steering chip."

"Fine," said the big man gingerly.

"Oh, one more thing," I said as I rose to my feet.

Ariella looked as though she was chewing on her mask with a vexed look on her face before I spoke.

"What other car are you offering?"

The big man wiped his handkerchief across his sweaty forehead, stood and gestured for us to follow him to the front of the showroom, which we did. He walked to the special display area just outside and there sat the metallic blue BMW 230i I had first considered buying.

"My daughter told me you were interested in this car. It has been fully inspected and serviced plus we put all new tires on it. I will give it to you for half price," the big man said beaming with an odd mixer of pride and hope.

I didn't say anything I just walked around it, hick a tire or two and opened the hood. While I was standing there looking at the spotlessly clean engine he said "I'll even give you a one-year warranty on everything."

We shook hands and he handed me two smart remote-control fobs.

Ariella insisted we needed to talk so I told her to get into the car and I drove it around a few blocks and came back on to Wilshire. We talked only about the car then stopped at Fromins. She ordered coffee and some kind of dessert. I wanted a lightly toasted plain bagel, cup of matzo ball soup, and a glass of lemon Amla ice tea.

"You did a great job. I will be sure to let the insurance company know how happy I am they sent you."

"You realize the written agreement hasn't been signed yet and it will contain some very serious language about liability and any future medical bills that may stem from the accident for both you and your lady friend?"

"Yes, and I have complete confidence in your ability to get it done spot-on."

"Thank you. Now tell me, how did you know when to push his buttons?"

"That kind of judgement just requires careful observation and tuning into body language and other unspoken signals," I said.

"You were watching him that closely? I'm impressed."

"No, I was watching you. You told me when the moment was right. I do my best when I adjust my approach on the fly and you made that easy to do."

"Wow, so you weren't just sitting back and hoping things would go well. Your brain was working."

"I've never been able to just float," I said as I took another bite of savory matzo. "I would appreciate it if you would stay on top of getting that computer chip report to me as soon as possible."

"What's the rush?"

"The crash may not have been completely caused by poor maintenance or a defective computer chip."

"That sounds as though you suspect the car was deliberately sabotaged. Do you?"

"Let's just say I want to make sure it wasn't."

CHAPTER 6

"Your calendar indicates you have a CAsLog shoot scheduled for today, is it still on? I mean, the pandemic warning and all seems to have put just about everything on hold."

"Yes, I know, but the shoot is still on and I'll be leaving shortly."

"Are you taking the Beemer or the Benz?"

"Does it matter?"

"Just wondering."

"I guess it depends on which one is parked outside."

"Right. Well please take my stuff off the front seat and put it in the Beamer. Thank you. I love you."

"Will do and I love you too. Bye."

The drive to the west side studio was short and uneventful. A pleasant change from the past few days. No car problems or wrecks, no plummeting sculptures, and no mysterious red heads. I arrived on time and my crew was set up and ready for me. I put my mic and mask on as we all went right to work.

As the artist and I stepped carefully into the middle of a large arabesque arrangement of colorful glass tubes and my production crew strived to follow us, I said "Thank you for inviting CAsLog to your expansive studio Arash Dentelle. Let's walk through your works as we discuss your intriguing approach to neon art."

Arash smiled, nodded and put his hands together in a gesture of prayer before putting on a mask and walking proudly between two very tall cork-screw shaped deep purple tubes. "I am honored to have you here Mr. Terra. Please do follow me into the heart of Kohinoor."

Arash is tall, lean and of tan complexion. His black hair, mask, eyes and clothing made him almost disappear with the neon on and the studio lights off.

As I followed him, I became increasingly concerned about how the crew was going to film us without bumping into or stepping onto the maze of fragile tubes so I stopped and looked to Tilly for assurance we were ok in terms of lights, camera and sound. She quickly picked up on my anxiety and gestured for me to stay put. I did. Arash also understood and walked back to stand alongside me.

With every inch of every wall, the entire floor, and the dome-like ceiling completely painted with the new Black-hole Black it was difficult to find a safe way through the maze of glowing tubes and electric wires hanging everywhere and crisscrossing the floor. I was becoming worried about any of us making a wrong move and causing CAsLog to incur a large insurance claim or lawsuit. I proceeded cautiously.

"There's been renewed intensity in recent years about neon as an art medium. It's been featured at several of the major international art fairs and a couple of important contemporary art museums have mounted impressive exhibits so I was delighted when I discovered your work right here in L.A."

The glaring light was making it difficult for me to read his eye expressions so I spoke in the general direction of the camera in hopes Tilly would let me know if things weren't going well. "You don't make neon that just hangs on the wall or in a window, your pieces occupy entire rooms. What has led you to do this?"

He nodded, stroked his hair and spoke with a lyrical accent, like poetry set to music. "Neon lighting is nothing more than electrified glass tubes that contain rarefied gases at low pressure. The color of the light depends on the gas in the tube. For example, neon, a noble gas gives off l'orange while Hydrogen is ruse, yellow comes from helium, and blue from mercury. But all of them are also affected by light reflections, from each other and from you and me. Look we both look deep purple."

"Ah, ah so we have become part of the artwork," I said still worried about how to move in any direction.

"Yes, absolutely, however, more importantly the use of space is conditioned by economics and there's politics connected to it as well which is the real reason why it's interesting to occupy it. I'm branding this space as my own."

"Even if it's only until the exhibit closes?"

Arash looked pleased by the question and held out his arms like Moses speaking toward heaven. "Oh, the aura last much longer than that. Once you've seen and walked through one of my neon installations, in your mind I will own that space forever. Each time you think about it you will think about how I made it mine and shared my energy with you. Even the audial buzz of the neon will remain with you forever."

Tilly began using hand signals to direct me to walk to my right and then turn to my left and stop. I did and it worked perfectly for Arash and I were now swathed in a completely different array of colors and shapes.

"Most neon tubes are straight and typically not very long, but you make yours much longer; twist and bend them in every conceivable direction and use a variety of tube thicknesses too. Why is that?"

"Neon was perfected by George Claude a French engineer and inventor, who presented it essentially in its modern form at the 1910 Paris Motor Show."

"Yes, I recall reading about that, in fact, he is known as the Edison of France," I said.

Arash looked a little perturbed that I had interrupted him, but wasted no time in his response. "That is correct and he wanted to use it to brighten up all of Paris including the Eiffel Tower."

Straining to see his eyes through the jarring light I spoke in the general direction of where I thought he was standing. "So, was that your inspiration to work on such a large scale? Oh, and what does Kohinoor mean?"

"It means Mountain of Light," he replied from a direction I didn't expect.

"Mmm, how appropriate. Uh, you are French and,"

"Persian."

"Persian as in Iranian, correct?"

"Yes, my family and I moved to Paris when I was a child of fourteen. I came directly from Paris to Los Angeles when I was 23."

It seemed like an appropriate time to shift our position so we worked our way through Kohinoor and entered the next large piece titled Esteri Jahan which I believe he said meant star-like universe.

"So, you must really enjoy places like Times Square in New York and the entire city of Tokyo?"

"No, not especially. I prefer neon that is more alluring and charismatic in design."

"Mmm, so you were born in Iran, migrated to Paris with your family when you were 14 and then came here to LA at 23. This means you spent your childhood and adolescence in one country and culture and your teenage years in another. And now, as an adult you live here. Is that correct?"

"Yes, it is," he said as he scanned Tilly and the crew for their reaction.

"Well, based simply on the sights, sounds, and smells of Iran and France, do you think you have two sets of memories and preferences that do not fit together and may not relate to L.A.? Do you feel diasporic — like one who inhabits an in-between space? I mean, in many ways how you use space in your sculpture work seems to reflect that history."

Everyone laughed at my comment including Arash and our congregated anxiety eased a bit, but just as swiftly the jovial mood morphed into fear as the entire space went black and a grousing grumble of dismayed panic overwhelmed us all.

"Shit. Damn breaker switch went off again," shouted Arash. "Don't move. I will go to the box and fix it."

Though I couldn't see anyone I heard Arash walk away from me when the cameraman spoke. "I'll turn-on the camera light."

That helped a great deal. We could all see each other and the tangled web of tubes surrounding us even though they now looked murky and vaporous instead of ethereal.

The extreme change in the visual effect of the space gave me an idea. "Get some shots of me while I walk around in this odd shadowy light."

"Careful James. We don't need an accident now and we certainly don't want to disturb his 'diasporic' use of space," said Tilly. "Can you see where the in-between spaces and electric cords are?"

"Not really, but I'll…

The sound of shattering glass was thunderous and piercing, but a quick glance around confirmed nothing around me or the crew was broken. A second smash of glass shrieked through the space followed instantly by a wail of pain from Arash. The clatter was coming from the far end of the large building. I intuitively found my way to the main door and opened it wide to flood the space with natural light. The crew gingerly walked through Esteri Jahan and Kohinoor to get to me and I told them to stay outside while I went back in to locate Tilly and Arash. I found him just beyond the end of the studio area on the floor surrounded by a sea of glass shards and eerie clouds of noxious gas. He was bleeding and seemed afraid to get up. Tilly was not in sight, but I could hear her talking on the phone to emergency services. I assumed she was in the office or outside.

"Did you see him?" said Arash as he gingerly pulled bits of glass from his palms.

"See who?"

"The guy that threw me."

"No, no one came into the studio. Who was it?"

"Some Ninja looking creep wearing a black helmet."

"Do you mean a motorcyclist?"

"Yea, _ucking asshole."

"He threw you? Are you saying he picked you up and literally tossed you into the tubes?"

"Yes, damn it … judo style. That's exactly what I'm telling you."

"Was one of your works standing here? I mean this seems like too much glass for such a small area."

"It was a storage rack of surplus tubes. There were at least a hundred of them stacked here."

"I see. Oh, um, the amount of blood oozing out from beneath you is looking serious. We've got to get you up, but don't move, let me find a broom or something to sweep some of this glass away first then we'll get you up so we can stop that bleeding."

"Be quick. The broom is behind the office door."

Before I could move Tilly was there with the broom in hand. I took it and swept hundreds of pieces of jagged glass away from Arash. "See if you can find something we can use as bandages," I said to Tilly.

"Towels in bathroom, just past the office," said Arash.

The enlarging puddle of blood surrounding him was making it difficult to sweep the glass away. "Let's get you out of this mess. Give me your arm. I'll lift you up and we'll walk to the bathroom."

Arash looked livid and locked his jaw with chilling determination. "Right, let's do it now."

I grabbed his right arm and pulled him up while bracing his back with my left hand. Glass fell off him in all directions as we walked cautiously out of the chaos, but he wasn't very steady so I repositioned my left hand and instantly felt a sharp splinter of glass pierce my palm.

When the paramedics arrived, they immediately cut all of his clothing off and swiftly put bandages on the multitude of cuts covering his entire body.

My hand had a new life line serrated across it with a notched puncture that throbbed like hell even though the medics had applied a pain deadener and wrapped it tight.

I assured Arash we would continue the shoot at another time and told Tilly I would find another artist to use for the trilogy show even though I had no idea who it would be. She didn't look convinced, but said she and the crew would wait to hear from me. I was convinced she would contact Liz the moment she got into the van.

"How did you manage to find your way to the office in the dark?" I said.

Tilly looked amused and said, "I just put my cell in light mode."

"Of course, light mode, I knew that."

"Sure, you did."

I hung around to listen to what Arash had to say to the police about the attacker. He also told them he had no enemies he knew of other than perhaps his girl-friends former lover who didn't drive a motorcycle and wasn't very athletic. The police told him to think about it overnight and to contact them if a name came to mind. He looked like a mummy as the paramedics placed him in the ambulance and drove off with sirens blaring.

I made sure the studio was locked then headed west on Ventura Blvd. and headed south on the 405. As traffic was very light, my mind kept rerunning everything said and not said during the abruptly curtailed filming with Arash. At the forefront is 'what does understanding of his life story bring to bear on appreciating his artwork?' It's a timeworn question, but still not an easy one to answer. His biographical history will be of interest to followers of CAsLog, but I didn't really have enough time to get him to enrich our understanding of what drives him to use neon. There was no critical interpretation. What was gleaned will only narrow and distort the viewer's grasp of him. We will definitely have to schedule another shoot.

I got off the freeway at Lincoln and went straight toward the Indigo Club. I was eagerly looking forward to listening to some real blues, especially since my mind and eyes were fixated on the motorcyclist following me ever since leaving Arash's studio. He fit the general description Arash gave the police of the man who had attacked him and seemed determined to stay just a quarter mile behind the s550.

When I got into Santa Monica, I pulled into the public parking garage next to the club and backed into a space where I could see any vehicle coming up the ramp. I sat there for a solid twenty minutes, but only cars came in so I used the time to contact Cisco and fill him in on what had occurred. Once again, he said he would check the traffic cameras to see if any of them captured a photo of the illusive stalker.

Once more I had the uneasy feeling, I was the intended victim of the glass hurricane, but why? I needed a cold one and to see the warm face of my friend Spider.

As I entered the club Spider was adjusting the sound system while listening to Buddy Guys most recent CD. It sounded so good I just reached over the bar for a bottle of brew and Spider waved two fingers at me, so I grabbed an additional bottle. We slid into our favorite booth.

"Hey good to see you looking almost normal for a change," he said.

"You're right I'm almost there, but surprises keep jumping out of the dark at me.

"Mmm, out of the dark uh. Do you mean that figuratively or literally?"

"At this point I'm not sure. Could be either way or both."

It took several of Buddy Guys songs before I completed telling Spider about all of the Ninja intrusions and thoughts I had during the past few days. He finished his beer as the music system changed to Eddie Kirkland.

"Most of the public's understanding of Ninja comes through exploitation action movies, and cartoons," Spider said. "Whether seen as deadly assassins or mystical warriors, most folks believe all Ninja are highly skilled and have exceptional physical abilities."

"That's true and I'm beginning to believe it too."

"Call anything Ninja and everyone gets the message—Ninja artist, Ninja gallery director, Ninja collector. But even with Ninja dust on them they automatically seem shadowy, obscure, impenetrable and most likely villainous," he said.

"Or at least able to straddle both sides of the ethical line," I replied.

"Yep, Ninja has become another N-word like Nazi and"

"Don't say it my friend. That word doesn't need to be anywhere near our friendship. Besides I get your point and you are right. By-the-way, one of my Ninja's turned out to be a young woman in love not an assassin," I said hoping to change the subject. "What's happening with the club? Are we going to close it?"

"Yes, I believe we should. We don't want anyone to catch this thing just because they came here to relax," he said as he slumped down. "This is meant to be a good time place."

"Right. What about the staff. How long can we keep them on the payroll?"

"I'm not sure, I'll speak with Irving about it. Are you going to need any cash?"

"No man, Nicole and I are good. Just take care of yourself and the staff. I'll check with the bank. Hopefully, this thing and all the political shit will end quickly."

CHAPTER 7

"What are your plans for today," Nicole asked as Duie and I returned from our early morning excursion out on the deck filling our lungs with a mix of salt and spring scented air. "I assume from the way you're dressed you plan to work in the studio. Right or is your hand hurting too much?"

"I'm not sure what I want to do. My hand is stinging and feels swollen and my ribs are still too stiff for doing any real painting. What I should do is concentrate on plotting out the Money Mirage special edition for CAsLog."

"Is there anything I can do to help," Nicole said softly as she snuggled up against me and played with the hair at the back of my left ear.

"If you keep doing that, we'll end up back in bed and I won't get anything done for at least two hours," I said as I turned and kissed her welcoming lips.

"Well, you know I'm always willing to do anything you want," she said as she wrapped herself around me and began riding my leg.

With that action, Duie, who had been snoozing near the sliding glass door, jumped to his feet and began wagging all over. I was beginning to feel the same way.

"OK, OK what is it that you want from me?" I said as I watched her hips move to and fro ever so rhythmically.

She increased the cadence of her words to match her hip action. "I have a meeting scheduled with Luc Blondin to discuss why the insurance company for the Spring Fling Garden Tour isn't going to cover the cost of his damaged sculpture."

Her undulating hips and fluttering eye lashes brought a rush to my head hot enough to make the tops of my ears feel singed. "Yes, yes, I'll go with you."

She slid off my leg, gave my manhood a squeeze and started toward the garage.

"Wait, I need to change, if I can manage to walk up the stairs."

"Ha, ha. Oh, I'm sorry. How about if I go up, pick some things out for you and bring them down here. Will that help?"

I flashed her a big smile and hobbled toward the studio. "Fine, but it'll probably take longer than that for everything to settle down."

She and Duie were both up the stairs and out of sight before I turned to watch them go, which was OK because despite how hot and pumped I was feeling, I did want to meet Luc Blondin.

Sitting in the front passenger's seat of the Beamer was a new experience for me, but I was happy to let Nicole take the wheel so I could just let my body rest. "So where are you taking me?"

"It's called Sawtelle. I hope you know where it is cause, I don't have a clue," she said as she backed the Beamer out of the garage.

"Yep, I know it. Just head up Pico."

Sub-communities within Los Angeles are designated by blue identifier signs, but many of the names are inauthentic and have since been changed even though the signs haven't. The Sawtelle area is such a place. Parts of it are called by a variety of other names. The area on either side of Sawtelle Boulevard in West LA has had a concentrated Japanese American community for several generations and as a result is often referred to as Little Osaka or Japan-town especially the stretch between Santa Monica and Olympic boulevards. However, there's no identifier sign with either of those monikers anywhere near the area.

"Historically the Sawtelle name applied to a wider area that is more commonly recognized today as West L.A."

"Oh well I know most of West L.A., but I'm not familiar with Beloit Avenue in Sawtelle. Do you know it?" Nicole said.

"No, I don't. Community boundaries are a little squishy over there so just head up Pico and turn left on Sawtelle. I'm sure we'll find it."

"OK, that's not far and won't take long. Plus we're a little early so I'll drive slow and take the bumps easy."

I was rubbing my ribs again and holding my bandaged left-hand palm up while feeling like I'd lost some kind of battle. That thought reminded me of the Wadsworth Hospital and the old National Home for Disabled Veterans both of which are associated with Sawtelle.

"Hey, I just remembered. I think Beloit is near the Nuart Theater. There are some old rooming houses along there. I'll bet Blondin lives in one of them."

Nicole twitched her lips left and right while looking at me out of the corner of her right eye. "I don't recall you ever talking about the Nuart."

"Oh, I used to know a girl who worked there and she was a history buff so she knew a lot about the neighborhood."

"I see. Is she still around?"

"No, I think she moved to North Hollywood or Studio City. I can't remember."

"Good."

"Right. Well anyway, she lived in one of the old cottages and told me war widows from across the country used to settle there, temporarily in hopes of meeting and marrying a war veteran with a pension. Today, however, those places are probably worth a small fortune. Didn't you tell me Blondin is a hospital orderly?"

"Yea, that's what he told Nellie and I. What else did this old girlfriend tell you about the history of the area?"

"Oh, a bunch of stuff about the old Soldier's Home. It's why there is a large national cemetery on Sepulveda Boulevard. The first veteran buried there fought in the Civil War."

"Wow that is going a way back."

"There were also gambling and prostitution joints situated just outside the Soldiers Home gates and on Pension days, when the men got paid, the area was flooded with thugs, gamblers, and ladies of the evening."

"I see and what does your old girlfriend do for a living?"

"Ha-ha, she earned a Masters in Library Science from U.C.L.A. and got a job as a Librarian."

We both laughed out loud.

"She did her thesis on the widow's-row of cottages built and operated by the Ladies of the Grand Army of the Republic which stretched for three miles down Nevada Avenue to Palisades Park on the bluffs."

"Nevada Avenue, I don't know that street, where, is it?"

"It's now known as Wilshire Boulevard."

"Geez, that's fantastic. How do you remember all of this stuff?"

"I pay attention when a pretty woman speaks to me."

"I'll remember you said that."

The Soldier's Home, Sawtelle and the city of Santa Monica were all developed on a former rancho that was controlled by John P. Jones, for 30 years a U.S. Senator from Nevada. He founded Santa Monica and used his clout to establish the Soldier's Home, which in turn provided buyers for lots in Sawtelle and customers for the town's business establishments. Like a lot of things around L.A., it was all a big real estate scheme.

Constructed in the early 30s, the section we were heading for consists of six properties directly north of Pico Boulevard and immediately south of the City of Beverly Hills. The area topography is flat and the houses are designed in lavish interpretations of the Spanish Colonial Revival style. Each building is either a duplex or four-plex and all had been completely renovated including well-manicured gardens. When we found the correct address, it was one of the duplexes.

"This place looks way beyond the reach of a hospital orderly."

Nicole raised her eye brows, lifted her shoulders and hid her upper lip. "Maybe, he's just renting. Nellie and I didn't talk to him much about his personal life. I guess I just assumed he's a starving artist. He doesn't give the impression of having any money."

"Well, there's only one way to find out what's what."

The duplex had what realtors call strong curb appeal and there was a driveway directly in front of the house which seemed odd because there was no garage, but Nicole drove onto it anyway and parked the car. To the right of the driveway was a small porch with a Mexican style planter filled with daffodils, rhododendrons and even tulips. The rounded arch front door sported an old-fashioned metal knocker. We both put our masks on as we approached.

When Nicole reached for the knocker, the door swung open revealing a tall, lean, blond headed man who looked to be in his late 20s. He was dressed in faded blue jeans and an old worn army shirt that looked as though it had never been ironed or cleaned much. To complete the ensemble, his combat boots were mucky and tarnished. Plus, his mask was some kind of molded plastic tactical thing.

"Oh, hi Luc. I hope I'm not too early. Ah and this is James Terra."

He stared directly at my eyes and then scanned my general appearance before speaking in a brusque military cadence. "Yes, I recognize your name Sir and I'm glad to see that you're alright. Please both of you come in. Sir did that happen when my sculpture fell on you?" He gestured toward my bandaged hand.

"No, no, that was the result of helping somebody else in need of assistance," I said as I adjusted the dressing.

His attitude was pleasant and welcoming, but a little cold-shouldering and the room was anything other than affable. It was small and had a hardwood floor with a well-worn path from the front door leading directly toward the kitchen. To our right was a rounded arch front window shrouded by a plastic curtain decorated with a tropical floral pattern like something you'd see in a 50s era film.

"Please be seated," he said as he pulled an old wooden stool away from an even older looking easel and sat down.

Nicole looked a little edgy and reluctant to sit, but I pulled her arm gently and we both sat on the only other available seat, a small, dilapidated and stained sofa that had its best days long ago. We both were surprised at how old and shabby everything looked inside because it didn't match the spiffy outside appearance of the building.

"Well, as you know Luc, the insurance company for the Spring Fling exhibit has denied our claim for damages to your sculpture because there was no evidence of vandalism and the owners of the house wouldn't allow us to leave the mess there long enough for a comprehensive investigation. So, I'm here to see if there is some-way we can resolve the situation."

"Can't say I'm surprised by their decision. What did you have in mind?"

I sensed Nicole was nervous despite looking completely calm except for fussing with the ring on her right hand. It was time for me to make a move.

I stood up and walked to the easel. "I don't recall reading anything on the web about you making paintings as well as sculptures. This looks like a self-portrait. Is it?"

"Ah, yes sir."

It wasn't much, but it eased the tension building up in Nicole and I could see how relieved she was by the way her eyes smiled at me.

Several other portraits were sitting on a long wooden wall shelf.

"And these other portraits? They obviously are not you, but they do look like men close to your age."

"Yes, sir. They're all soldiers from my unit."

"Oh, how wonderful," said Nicole in a very feminine manner.

"Not really, they're all dead."

Nicole quickly bowed her head as her eyes filled with tears and pain. She looked like a lost kitten.

"My portrait should be over there with theirs," Luc said as he shied away in what seemed a practiced movement then turned and looked directly at me for a very long ten seconds. "You know, traditional portrait painting is an attempt to duplicate a visual appearance. I'm not doing that I'm trying to bring to the surface what I feel about these brave men and to extract the psychological internalized mortal presence of each of them."

At that moment, both Nicole and I were stunned. This guy didn't look or seem like a man who would summarize centuries of the very best about portrait painting into one short statement. But there it was. He did it and did it well.

"OK, and you do so while making kinetic sculptures too?"

"In a way yes. Look, for some, life is harsh when you grow up poor and joining the army feels like your only option. To say nothing about how having to fight in unpopular wars, makes your attempts to communicate to the general public about how you feel about the hell you've been going through."

We all froze while time suspended itself for a moment or two.

"Oh, I'm sorry, I shouldn't speak so ugly in front of such loveliness."

Nicole looked surprised by the apology, but managed to blush anyway. "It's OK, I understand. My father and my uncles all still have very strong feelings about the wars they fought in."

Again, silence seem to crowd the small space and suck away all of the breathable air. Nicole walked deftly over to get a closer look at the portraits and then turned toward me. A dim light appeared behind her eyes.

I read the gesture as a signal for ideas. It was time to redirect everyone for as interesting as the conversation was, it wasn't getting any closer to solving Nicole's dilemma.

"Impoverished you said? This is a pretty upscale neighborhood certainly not disadvantaged. I mean even if you are a renter and not an owner. Living here still requires some serious funds."

"Right, you are sir. These houses all belong to a former in-law of mine. I'm just the caretaker, occasional gardener and all-around handyman."

"I see, so where do you create your sculpture work?

I was hoping we could get away from the ever-shrinking room and go outside or to a back studio garage anywhere where we could all breath.

Looking wary, Luc straighten up and said, "OK, all though I don't see how looking at more of my sculptures is going to solve finding funding to repair the one that was sabotaged."

"I see, well Luc I think you're a damn good painter. I'm not overly fond of your sculpture work, however, with that thought in mind, I'm interested in doing a segment about these portraits on CAsLog. How do you feel about the idea?"

The look in Nicole's eyes was an odd mixture of surprise, pride and gratification while Luc was obviously studying me like a sniper considering whether to pull the trigger or not.

"Before you answer," said Nicole. "I was hoping you would be able to show us how far along you've come in repairing the sculpture because I would like to add it to my art collection."

Luc swallowed hard, inhaled deeply and smiled with cautious eyes then gestured for us to go through the kitchen toward the back door.

The backyard was narrow and long, but not large. There was a lone orange tree within arms-reach of the concrete landing we were standing on and the rest of the space was taken up with partially dismantled stoves, refrigerators, washing and drying machines, and an assortment of toasters and other small appliances plus piles of scrap metal. After quickly scanning the ram-shackled mess I spotted the debris from the errant whirly gig near the back gate. It wasn't vertical yet, but I could tell much of it had been re-assembled.

Nicole looked confused, but managed to move through the rubble with a degree of cautious grace and poise. "So, your raw materials are gleaned from the houses you care for? Recycling is commendable."

"Well let's say it's a lot less expensive than buying pristine sheets of newly rolled steel," said Luc. "You know it's not necessary for you to buy this sculpture. I was going to redesign it after the exhibit anyway and you should never buy art you don't really want."

Nicole turned and stood face to face with Luc and gave him a sweet nod. "OK, but I do like kenetic sculpture and have planned to add several pieces to my collection so will you agree to show me any new piece you complete before you show it to anyone else?"

"Yes mam, you got a deal."

"I must say I'm surprised at how unorganized this is," said Nicole, "I would have thought as a former soldier you would prefer less chaos."

"I like it this way, in fact I deliberately cultivate the mess," said Luc. "It's more interesting, more stimulating."

"Creativity is about connections and you can't make them if everything is cordoned off and separated," I said.

"What about your tools," asked Nicole. "My father always kept his tools in perfect order. If any of them was even slightly eschewed he would become very annoyed."

"Oh, well yeah, I keep mine organized," replied Luc.

"Isn't creating more efficient and therefore more productive when you're organized?" said Nicole.

"In art equating productivity with creativity is like trying to mix oil and water," I said. "In fact, an artist can often be more creative when least productive."

"You mean like when you sit out on the deck admiring the scenery instead of working in the studio?" said Nicole with raised eye-brows.

"State of readiness is what is important," said Luc. "It keeps your entire nervous system fired up and that's something all soldiers, uh and artists are aware of."

"Mmm, yeah James gets fired up and ready to go, that's for sure. But I think you're talking about *mise en place*, that's what the French chefs call it," said Nicole. "Keep everything just as you like it so you can work whenever you want."

"You take advantage of the chaos by searching for the grace within it," I said. "By letting the assortment of materials sort-of cross pollinate. One odd bit gets shoved next to another and you see a connection that wasn't there before and your enthusiasm turns to passion."

Before we all could enjoy the suggestiveness of the moment a voice rang out from inside the house.

"Hey, babe where are you?"

We all turned to see a perky looking young woman in short-short blue jeans and carrying a bag of groceries step out onto the landing.

"Oh, I didn't realize you had company.

"Maggie this is Mrs. Volkov and Mr. Terra. They're here to talk about the accident."

"Please call us Nicole and James and we're here to look at all of Luc's work. I especially like his portrait work," I said. I never realized before how much I dislike hearing Nicole referred to a Mrs. Volkov.

"See I told you they are good," said Maggie with a big grin.

"Maggie was my teacher," Luc replied with a bowed head.

"Oh, wow, where do you teach," asked Nicole.

"At the VA," replied Maggie as she set the bag down and quickly took out a mask from her back pocket.

"I didn't realize they have an art program there," I said as I took a closer look at one of the portraits.

"It's not a program it's art therapy sessions," said Luc with a gesture of stiff pride. "And it's been very helpful to me. In fact, it helped me to readjust to civilian life."

Luc put his arm around Maggie and they looked into each-others-eyes.

"Well Ms., ah, Maggie that's a very important skill to have," I said.

She turned to face me and put out her hand. "It's Mayye … Margaret Mayye. A very old English name. Oops, sorry." She withdrew her hand and offered her elbow instead.

"Maggie Mayye, that's a name I hear often."

"You do? Where?"

"On my phone," I said. "I use one of those juke box ring-tone programs on my cell."

Maggie's youthful face lite up with a marvelous glow. "Of course, so you use the Blues one and it plays Rod Stewarts famous hit."

"Yep, and I love it every time I hear it."

"So does my grandfather, although I think he probably likes the story behind the song even more."

Everyone laughed, but I knew darn well Nicole had no idea what Maggie was referring to and I could have done without the reference to her grandfather, it just reminded me of how old I'd been feeling lately.

"Well Luc, Nicole and I have to be going. You'll be contacted by my assistant Tilly soon. She'll work with you to set a date for the CAsLog crew and I to interview you," I said as Nicole and I moved toward the front door.

Luc looked directly at Maggie and said "Can Maggie be there too? I'd feel a lot more comfortable."

Nicole turned and gave me a sort-of 'you better get this one right' look.

"Why yes, of course she can, assuming we can find a day and time that works for all of us … and this pandemic thing doesn't end up causing us to cancel everything."

Nicole gave everyone her best eyes smile and said, "I'm sure it will work out fine." And with that we said our good-byes and headed out the front door.

We had barely got to the car when Maggie came running out of the house.

"Can I get a ride with you guys? I've got a therapy session that starts shortly, my car is in the shop, and Luc has got to change an air conditioner filter in one of the other houses."

"Certainly," said Nicole. "James won't mind sitting in the back. He hasn't fully recovered from his encounter with Luc's metal hurricane yet."

"Oh, I'm sorry," Maggie said as she flinched and looked anxious. "Luc feels terrible about what happened."

"I'll be fine. I'd like to know more about the Art Therapy program anyway, so you can fill me in on the way."

We all got into the car and Nicole drove toward Wilshire.

"So, Maggie what aspects of the program do you think I should know about?"

"Well to begin with, did you know doctor's prescribing arts activities to trauma patients has led to a dramatic fall in hospital re-admissions and saved the health industry a ton of money?"

"Uh, no I didn't."

"Yep, the arts can help people take responsibility for their own health and wellbeing in ways that are crucial to the health of the nation," she said with obvious gratification.

"The nation, how so?"

"Without being cynical, when it comes to working with former solders, this program isn't window dressing. Patients with a wide range of conditions, from chronic pain to deep depression benefit greatly from an eight-week course involving drawing, painting, poetry, ceramics and even mosaic."

"Wow, I'm impressed by the breadth of the program. Do you teach each of those subjects and did Luc learn all of them?" I asked. "And how does the program save the hospital money?"

"A cost-benefit analysis showed a 35% drop in second doctor consultation rates and a 27% reduction in additional hospital admissions." Maggie's eyes were beaming. "Plus, as much as 86% of patients completing the program reported a lessening of their symptoms and improved sleep."

"That is impressive," I said, "And was Luc in that group?"

"Sorry, I can't answer that. Patient confidentiality. You know," Maggie said.

"I've read making and consuming art lifts one spirits and helps to keep people sane. Art, like science and religion, helps us make meaning from our lives, and to make meaning is to make us feel better," said Nicole. "At least, that's what it said in an article in Vanity Fair, I think it was Vanity Fair. Any way I sure enjoy owning art and having my own artist right at home with me is great."

Nicole was actually blushing, the top of her ears had turned red.

"Thank you and I love you too," I said. "Now, getting back to Luc. While I understand that you can't give me specifics about why he needed therapy, can you tell me something to help me to understand why he creates such divergent art? I mean the stretch from very giant whirly-gigs constructed from used washing machine and refrigerators to using small brushes of oil paint on canvas to render very humanistic portraits is a challenging to grasp.

"Have you considered to him the expanse is not so great? Perhaps they're one and the same and creating one allows him to create the other."

"Well, CAsLog viewers certainly don't need to know everything about an artist to appreciate their output—whether they abuse drugs or drink to access; or who they sleep with or vote for—but their inquisitiveness for such details is understandable" I said.

"How do they feel about so-called outsider art? I mean art made by those distant from the ordained art world?" Maggie said with an edge to her voice as she turned to look at me.

"That's an even thornier issue and can present difficult choices to make," I said. "Like which details are relevant, rather than just salacious? And finding the dividing line between honest clarification and illumination can be tedious for the viewer to sit through. Keep in mind most of our Logs are only 15 to 20 minutes long."

"Why did you bring this up? Do you think Luc is an outsider artist? I mean I read his resume and as I recall he attended a college in

Tennessee before joining the army," said Nicole as she neared the VA hospital.

"Oh, art's relationship to mental health as always interested me. Plus, I just feel each artist's situation is unique, and should be approached as such. I don't mean to make you guys uncomfortable," Maggie said. "And by-the-way, Luc taught himself to paint and developed his own affinity for portraits."

"He developed that style on his own, the impasto brushwork, the strong chiaroscuro," I said. "You didn't teach him any of it?"

"That's right," she replied. "He faced the anxiety and all the insecurities on his own. I don't know why he said I helped him."

"Perhaps he just doesn't want to be thought of or labeled as self-taught," said Nicole. "Besides wouldn't creating new work help him to transcend his fears and push him to become even better?"

Maggie didn't answer and neither did I. Nicole drove to a stop in front of the main VA administration building.

"This is good, I'll get out here. Thanks for the ride. Bye." said Maggie as she slid out of the car and ran across the lawn toward another building.

"You know, at no time did Nellie and I ever think Luc has a mental health issue or that he is an outsider artist," said Nicole as she continued driving west on Wilshire Blvd.

"Yea, qualifiers can have a strong effect on all of us," I said as I relaxed in the back seat. "You said he works as an Orderly at the hospital. Are you sure he isn't a patient?"

"Why? Do you think he shows signs of schizophrenia or bipolar disorder or something?"

"No, but I'll have to know before I can make a CAsLog about him. I mean making a case for the artistic merit of his painting and sculpture could place me in a difficult position," I said. "I have to be careful about what salient details are relevant. Especially if I'm going to imply his artwork is exceptional. The whole thing could get complex.

"Oh, come on. He's a war veteran. Cut him some slack? Besides revealing the full range of influence's he has had would be very thought provoking."

I made myself a mental note for this was a side of Nicole I'd never seen before and I had no idea she had such strong feelings for Vets.

"Hey, I could grow to love his. It's downright relaxing being driven around in a fine car by a beautiful lady," I said.

Nicole continued west on Wilshire Blvd. toward Santa Monica while I enjoyed the scenery. As we drove past a section of the National Veterans Cemetery, I recalled something I read recently.

"Did you know most suicides happen in late spring and early summer," I said.

"Geez James are you trying to scare me to death," said Nicole as she drove the car to the side of the road and stopped. "If you're that depressed, please tell me why."

"Oh, no, no, I was just thinking I don't have any feelings like that so I must not be crazy or even disturbed, cause I'm making it through spring just fine despite enduring two car crashes and having a metal whirling dervish fall on me. I'm sorry I didn't mean to frighten you."

"Don't do that again," said Nicole. "We need a degree of normalcy in our lives right now so if anything is ever bothering you, please talk to me. Don't let it stew inside you. OK?"

"I will, I will, although you know there are times when I feel like I want to leave myself behind. To be in a different place, with new scenery, new people. You must feel that way once-in-a while, uh?"

Nicole started driving again, but kept one eye on me in the rear-view mirror.

"I like to think of myself as a self-reliant woman," said Nicole with one eye on the road and the other still focused on me. "All though occasionally I feel like I'd like to be an alley cat."

"Wow, maybe we should get you a costume and you can hide under the furniture and I'll come looking for you … here pussy,

pussy," I said with a grin as wide as Wilshire Blvd. "And if I'm successful finding you, I promise I won't go looking for myself."

She smiled and winked at me in the mirror.

"You know, alley cat seems more like Merra's style than yours," I said with instant regret. "You're more like a soft kitten to hold, cuddle and caress."

She stepped on the gas causing me to lurch back in the seat and my ribs gave me a sharp bite.

"One of those portraits had something in it that was not in any of the others, did you notice?" I asked in hopes of changing the topic.

"Uhm, no, not that I recall," said Nicole. "Which one?"

"Luc's," I replied.

"He put something in his own self-portrait, but not in any of the others? What?"

"A fly," I said.

"Are you kidding? Do you mean a real fly or a painted one?" Nicole said.

"A very good trompe-l'oeil one," I said.

"Really, that is intriguing," she said. "I wonder why?"

"Well, when seeing one in a portrait, serious Art History buffs instantly recall in medieval painting and in a lot of Renaissance ones too, a fly is painted on Jesus Christ's crucified body as a symbol of redemption, because a fly represented sin and Jesus was without sin," I said.

"And so," said Nicole with a tilt to her head. "a fly painted on a layman signified sin without redemption."

"Right, which meant the person was going to hell," I said.

"I see and you really think Luc knows that history? Hey, are you saying I'm not a true Art History buff?"

"Oh, no, no I just meant maybe someone, like say Maggie explained it to him."

"Well, whether she told him or he read it in a book, doesn't matter, the real point is he probably knows the significance of it or he wouldn't have put it there. By-the-way, where in the painting is it located exactly?"

"On his left shoulder," I replied. "And it took some real skill to paint it so realistic looking."

"I wonder why he feels he is going to hell," noted Nicole as she slowed down in the heavy mid-day traffic bogging us down.

As we approached the next main intersection it became apparent why traffic was crawling at a snail's pace.

"There's the problem," said Nicole. "That hot shot in the red convertible has rear ended that Range Rover and their both just standing there shouting at each other."

"Maybe if you move into the left lane," I suggested.

"Screw that I'm going down to Pico instead," she said.

She made a quick U-turn then an even faster right and headed toward Pico.

"Hey let's not create another reason for the car insurance company to up our rates again, OK?" I said. "Speaking of insurance do you know, off the top of your head, what the total value of your art collection is?"

"Well, I can tell you this much, the insurance premium went up after I got full ownership," Nicole replied with a hiss of irritation in her voice. "Damn brokers couldn't give me any reason for the increase either. Most likely it's just because I'm a woman."

"Did they make you get it re-appraised when you took ownership," I said.

"They tried to, but I told them to just keep everything at the same level it's been at for the past seven years."

"Why did you do that?"

"Because there were just too many things unsettled at the time. You know, after the divorce it took some time to get my alimony checks flowing, get the beach house and other things into my name so I didn't want to spend a big pot of money for a new appraisal. Especially since Patterson left on his business trip to China without completing the transfer of my share of all the stocks and bonds. Why are you interested? Do you need money for something?"

"Oh, no, no, I'm was just thinking about ideas for the special summer CAsLog that's all."

"Tell me again who the artist is you decided to use," she said.

"Snookz Jefferies."

"Wow, you finally got him to agree to be in a CAsLog. Congratulations."

"Mmm, thanks, but the credit really goes to Terratan Landchilde. He's the one who convinced Snookz."

"Did you tell Liz yet?"

"Uh, no I didn't, not yet anyway. Did you know there's a growing number of lenders willing to put up cash against high-quality art collections? The art-lending market has expanded to an estimated $20 billion of loans outstanding in the U.S. alone."

"Wow, that's going to be a very different CAsLog episode for sure," she said. "Given how murky the art market is right now and how often I've heard collectors talk about leveraging their collections against business deals, you might upset some touchy nerves around town. Especially now when business is coming to a complete stand-still."

"Yea, you could be right," I said as Ninja images flashed before my eyes. "Opting to leverage in order to gain liquidity for other investments and to buy more art is definitely the dark side of the art community and with banks stopping everything now could cause some to panic."

CHAPTER 8

The guitar solo from *If I Had A Harem* by Prince glided me out of my slumber as I laid snuggled up against Nicole in our comfy warm bed.

"Please answer that, Blues in the morning is just not my preferred way to greet a new day," said Nicole as she handed me my cell and pulled the pillow tightly around her head while rolling away from me.

"It's reveille, a rally cry, a, uh, oh, hello Cisco, how are you this fine morning?"

"At least I'm out and about enjoying the sand and surf which is more than I can say for you."

"What … uh, where are you?"

"Enjoying the view from your deck."

As I jumped up and slipped on my shirt and pants, I was hoping he wasn't referring to Merra. "View, is there something special in sight?"

"Do you mean besides the clear blue sky, serene waves, and pristine sand or are you only referring to the red head in the polka-dot bikini?"

"Damn, uh, uh, I'll be right down."

"What's up?" mumbled Nicole from beneath her shadowed pillow headdress.

"Oh, nothing, it's just Cisco outside. I'll go down and see what he wants. You go back to sleep."

Duie was dancing about feverishly waiting for me at the foot of the stairs. I rushed down while striving to zip up my pants and get my hair off my face at the same time. I planned to slide the door open slowly, but Duie knocked it flying as he charged past me and Cisco, heading straight for Shotala.

"Hey Cis, good to see you man. Something happening?"

"You really are a lucky SOB ending up in a great place like this, with a fine lady in your bed and all this beautiful natural scenery right outside."

He was smiling like a Cheshire cat as he watched Merra strutting her stuff in an ostentatious manner while heading toward the volley ball court and trying to coax Shotala to follow her. When she turned to face Cisco and I, she bent over a bit and adjusted her breast and the tie strings on the top of her scanty, florescent lime green, bikini with strategically placed black polka-dots.

Cisco lifted his shades, "It's going to be a hot one on the sand today, hey buddy"

"Yea, let's walk into the breeze coming from the pier," I suggested. "We both need cooling off."

Merra smiled, put on her mask, waved and turned south as both dogs followed her. Cisco watched her for a moment, adjusted his shades again and spoke with a shrewd smile as we faced into the morning breeze.

"Look unless Luke Blondie or whatever his name is does something illegal in Santa Monica I can't investigate him or the art accident at the Brentwood garden tour, but I can look into the illegally imported Roadster. The dealership is well within my jurisdiction. Do you think it's worth doing or not?"

"Probably not, however, don't you have some good contacts in the County Sheriff's Malibu office?"

"Yea, they handle enforcement services for most of the area along the coast. Why?"

"I just can't figure any reason why someone at the car dealership would deliberately have sabotaged the Roadster just before I bought it. They didn't really have an opportunity to do that before I drove it away."

"Ok, so when would some body have had an opportunity?"

"At Nells during my talk and maybe when Nicole went to the deli while I was at Kirill's Malibu beach house. I doubt anyone would have touched the car at Nells because I left Duie sitting in the front seat and there were security personal and parking attendants everywhere."

"Ah, I see, so you want me to have the Sheriff's office check if there were any parking lot surveillance cameras at the market right."

"Yep, it's a long shot, but we know for sure there weren't any on at Nell's."

"Ok, I'll contact the Sheriff's Lost Hills office. What are you going to be doing," Cisco said as he turned and gazed back down the beach toward the volleyball court.

"Well, first things first, I have to go find Duie."

"Sure, you do, just don't get lost, I mean I wouldn't want you to get disorientated by staring at spots before your eyes or anything. Especially big, black spots floating in lime green."

He smirked a bit and I shrugged while scrutinizing the beach trying to spot Duie just as Merra spiked a ball hard at her opponent who swiftly dove into the sand. The whole image made me flash again on the falling metal wonder.

"Hey, by-the-way, I was told someone altered the label on the whirly-gig by writing *In-coming* across *Untitled*. Do you think it's worth having it checked for fingerprints?"

"I doubt it," he replied. "You're beginning to sound a little paranoid and anyway why are so many artworks called *Untitled*?"

"Yep, lots of artists don't like to title their works." I'm always amazed at how Cisco's interest in art oozes out of him at the oddest times. "Even Picasso insisted on no titles preferring to let the art speak for itself."

"Sure, I get it, art is a visual language in itself. But, having so many thousands of works all labeled *Untitled* isn't practical. In fact, it's got to be a numerological nightmare," he said.

"I've always felt titles provide one more opportunity to communicate directly with the viewer and help them in understanding and appreciating the work. Of course, historically artworks were not titled," I said.

"Really, that explains a lot about history," he replied while straining to get a better look at Merra and her friend bounce the volley ball and themselves back and forth.

"Yep, it wasn't until artworks were sold or left their place of origin titles were necessitated. Most works depicted familiar stories from the bible or popular myths which everyone knew. A title would have been considered redundant," I said. "Titling started with museums and commercial galleries. It made it easier to keep track of things."

Cisco's gestures implied he was genuinely interested in the altered label, but made me wonder why. "Should I see if Nicole can find the label so you can check it out," I said.

"Ah, let me think about it," he said.

"You know it was Conceptual artist Felix Gonzalez-Torres who started using titles to really help the viewer."

"Like what," he asked.

"Oh, they were always emotionally charged titles, like *Death by Gun* and of course the art was completely abstract," I said with a chuckle.

"A Conceptual Latino, mmm," he said with a grin. "Speaking of conceptual I've got to stop ogling the scenery around here and check in with the Captain, or my job will just be an abstraction."

"Ok, well keep in mind Duie's namesake, Marcel, famously said a "title is an invisible color that wiggles its way into resistant artworks or something like that," I said.

"Right another fancy dodo chess-move," he said with a laugh.

Cisco headed back toward the house then turned onto the path that passes between Nicole's house and Merra's and leads to the street where his car was parked. I took a long look toward the

Volleyball Courts, but couldn't see Duie, Shotala or Merra anywhere in sight. I decided there was no getting around it, I'd have to walk down there to find my love hungry mutt and once again evade Merra's charms.

I hadn't gone too far past the house, when Nicole spoke from the terrace deck.

"Where are you going?"

"To find Duie. He took off after Shotala. I'll be right back."

"No need, they're both up here."

As my head whipped around way too quickly and the sun glared directly into my eyes, I squinted to discern there were two women standing side-by-side on the terrace. Their facial expressions weren't evident, but something in their demeanors made me believe everything was alright even though I suspected the other woman was Merra. I rushed inside not completely sure whether to panic or not.

By the time I was inside, Nicole and Merra were coming down the stairs heading straight toward me. Merra's bikini was stunning and Nicole's synthetic one with translucent multi colored daisys was extremely rousing and uplifting.

"We're going out to soak-up some rays," said Nicole. "You my dear have to phone Terratan Landchilde."

"Why, what do you mean?"

"He phoned in somewhat of a fluster and wants you to call him back right now."

"He didn't say what it concerned?"

"Something about Snookz somebody," said Merra.

"How do you know that?"

"I answered the phone while Nicole was dressing, that's how."

"Right. OK, I'll phone him. Ahm, you ladies are going to stay on the beach, right?"

"Maybe, maybe not. We'll see."

I was feeling a little piqued and irritated at the same time. Obviously, once again Snookz was going to do something to screw-up my CAsLog plans plus he's causing me to miss out on enjoying the company of two lovelies.

As I reached for my cell it went off with a Susan Tedeschi blues number which I always enjoy and wanted to listen to far more than answering the call, but I could see it was Terratan again, so I answered. He told me Snookz was leaving for an extended stay in Cape Cod because of the pandemic. Which meant if he was going to be on CAsLog the shoot would have to take place almost immediately.

As I pondered the dilemma, I felt my internal frustration meter rising, but the sight of Nicole and Merra rubbing sun tan lotion all over themselves generated a broad smile across my fretting face. At the zenith of my grin the cell went off again. This time with Joe Bonamassa and Beth Hart's *Close To My Fire* which was even more fitting to the morning and since it was Cornish Tweed this time I felt I could spare a moment to enjoy the sounds and sights of my small part of the world. There's something irresistible about watching beautiful women caress themselves with smooth creamy lotion. It is down-right hypnotic.

I'm not sure how much time elapsed before I contacted Cornish, but when I came out of my trance the ladies were now rubbing lotion on each-others backs and Cornish's voice was screeching from my cell. When I finally said hello, I was pleasantly surprised to hear him tell me he had completed his evaluation of the Snookz paintings so I let Terratan know and set up a time for the three of us to meet. I then sauntered out to join the ladies in the morning sun.

Best to be casual I said to myself. "So where are Duie and Shotala?"

"She's up on the terrace and he's in your studio. They need to stay apart for a few days and not get too heated up. Understand?"

"Ah, right, got it."

"You look as though you need to cool down a bit too. Was there a problem with Terratan?"

"No, not with him. It's Snookz again."

"Oh, what has he done now," said Nicole. "He's not backing out of doing the shoot is he?"

"Not if I can help it," I said as I stepped in front of the chaise lounges to better see both of their faces.

"Hey, you're blocking our sun."

"Oops, sorry I wanted to see your lovely smiles."

"Yea, sure we believe that's what you were looking at."

I pulled a chair to one side and sat down. The view wasn't as good, but still well worth a gander.

"Is there anything I can do for you two, perhaps a cold drink?"

"Not right now, we're fine," said Nicole with a sweet smile.

"I must say it's good to see the two of you relaxed and not skirmishing. Did you sign a peace treaty or something?"

They looked at each other and spoke simultaneously, "yes we did."

"Well, it's really Duie's fault. He seems to like us both and he obviously loves you," said Merra. "So, while you were talking to your friend Cisco, we had a heart to heart too."

"Besides talk between long time pals is curative and always the best kind of therapy," replied Nicole. "Friendship is like art. It gives value to existence. You agree with that, don't you?"

"Mmm, maybe, but are you sure Shotala didn't have something to do with Duie's joyous behavior?"

Merra smiled seductively while titling her head down so I could see her eyes behind her sun glasses. "Under the circumstance I can understand why you would say that, James. But if I've learned anything about friendship in the past few years, it's to hang in there, stay connected and don't walk out because a close friend is a large part of the super glue that holds one's life and convictions together. Next to full-on love it's the most powerful elixir in the world."

Nicole sat up quickly, snapped her sun glasses off and aimed a sharp stare directly at me. "Is there something going on between you two that I should be aware of?"

"Not really," said Merra. "I teased James a little, you know, just as a test to see how committed he was to your relationship. He passed with flying colors."

"Oh, so I'm some kind of guinea pig," I said without too much thought or concern. "Well, you ladies enjoy your day. I've got better things to do with my time than to sit around here chitchatting."

I bolted off the deck, walked straight through the house to the garage and drove the Beamer away without even looking back. I could feel my temples throbbing so it took a couple of miles or more before my blood pressure eased up.

"Not one of your better decisions James," I said out loud just to judge how high my frustration level was.

As I vented, to my surprise I felt wet licking behind my right ear and when I looked in the rear-view mirror Duie was smiling back at me.

"Hello pal, it's good to see you too. I think I may have made a fool of myself though. Too bad you missed it."

Duie gave my ear a few more swipes with his tongue then scampered over the front passenger's seat headrest, took his stance as point guard and stared straight ahead. "What do you say we stop by Palisades Park for a while before going to this damn meeting? You'd like that wouldn't you boy?"

Duie's tale wagged as he put his front paws on the dash then stretched his face forward with a look of determination. His understanding of the moment was spot on.

"Hey, we're not in the Roadster so there isn't going to be any wind in your face?"

He turned to look at me and tilted his head as to say, "What?"

Palisades Park was just what Duie and I needed. We sat on our favorite bench and watched an endless, but much smaller than normal, parade of humanity pass-by. Young, old, heathy, infirm, happy, melancholy, prosperous, pitiable and in all shapes, sizes and colors. Duie greeted each who approached him with a friendly wag and a gentle sniff. He made no assumptions about their motives or character. Perhaps that was because his world is safe, pleasant and maybe even serene. He had no reason to question anything. I however, felt an over active need to question everything in my life. Including why should I care about the valuation of a few Snookz Jefferies paintings? My ribs and knees hurt. My head throbbed and the bullet scars scattered about my body all wrenched in a way I didn't like, but watching the Palm trees sway in the morning breeze brought my face to a full-on smile even though it was completely hidden behind my black mask.

"Hey, that crow seems to know you. I think he's talking to you," said an old woman sitting at the far end of the bench. "You must come here often."

"Yea, I guess I do. A couple of times a week anyway," I replied.

"Well, that bird knows you. Do you feed him?"

"Oh, I sometimes have walnuts or almonds in my pocket and I throw him a few," I said. "He has intelligent eyes and always looks alert. I like the way he's watchful and doesn't fly off. Even Duie likes him," I said as I petted Duie who was keeping an eye on every move the bird made.

"So, he doesn't scare you?" she said.

"No, why would I be frightened of a bird?"

"Well, they can be intimidating, especially the big ones like him," she said. "They get a lot of bad press."

"Did you ever consider it might be a female?" I proffered.

"Oh, that's a nice thought. Isn't it? Yes, she could even be a mother," she said with a twinkle in her eyes. "She probably likes you because you've been nice to her."

"Sometimes when I walk out onto my deck at home, there is one perched nearby and I often wonder if it's the same bird," I said.

"Have you tried giving it some nuts?"

"That's a thought. I should try that," I said.

"I read once that crows can differentiate between human faces. That means they know who you are, so to speak. Maybe she follows you home," she said. "Do you walk or drive home?"

"I prefer to walk," I said. "But I usually look at people, not at birds."

"Well, they can tell the difference between your face and your neighbor's. And even the difference between your face and your wife. And they don't just remember your features, they assign you a specific identity." Her smile deepened the pleats and creases of her elderly face.

"I'm not married, but I do live with a woman. The former Mrs. Patterson Volkov," I said.

"Mmm, well ask her if she's ever noticed a crow hanging around," she said.

"I will, in fact, there are several things I should ask her," I said as I picked up Duie and started toward the car. "Nice talking with you. Take care of yourself and start wearing a mask."

***

Tweed's lab and office are located in San Marino near the Huntington Library and Cal Tech so I took the 10 to the Del Mar Ave. exit and headed north. I was the last one to arrive and when I entered the oddly shaped industrial looking building, I found Tweed and Terratan studying and talking about the Jefferies paintings standing on several tables in a rather small non-descript space.

I stepped between them and gave the paintings a once over before speaking.

"Good morning gentlemen. If we accept, for the moment, these are all genuine Snookz Jefferies paintings, is there anything else about them or associated with them that increases their value?"

Tweed squished his face and shook his head in total disbelieve at what he was hearing. "Absolutely, several things in fact."

Landchilde smiled broadly as a faint blush surfaced beneath his pale, mature cheeks. "Figurative art has been popular for centuries and in spite of the domination of abstraction during the past century, especially now with the advent of world-wide NFT algorithm fever generating an onslaught of geometric abstractions, paintings of figures in a landscape settings have garnered increased market performance for a solid quarter century now."

"Yea, it's a renaissance of sorts. Take a look at this data," Tweed said as he handed me a couple of printed charts from a pocket sleeve in the report he was holding. "Since the beginning of this century there's been a major shift back towards representational art."

The data clearly showed there had been a dramatic increase in the selling of figurative art at auctions internationally.

"Well, I guess the accolades these artists have been receiving in the art press is certainly being echoed in the marketplace," I said. "According to this there's been a little fluctuation, but their value has been essentially consistent for over twenty years now. That's impressive."

Landchilde cleared his throat and adjusted his bright peach colored neck-tie. "The big-ticket figurative paintings, those selling for prices in excess of a million, are in real demand and there's no sign of a devaluation on the horizon, suggesting demand is on pace with supply."

Reaching for a black folder, Tweed stepped forward and looked back and forth at us both. "The overall sales figures show a few big names are dominating the figurative art auction block and Jefferies is one of them, but…"

He let it hang there as he decided to hand the folder to me. "But what," I said.

"Oh, I'm never comfortable speculating. It's just, I feel the only thing keeping his prices high is the low volume of work he makes available but, that's just a guess. I don't really know whether it's something he consciously does or not."

"It would be hard for him to control the number of his paintings which might come up for auction, but he certainly can control the amount of new works he makes available through his dealers and privately. I wouldn't say he has a prolific output or a significant presence of his major works on the primary market—compared to others in particular and that might account for the higher average prices his works command. His paintings routinely fetch well into the mid-to upper six figures at the major art fairs," I said as I glanced through the folder which was the report, I'd hired Tweed to write.

I handed the report to Landchilde and turned back toward Tweed. "So, without taking time to read the full report now, what are your major conclusions about the authenticity of the works?"

Tweed took a few steps back and forth in front of the paintings and nodded his head in a gesture of acquiescence as he spoke. "They're all originals, but the three large ones are copies."

I felt a tweak in my side as I inhaled deeply. "What? Are you saying Jefferies copied his own work?"

Landchilde chuckled as he folded the report open to a page near the end and handed it to me. "Yes, he did. He sold the first versions quickly for very little money. He was desperate and after the good reviews started rolling in, he realized how foolish he'd been so he made the second versions and sold them quietly at much higher prices. Not uncommon, lots of artists have done so."

"Wow, that will make for a very captivating CAsLog segment," I said.

"Maybe, but at the moment we don't know if Krill is aware he owns copies," said Landchilde.

Tweed's nervousness was beginning to bother me. "How did you determine they are copies? Is there something different about the paint he used or the canvas?"

"No, I found them while doing research online. Some enterprising fan of his has posted a copy of his entire catalogue raisonné and they're in it.

A catalogue raisonné is a comprehensive, annotated listing of all the known artworks by an artist and each work is described in such a way that it may be reliably identified by third parties.

"It takes years to complete a catalogue raisonné, isn't Jefferies a little young to have generated enough works to merit the cost of producing one? Who paid for it," I said with too much huff. "I mean come on it took over 11 years to complete the Robert Motherwell catalogue."

"Yes, that's right. But keep in mind it was paid for by the foundation he established," replied Landchilde.

"And Jefferies' catalogue was also paid for by a foundation," said Tweed. "The Snookz Family Foundation and Charitable Trust to be exact."

"Who the hell are they?"

"Well, they usually fund think-tank stuff so most of the contributions they receive come from political types," said Tweed.

"Geez, this quagmire is getting hairy."

Tweed gave out with a Cheshire cat smile and said "Yeah, that's what I felt too so I dug a little deeper, no pun intended, and looked into who's on their board."

"And?"

"And it seems the board is made up of several very conservative Wall Street investors who just happen to be Jefferies family members and in-laws."

"Ha uh ... and they sell his works to very private investors, hence the need for a catalogue raisonné they can control," said Landchilde.

"I believe so," added Tweed.

Cornish's fiddling with the ball point pen in his hand, flipping it in the air as if he expected it to magically turn into something else, was beginning to irritate me and the wary look on his face was doubly unsettling.

"Cornish you seem a little leery. Is there something more bothering you?"

The moment those words left my mouth, Terratan's relaxed posture immediately stiffened and Cornish let the pen fall to the floor following it with his eyes as if they could incinerate it.

Terratan walked over and put his hand on Cornish's shoulder and smiled as he spoke.

"You're with friends now lad. If you have doubts about something or if you're just not sure, it's better to bring whatever it is forward. Doing so later will be far worse for everyone."

"Well, it's a very small thing and I, um, I could be wrong. You know, maybe I'm being picky," he said as he continued staring at the floor.

"Hey, if it turns out to be nothing you've already convinced us you are man enough to accept responsibility for your judgements. Now tell us what's needling you," I said.

"I didn't put it in my report because it could be it's just a quirk of mine, it really doesn't mean anything," he replied.

"Right, we got that. Now what is it," I said.

"When it comes to testing paint to see if it is consistent with what is known to have been used by an artist, I was trained to take only a minute portion," he said.

"OK and?"

"And one of these paintings shows signs of having had much larger amounts taken from it," Cornish said as he looked up through the tops of his eyes and pointed to one of the paintings.

"So why would someone take more than they need?" asked Terratan. "And were you able to determine how long ago it was done?"

"Well, that's the thing the possible answer to both of those questions could pose a problem," he said. "The samples were taken recently and the only reasons you would need so much is if you bungled the tests and/or you were trying to duplicate the paint," said Cornish.

The three of us nodded our heads as a chilly silence settled around us.

"But, I could be wrong. Maybe somebody was just sloppy," Cornish said. "Maybe the owner of the paintings or the shipping company accidently scrapped something over it."

"Yeah, that sounds like a possibility, but what is important is you brought what ever occurred to our attention," I said.

"And not putting it in the report was also the correct way to go," said Terratan. "James and I would, however, like you to write an amendment to the report listing the location and condition of the spots as well as your thoughts about what might have caused them."

A feeling of calm returned like warm sunlight coming out from behind a dark cloud and I'm sure it was visible in my general demeanor as I turned back toward the door. "Well gentlemen we've made an excellent start. Cornish, thank you for completing your report efficiently, comprehensively and in a timely manner. Terratan, again your guidance and wisdom have been sage. I owe you a great debt of gratitude.

"James stop, right there. You are not going anywhere until you explain what we are doing next," said Landchilde. "And why you seem so relieved."

"Yes, relieved. You are quite right, I am. Well, we now have some possible leverage over Snookz and a fuller, more precious story to tell for CAsLog."

Landchilde stood stiff backed and steely-eyed again. "OK, ok even though I don't care for the word 'leverage' and do understand you mean it in a positive way let's be clear we haven't discovered any crime here … right?"

Tweed was also stiff as a board. "And we're not talking about committing any crimes … are we?"

"You guys are true gems and I'm proud to know you both. Right, we haven't found any crimes and we're not going to commit any. At least not that I know of at the moment. Speaking of which, where do you keep these paintings at night. Surely you don't leave them in this unsecured lab office."

"I have a very secure walk-in vault arrangement with the private tech firm next door," said Tweed. "Their projects are far more valuable than these bits of art. They even have a 24/7 armed guard service monitoring the building."

"Great. What do they make?"

"Whatever it is, it's very hush hush and requires top government security clearance," he replied. "I'm very grateful they allow me to use their x-ray fluorescence equipment plus infrared and reflectograph non-invasive stuff to study all the various strata, from surface paint films down to the canvas ground layer of each painting. Of course, I did the chemical analysis here."

Landchilde smiled at Cornish then stepped forward and shook my hand. "James for a moment there I was beginning the think we had lost you to the, what is it the kids say, to the dark side."

"No, no. I guess I've just been a little irritated lately," I said.

"Well, who wouldn't be with two car accidents and a near miss with an oversized whirly-gig."

"I know about the falling sculpture, but two car accidents. I'm surprised you're walking," said Tweed.

"So do we have a filming date set with Snookz yet?" asked Landchilde. "And do either of us need to be there?"

"The decision has been made. We're going to film you two at the station and edit your comments into the final screened version of the program. So, I'll be interviewing Snookz privately and in a quiet place away from people. This pandemic thing has frightened him and my crew. Oh, and each of us should wear a mask at our next meeting."

"I told Tilly to move the filming date forward as much as possible, but I'm not sure if she has had any luck coordinating with his assistant. By-the-way, Did Kirill mention what he needs the loan funds for," I asked.

"He made an off-hand remark about doing more renovations to his house, but I sensed he wasn't interested in discussing it further."

I looked out the office window at the building next door and could easily see their security cameras, guarded gate, and barred windows.

"This looks like a rather expensive complex for a newborn business such as yours to be in," I said to Cornish. "Are you doing that well. I mean are there really so many clients here in need of your services?"

"You're right the rent is not cheap, but I have a guardian angel so to speak," Cornish replied. "Perhaps sponsor would be a better term for it."

"And who is he, pray tell?" said Terratan.

"My uncle. He and his partner own the tech firm next door and the entire complex," said Cornish. "He is my mother's brother so he gives me a good deal on the rent and makes it possible for me to store the paintings in their lab vault."

"Keeping it in the family," said Terratan. "That's wise thinking my lad."

"Well, I really wanted to be closer to the art community on the west side, but rent there is even crazier, plus I wouldn't have a vault available to me," he said.

I bumped elbows with both men and let them know I would keep in touch concerning shipping the paintings back to Maytor Kirill. When I got outside, Duie was right where I had told him to stay on the small strip of lawn in front of the car. I can always rely on him to listen when I speak. A very gratifying feeling.

CHAPTER 9

When the crew and I arrived at Meditation Park no one was around except a bearded fellow polishing a sleek new Prussian Blue Jaguar. Tilly studied the lean looking man for a moment then turned to me, with consternation engraved across her forehead.

"Well, are you going to speak to him first or do you want me to?"

"Speak to who?"

"You mean you don't recognize him. Take a hard look, that man behind the face mask whiskers is Snookz Jefferies."

I felt as though the look of bewilderment on her face had just crash landed onto my mug. Rolling down the window I leaned out to get a closer look as the sound of a radio announcer barking something about a virtual soccer game emanated from the shiny car while the hirsute wonder continued casually buffing.

"Hey James, good to see you man. Want a cold one?"

The words were welcoming, but his tone sounded more like some Old Testament prophet and definitely reminded me of the Jefferies I knew. I held up one finger and said "just give us a minute or two," as he waved a bottle of beer.

Tilly looked more confused than ever. "I thought you said this guy could be difficult. How long has it been since you've talked with or even seen him?"

"You're right it's been a while. Just take the guys and the gear over by the picnic table near the pond and set up there. OK?"

"You're the boss."

Jefferies had arranged the time and place for this meeting through Landchilde and Tilly so when I thought about when I had last seen him, I realized it had been well over a year, but he only sported a small mustache then.

Tilly and the crew offloaded the gear from the van and headed toward the pond while I ambled toward Jefferies' new chariot. The F-type sports coupe is a pure Jaguar and in that deep blue color it looks like it could pounce on anything in its path.

"Nice looking wheels."

"Yea, it's a pulse-quickner that's for sure. This one is a supercharged 3-liter V6 that delivers 340 horses. Get in and we'll take her for a spin."

"Oh, no, no we've got to do the shoot while the light is good."

"You sure, it's got suede seats, rides on 18" wheels and delivers sheer exhilaration. It's super smooth. Gets to 60 in 5 seconds. Plus, thanks to Covid there isn't much traffic anymore."

I was beginning to feel as though I was back at the car lot on Wilshire, but the sales patter wasn't coming from as pretty a mouth or any mouth I could see.

"Let's take the beers over to the table under that tree near the pond," I suggested.

"Right straight to business. OK, James, but we're going to finish our beers before getting in front of the camera."

Snookz's jovialness was probably due to having imbibed several beers. The nearby trash bin was sparkling in the clear spring sunlight with empty bottles and the moment also revealed why he had always turned down my invitations to be on CAsLog. Under all the facial hair and odd-looking face shield his face was etched in fear, dread, anxiety and sheer panic. He was obviously terrified to be on camera and to have anything he might say be permanently recorded. Over the years, I've met several individuals like him, scared to death of being filmed.

He was noticeably physically fit, projected vigor from his towering 6' frame and had a youthful handsomeness to his bearing. That said, I was still a little surprised when we sat down and raised our beers in a gesture of mutual salute for his hand was trembling uncontrollable.

"Hey did you make that shield yourself?"

"No, one of my studio assistants did."

He threw his head back and took a long swig from the bottle. I gave Tilly and the crew a signal to start filming quietly - they did.

I quickly concluded I would record a voice over formal introduction after Snookz left and decided to keep our conversational candor warm without being too familiar so I set my transmitter mic on the table and positioned my notebook in front of it hoping he wouldn't notice.

"It's nice to be away from the hustle and bustle. You made a good choice in selecting this place for the interview. Do you come here often?"

"Yes, I enjoy driving away from the city and on through these hills and then pulling in here. It's a peaceful place. I often just sit and listen to the silence and occasional bird."

"Do you carry that ambience with you when you return to your studio and paint?"

"Not really. As you know my work involves depicting people. People playing mental and physical games with one another. Bird songs, soft shadows and gentle light would be out of place in my work."

"And what about the people who collect your work? What do they tell you about how they see it?

"There's a bag of worms for sure. Some are awestruck and enthralled by the suggestiveness of the tableaus, others savor the benevolence and altruism of the settings and then, of course, there's an entire group who only think about the investment they're making."

"Mmm, yes that third group are hard to pin down. What do you mean by investment?"

"They're hoping my work will go up in monetary value, the quicker the better according to them."

He took another long draw on the beer and smiled at Tilly who pretended to be checking her light meter. His attention then shifted to the camera and he noted it was on.

I quickly made a gesture to everyone and said "OK guys, is everything ready to go?"

"We're ready," said Tilly.

Snookz finished his beer and said "Should we set these bottles out of sight?"

"I'll take them," Tilly said as she quickly gathered them.

"Does having your art considered as an investment bother you?" I asked.

"Oh, I don't mean to make it into a manifesto, but it is after all my life's work and the thought behind each painting is the real value not the painting itself."

"Let's keep this casual and see where it goes," said Snookz.

"All right. I have no problem with that. Perhaps we could start with some basic questions keeping in mind we'll be able to edit later if need be."

Snookz looked uncomfortable as he adjusted his posture and pulled at his shirt collar. "Uh, just keep the questions direct and uncomplicated and we'll have no problems."

"OK, well let's start with why you chose to make copies of Saints of Sand & Surf from your very first solo exhibit."

Snookz sat straight up, entwined the fingers of both hands and stared at the sky before titling his head down and looking at me through the tops of his unblinking eyes. "Damn James. Landchilde assured me this was going to be about how values are set for my new paintings. Not a history lesson."

"We need a comparison to start with otherwise our viewers won't have any reference to go by," I said in a calming tone. "Plus, those three paintings are currently being offered as collateral for a loan, so their present-day value is very pertinent."

His exasperated expression rose quickly to the tops of his ears as he closed his right hand into a fist and began short-jabbing it into his left palm while grinding his teeth.

I was feeling concerned, but a Blue Jay landed on the nearby boulder and caused a reluctant smile to manifest at the corners of Snookz's eyes. "Those who do not want to imitate anything, produce nothing," he said. "That's a quote from the great master, Salvador Dalí."

I must admit, I was totally unprepared for a quote of that nature and by the expressions on the faces of the crew and Tilly, so where they. However, I learned long ago to embrace steam rather than try to contain it.

"Yes, Dali was certainly a genius when it came to appropriation and dare, I say, plagiarism of his own works," I said.

"You are of course familiar with Giorgio de Chirico's many copies of his early metaphysical paintings?" he said.

"Mmm, yes," I replied as I quickly scanned the recesses of my grey cells for any bits of related data. "I certainly recall they were highly sought after by collectors."

"Right and only the very best experts of the day could tell the difference between the earlier and later works," he said with what appeared to be a big grin of deep satisfaction. "He called those copies 'true fakes' and didn't see anything unethical about having made them himself. He valued the idea of each more than the individual paintings."

"In other words, you're saying you own the idea. Is that correct?"

"Absolutely. One of my old art professors once told me about a collector, from Texas as I recall, who bought several Picasso's just after the second war. The experts told him their provenance was sketchy, so the collector took all of them directly to France and delivered them to Picasso. When he asked him to take a close look at them, Picasso replied "I don't need to scrutinize them because they look like my work therefore, they are."

Snookz, smiling broadly, relaxed and leaned back to get a closer look at the Jay. "I think of it more as a form of conceptualism."

"I can see that, but do you believe such an approach increases the monetary value of the work?"

"Well, the copies, as you call them, are not forgeries. In fact, they aren't really copies either. They're simply gleaned from the first versions and have dozens of subtle alterations. They weren't made at one of China's notorious art villages by talented copyist and there's no 'Made in China' label on the back. They were painted and signed by me."

"That's true and with regard to their authenticity they have been validated by two independent experts," I said. "And yet, they were not appraised as of the same high value as the first versions. Why do you think that is?"

"Really, so do you mean to say they are here in L.A.? I thought they were in Jersey City," said Snookz.

"Yes, they are here. Owned by a somewhat reclusive collector."

Snookz took a deep breath and watched the Jay hop behind tall grass and disappear, but Tilly rustled her clip broad which returned his attention to the camera.

"Undoubtedly, the appraisers place a monetary value on being first. It's the old virgin thing or perhaps more like the Mona Lisa."

Tilly wheezed and struggled to clear her throat as she thumped the clipboard.

"The Mona Lisa? Leonardo da Vinci's Mona Lisa? That's a leap," I said.

"Not really. Leo made at least two versions and all the experts agree the second one is the best one."

"I'm looking forward to hearing what the owner of the first versions of Saints of Sand & Surf will have to say about that. I'm certain the owner of the second versions is going to be thrilled."

"Take a look at that Jay over there. He just gathered two seeds and ate one. Now he's hiding the other one. He'll come back for it another time. Do you think he will enjoy eating the second more than he did the first one?" said Snookz. "Do you think he even gave any thought to which one came off the bush first? I doubt it."

"Perhaps more importantly, will the second one still be palatable when he returns." I said.

"Exactly, the first versions of Saints of Sand & Surf have had a torrent of exposure. Everyone in the art world is familiar with those paintings. Everyone knows exactly how they taste artistically, but the second versions have never been exhibited and have never been scrutinized or reproduced in magazines or on line. The subtle detail changes within their overall smile, if you will, guarantee they will taste different than the first versions. If only because we are now different also."

"You know, in haute couture fashion, copying is now considered acceptable. Even the most quintessential designers do it. Most of them include at least one garment in their line-up that has appeared in another designer's collection first."

"Ah, no I wasn't aware of that," I said. "It certainly used to be the cardinal sin of fashion.

Major brands usually zealously guard their trademarks."

"According to social media, copying anything is no longer verboten. It's the coolest thing to do," Snookz said as he winked at Tilly.

"Well, I will admit social media does have a unique hold on contemporary discourse dislodging a great many gatekeepers and causing a complete re-evaluation of knockoffs in general," I said as I felt we were drifting off course.

"I've been thinking for some time now about creating something new from pieces of works I've held back over the years. I have a great many of them in my storage vault."

"Are you saying you would actually cut out a portion of one of your old paintings and glue into a new one?"

"Maybe, I like the idea of collaborating with my younger self. Sort of Jefferies on Jefferies."

With that declaration Snookz walked to his sparkling four wheeled steel animal and said "Being an artist is 24/7, there's no moment that you're not one. Oh, which reminds me, do you know any upper echelon collectors who specialize in works on paper?"

"Ah, off the top of my head I can't think of one. Why do you ask?"

"Oh, I've been thinking if we have to quarantine ourselves maybe now would be the time to make some etchings."

"Well, is paper at one with your nature? If it isn't I wouldn't advise spending time playing around with it," I replied.

"Yea, you're right. That's why I was thinking I'd make etchings at least that way I'd be able to use oil-based inks which is something I am at one with."

"What about scale? Everything I've seen from you is too large to be turned into an etching."

"Hey, you're right again. Thanks, Sketchy," he said as he set his mic on top of a small post, got into the Jaguar and rode off onto Sunset Blvd heading west toward the beach. "Good to talk. Stay healthy and take care of yourselves," he shouted out the window of the Jag.

"I can't wait to see how you're going to edit this and manage to insert Landchilde and Tweed's comments into a cohesive CAsLog segment," said Tilly.

"It's just the kind of challenge I live for, in fact, I'm thinking this segment deserves a full hour. What do you think?" I said.

"I think Liz will have something to say about that and I'll be surprised if she gives you 30 minutes."

"Hey, did the mic pick-up everything he said" I asked the sound man. "Including the stuff at the end?"

He looked at his gauges and gave me a thumbs-up.

"Great, that'll be helpful."

"Well let's start pulling the whole thing together here and now. I'll stand in front of the water fall and give a food-for-thought summary of where we are to date. Ok?"

Tilly and the crew shrugged their shoulders and headed for the indicated spot as I took a short walk around the grounds. I didn't get far.

"We're all set, but since there is too much stochasticity noise coming from the falls, you'll need to use the hand mic and hold it close to your mouth," said Tilly.

"Will do."

I took off my small transmitter mic, grabbed the hand mic, headed for my spot and took a few deep breaths before facing the camera.

"Like actors, authors and musicians, most artists have little control over who enjoys—or doesn't enjoy—their work. However, actors and musicians can sell multi-products such as downloads, CD's, books and tickets to performances. The visual arts work differently. Galleries typically sell unique one-of-a-kind paintings, drawings, sculptures, photographs to collectors and museums. This arrangement causes artists to be careful about their sales. In other words, they and the galleries who represent them feel collectors must meet certain financial and reputation standards, as well as have plans for exhibiting the artists' work. And though placing art has traditionally been the gallery director's responsibility, today a number of artists seek to exert greater control over their own legacies. For example, Abstract Expressionist painter Clyfford Still is the most famous artist to exercise this challenging practice. He handled most sales of his artwork himself without the aid of a gallery or agent. Today, Los Angeles based artist Snookz Jefferies actively seeks to influence how his paintings come to market and who gets to own them. Some would characterize him as adamant in wanting to sell only to collectors with close institutional ties.

That said, most artists' motivations, are more economic than ideological. They just want their work to go to those that like it and will care for it rather than treat it like a commodity.

On the other hand, artists whose works are in high demand like Snookz will set restrictions regarding who can collect their works based on their political views, the causes they are passionate about and even on personal grievances they may have with an institution or its sponsors. At the very least, these major artists are insisting on being consulted as to whom may buy their work.

So, is art a good investment? Well, it often outperforms other major asset categories like real estate and rare cars so one would assume most major investors would be throwing big bucks at this glamorous asset.

But, how does that correlate with what gallery directors and artists advise and is it true you should 'only buy art you love' not what you think might garner fantastic profits in a few years. That said, every season each of the top tier international auction houses offers at least one exceptional art collection, put together several decades ago for an insignificant sum, and now said to have gained enormous monetary asset appreciation. How does one determine the true value of art? Is it via researching the 100 Index in New York, Paris or Hong Kong stock exchanges? Or is there an invisible dark matter, only available to art community insiders and which has an enormous influence on the art market?"

The look of complete surprise on Tilly's and the crew's faces caused me to stop.

"Well, what do you think?" I said.

"Ah, with a little editing or perhaps some voice over we'll be able to use most of it," said Tilly. "Are we done now?"

"Oh, sure, you guys go on in. I'm going to stroll around for a while. It's very peaceful here. Plus, it's great to be outside and not needing to wear a mask."

"Maybe that's why it's call Mediation Park," said Tilly as she waved good bye.

As I headed up one of the garden paths I heard a motorcycle on Sunset Blvd., but I didn't bother to look back to see if it was a Ninja or not.

CHAPTER 10

"You seem preoccupied. Are you still reeling from your recent bout of mishaps or just musing about some painting," said Cisco as he walked over and sat down a few feet from me on the deck to watch the sunset.

"Just thinking about something Maggie Mayye said."

"Who's she?

"Luc Blondin's art therapist. She mentioned something about Luc needing to make both whirly-gigs and portraits. I can't seem to let go of that statement. There's something more to it than a direct observation."

"What's odd about it? I mean you make drawings, paintings and videos. Why can't he release his creative demon in more than one direction? Besides I recall you telling me once that crafting objects which only last for a finite period of time is an old tradition in art. Going back to that dodo group."

"Ha, ha ... you mean Dada. Yep, that's right. It's not a new idea, but I think it might run deeper in Luc's veins and demon might just be the right word for it. Especially the Dada credo about leaving little trace of its existence.

"OK, well I've never understood why they didn't document the stuff. I mean, according to you they struggled to come up with something they thought was meaningful then they just let it vanish. What's the sense in that?"

"Oh, oh, yes, yes, indeed. You know, Cis, sometimes you are justo en el blanco."

"What? What did I say? Hey and your Spanish is also right on target.

"When that damn whirling dervish knocked me over and covered me in shrapnel I heard a buzzing sound," I said.

"You didn't tell me that. Does that mean it had a motor in it?"

"Maybe, just maybe and it may have also been full of shell fragments."

"That would take gun powder to disperse. Did you smell any when it crashed?"

"Can't say I did and from what I saw of the resurrected sculpture he created from it's scraps, it won't do any good to have it tested. I mean the thing looks brand new now. But, I might be able to determine if he puts motors inside any of his sculptures."

"You plan on sneaking into his studio?'

"No, no. You know I don't break the law. That is, unless it's absolutely necessary."

"Que tan mentiroso."

"Hey, that hurts. The truth is sacred to me."

"OK, how are you going to determine if he uses motors and even if he does, what would that prove?" he said with complete satisfaction.

"When we do the CAsLog shoot I'll make certain part of it is done in his workshop and yard." I said with equal gratification. "And it matters because he claims to power his sculptures only via the wind.

"Hey, by-the-way, where is Duie? I'm surprised he isn't out here with you."

"Damn! I'll bet he's snuck-off with Shotala probably down at the palms and I'm suppose-to keep him away from her for a while. Know what I mean?" I said.

Cisco studied my expression for a moment and said, "Oh, yea, it's that time. I get it."

"Right. Let's walk, we can talk while I look for them," I said. "So, what did you want to see me about?'

"Well in a way, it's about Luc," he said with a shrug. "It involves the truck that knocked you into the culvert up in Coldwater Canyon."

Cisco's face was disconcerting at best as he bent down to pick up a small piece of sea shell.

"Oh no, it wasn't' Luc was it?"

"No, not him, but it was a Vet," said Cisco. "A few years younger, freshly back from the Middle East."

"Really, I'm sorry to hear it," I said. "So did you arrest him?"

"Yes, with the help of LAPD. He was caught driving the truck," he said. "Trying to help another Vet."

"What's going on? I've never done anything to a Vet or even said anything bad about them. Why are they targeting me?

"That's the point. They weren't targeting you. The whole thing was a real accident," he said as he pointed toward Duie at the palm trees. "The guy was rushing to get the truck back to the furniture store before it was reported stolen and he just made a bad move trying to pass you on a curve."

"That's all there is to it? Wow, what a relief," I said with a deep sense of internal release. "So, what happens now?"

"Well, you have a decision to make. Do you want to press charges or not?" he said.

"What kind of charge?"

"Reckless driving, leaving the scene of an accident and attempted murder are what the LAPD are proposing."

Before I could digest such a bad sounding pill, Duie came running to us wagging his tail like a helicopter which immediately made a series of war images flash before my eyes.

"No, definitely not," I said. "That's ridiculous. I mean come on the guys a Vet."

"I'm with you on this James. Let me handle it. I'll tell them you don't want to press any charges."

"Well, hold on a minute," I said. "Why did he steal the truck?"

"He was helping a fellow Vet move his family into a cheaper house cause the guy doesn't have a car and neither of them could afford to rent a truck," he said. "So, another buddy who works at the furniture store told them when the truck would be most likely free to appropriate. But he didn't think the boss was going to be back so early or something like that," he said as he rough-housed Duie a bit.

"Damn it, these guys can't get a break," I said.

"Look, if we can come up with something corrective or educative in nature, I can probably convince LAPD to drop the whole thing," he said as he looked up at the ferris-wheel on the empty pier swirling its colorful lights in front of the dark night sky.

"Alright, let's try this. Tell them I want the guy to successfully complete the art therapy program at the VA Hospital," I said. "You know, tell them I'm an artist and do the CAsLog TV thing. That should make the whole thing seem more acceptable to them."

"Maybe, but they'll still want him to sign something and they may expect you to be his sponsor," he said.

"Fine, fine, make it happen," I said. "I'm just happy to know the guy wasn't deliberately trying to run me off the road.

Cisco saluted and headed to his car. Duie and I sat and watched the empty Ferris-wheel twirling light show. I missed hearing the shrieking kids. Which made me think of Maggie Mayye and what her reaction might be when a couple more Vets show up for her program.

Before I could ponder the thought, John Fogarty's guitar riff from *Put A Spell On You*, slid out of my cell. The screen listed Terratan on the line. I answered with hello as he charged straight into speaking.

"You know James, this whole idea of yours to do a CAsLog about using art as collateral for a loan has made me be more attentive to some of the periphery activities of my current clients."

"So, I assume from that statement one of them said something off kilter."

"Well, I'm not sure if it is or perhaps, I'm just being a little too skeptical."

"OK, so tell me what it was and we'll talk through it," I replied.

"It's actually two things, from two different directions and they might be connected some-how. First there is the general feeling there's going to be a major economic shift coming soon especially if this pandemic thing actually grows world-wide."

"What's giving you such an idea?"

"The number of wealthy people I've encountered recently who are actively buying high end art and booking extended stays in luxury resorts."

"And what's unusual there?" I said.

"Most of what they're buying is unrelated to anything else in their collection," he said as he grumbled something about the lite-traffic he was driving in.

"Maybe they're just turning a corner and seeking a new direction," I said.

"Could be, but why are they in a rush? I mean, look these people usually take time before deciding to fork over six figures or more for a painting. Especially if it doesn't fit with everything else in their collection, and they have to sell large sections of their stock portfolio in order to get them. It's as though they feel a need to have the wealth in real assets. You know, diamonds, real estate, art."

"Well as you know art is seen as a value preserving asset," I said. "It isn't impacted by the risks one associates with the financial market."

"That's true it is a lower risk investment and when there is a recession it usually takes it less than half the time to recover than the S&P 500," he said as he cursed again about the car in front of him.

"Let's leave that for a moment. What is the other thing buggin' you?"

"I was asked if I know anything about some new works on paper Snookz is about to release," he said and finished what sounded like a drink. "Do you know anything about them?"

"In a way I do," I said. "At the end of the CAsLog shoot he mentioned he is thinking of making some prints, but I got the impression he hadn't fully committed himself to the idea. Hey, you are on the phone while drinking and driving. You better pull over and take a break before you end up in a culvert or jail."

"You're right James. I will. Talk to you tomorrow."

CHAPTER 11

"You promised so no more delays," said Nicole. "We're taking the Beemer and I'm driving."

It was a stunning morning, bright sun in a clear blue sky and I did agree we would take one day per week to get away from everything. No e-mail, no phones, no demanding deadlines, no nothing.

"OK, ok, what should I wear?"

"Put on your hiking shoes and a hat," Nicole yelped as she headed for the garage. "Oh, and bring a full canteen. I've got the snacks and Duie."

I put on my old boots, filled the canteen and found my straw hat. I was set, at least on the outside. On the inside my right knee was still troubling me, if I turned too abruptly, I'd trigger a needle-sharp pain in my lower left ribs and the concept of doing nothing for an entire day was short circuiting my brain. However, for loves sake I had a full smile on when I slid into my treasured 230i opposite my beloved Nicole.

She backed out of the garage and headed north on the 405 before I even finished thinking about everything I could be doing instead. She exited at Mulholland Drive and drove into the Santa Monica Mountains. The moment we got away from the freeway she turned on *Nocturnes* by Debussy.

"There, now you relax, enjoy the music and the scenery. I'll take care of the driving."

I reclined the seat a bit and laidback determined to think tranquil thoughts, but my mind locked onto Luc Blondin and wouldn't let go.

"You ever had any psychoanalysis," I said as carefully as I could without over powering Debussy's melodious tones. "Ah, what I mean is, have you ever paid someone to listen to your hopes and fears just to nudge you toward better personhood?"

"Well, I did go to an unlicensed healer to discuss chakras and cleanses once," Nicole said as she slowed the car down some. "There is no end of behaviorists and life coaches in this town. Do you feel you need one?"

Dubussy was followed by Gustav Mahler's dulcet *Symphony No. 4* and I have to admit I was feeling a bit soothed.

"Ah, no, no, I was thinking about Luc and wondering if Maggie gives all of her soldiers the same curriculum. You know, him wanting to have her present during the CAsLog shoot suggest he has more anxieties than meet the eye," I said.

"Yes, I do. Keep in mind therapeutic options are myriad. It's not one-size-fits-all. There are cognitive-behaviorists, nutrition coaches and of course that old standby psychedelic drug trips. If you've got a problem, there's always someone out there who will help you solve it."

"Yeah, that's true. There are even artist coaches, whose services are geared toward both professionals and hobbyists. Maybe I'm overthinking the whole thing."

"I'm sure Maggie presents artmaking as more of a process of self-discovery rather than a path to a lucrative career. And she strikes me as one who has a passion for helping vets become balanced human beings again."

"Maybe a little too much passion? Aren't there rules about her being personally involved with a patient?"

"Oh, come on James. Relax. Hey, we're here," she said as we passed over an old bridge and turned left into a parking area.

The sign read Peter Strauss Ranch and my mind flashed back on an old sculptor I'd met during my first year as an art student. He was talking about how this actor had worked out a deal to turn his home over to the Santa Monica Mountains National Recreation Area for cultural events.

"I've heard of this place. It has an amphitheater, a large round pool and hiking trails," I said. "And years ago, it had an annual outdoor sculpture invitational exhibition every summer."

"It looks quiet and lovely. Let's go to one of the picnic tables over there under those big oaks," said Nicole as she picked up her hiking bag and starting walking. Duie darted off toward the trees as well.

We sat in the shade, snacked a little and walked up the main trail to look at the views. It was refreshing and peaceful.

"What a great view and I've always enjoyed the smell of sage," I said as we reached a small overlook area with an aged handmade bench placed under a few grand old growth live oaks. "It's a little hazy, but the Poppies and Yucca are plentiful this year."

"Too bad the swimming pool hasn't been kept in good shape. I'd love a swim right now," Nicole said. "Did your friend tell you they made some of Ester Williams films in it?"

"No, he didn't. He did mention the place was originally called Lake Enchanto and there was a weekly radio dance show aired from the amphitheater during the 40s or 50s, I think. Did you notice the small creek we drove past near the parking lot?" I asked. "Maybe there's enough water in it to wade around and cool our feet."

"Ok, let's head there. Lake Enchanto, mmm, I like the name."

The hike down the return trail was much quicker than going up had been. We reached the creek in less than 20 minutes and started walking down stream. There were small pools of water here and there and just past an old, dilapidated retaining wall like-dam we discovered a nice spot with shade and a small sort-of swimming-hole area. Nicole wasted no time in removing her boots, jeans and blouse before walking right into it. I took off my socks and boots, rolled up my jeans to just above my knees and started toward a boulder large enough to sit on. The water was much colder than I had thought it would be which made me realize I should place my wallet with Nicole's clothing. When I finally reached the boulder, I was especially pleased I made it without slipping on any of the ultra-smooth rocks.

Standing in front of me in her panties and bra, Nicole sat down in water deep enough to wet her nipples and make her shiver and shake which was beautiful to watch.

"Are you happy we're together James?"

"Yes, very much so," I said while trying to maintain a hold on the boulder. "Are you, and what brought this on?"

"I am, absolutely. I just don't want you to feel as though you're trapped in our relationship."

"Trapped, what makes you use that term?"

"Well, you didn't exactly invite me to move in with you at the old studio and when you were discharged from the hospital following the shooting I more or less kidnapped you by bringing you to my place. You know what I mean."

"Mmm, but I didn't put up a fight about it either. Did I?"

She stood up and walked over to me. We hugged and kissed like teenagers. Within minutes she sat on my lap, my zipper opened and we became fully coupled, to wit in the heat of our spring fever we both slid off the boulder and landed in the water. The rush of cold besieging my exposed manhood made me quiver and shudder in a hasty scamper to seek dry land and warm sunshine.

"Are you alright? No stitches out of place or anything?" said Nicole.

"I'm fine and I'm sure glad the Beemer has that heated seat option we thought we'd never use. Ah, we probably won't use it today."

Standing soaking wet in an intimate natural setting on a beautiful sunny day revealed Nicole to be a true vision of loveliness.

"You are a goddess and I'm the luckiest man in the world to have been trapped by you."

She charged right into my arms and covered me in kisses that made my chest swell.

"Maybe we should check out the back seat in the Beemer," I said as we both rushed to get dressed. "I didn't see any Park Rangers about, did you?"

"Probably the pandemic is keeping them in the office."

When we finally got untangled and left the Ranch, we took Kanan Dume Road toward PCH. The road was littered with rocks, plant debris and mud from recent late spring storm-triggered slides which was making me concerned about possible damage to the Beemer and I sure didn't want us to be involved in another accident.

"Would you like me to drive?"

"Absolutely not. You relax I can handle this."

"OK, OK, just asking, but keep in mind the front of this car sits lower than your Mercedes."

"Right, I got it."

A blues blast from inside the glove box startled both of us and made Nicole pull over to the side of the road. It was coming from my phone and I didn't recognize the tune so I looked at the title on the screen. It read Allman Betts Band. I like it, but the text also showed the call was from Cisco so I had to cut it off and answer.

"How you doin' Cis," I said while gesturing for Nicole to keep driving.

She headed toward Pacific Coast Highway and was obviously planning to take it straight back to Santa Monica. This is one of my favorite stretches of highway to travel in LA. It makes me feel good, but I definitely needed to talk with Cisco.

"Yea and," I said.

Cisco proceeded to tell me the L.A. County Sheriff's Office was able to look at the surveillance video from the Malibu Market parking lot for the day Nicole had been there buying our picnic lunch. It showed several suspicious looking people in the lot, one of which crawled under the car while Nicole and Duie were inside the market. The others seem to be watching to make sure the guy under the Roadster wouldn't get caught. Unfortunately, when the person slinked-out he kept his back to the camera and was under the car for less than two minutes then walked quickly out of the camera's line of sight, so there was no video of the individual's face. It wasn't even possible to determine if the jerk was male or female. The only thing which might be of help is the statement given by the box boy who'd been rounding up shopping carts at the edge of the lot. When shown the video he stated he remembered the person because they wore a great outfit and rode a 'really cool' motorcycle. Cisco said he was going to check to see if the individual shows up on any other surveillance cameras along the highway and if the license plate number is valid.

"What are we listening to now?" I asked.

"Beethoven's *Eroica*," replied Nicole. "It was named the greatest symphony of all time by the world's top conductors."

"I thought his greatest was his Fifth, with that instantly recognizable duh-duh-duh-duuuh opening," I said.

"Nope, that one didn't even make it into the top 10," she said as she increased the volume a bit.

"Did any of those conductors know anything about the blues?"

"Oh, come on James, just listen to this. There's a lot happening. It goes way beyond the blues," Nicole said as she flashed a beautiful smile at me. "It's about the power and joy of being alive. Aren't you happy to be alive?"

"Yes, all things considered, I am. Especially with you in my life," I said as I leaned the seat back and closed my eyes to listen to the greatest symphony. "Hey isn't this tune over 200 years old?"

"Absolutely. That's remarkable and it's still number 1 with the music elite," she said.

The music was powerful, but all I could think about was finding the asshole riding the 'really cool' motorcycle. He or she needed some powerful duh-duh-duh-duuuhing on their head.

This solved another mystery and meant I wasn't paranoid or delusional, but it also opened up an even greater mystery to solve. What the hell is going on and why? And even more importantly, who is the target?

Damn it. Here I am thinking maybe I had a touch of post-traumatic stress disorder triggered by having been run off the road by a crazy truck driver, but no, there's actually some lunatic stalking me or worse, stalking Nicole and me as a couple.

"Well, did you like it," Nicole said.

I couldn't remember a single note. My mind was filled with irrational thoughts and visions of a monster dressed in a great outfit riding a really cool motorcycle. Ha, mmm, like the one that followed me from Arash Dentelle's studio and why can't I get that damn buzzing sound out of my head.

"Oh, yea, it was great. Do we have time to hear it again? Hey, what does *Eroica* mean anyway?'

"It's Latin for a heroic female," said Nicole.

"So did you select it for the music or the title?" I said and immediately smiled. Nicole looked at me with her dark eyes as if it was a dangerous question to ask. I closed my eyes and pretended to nap.

CHAPTER 12

It was Friday night and I wanted to listen to some live blues at the Club so I was thinking maybe I could convince Nicole to invite Merra to join us. When I finished a little more preliminary editing on the Money Mirage video, I looked around for Nicole.

"Hey Duie, where is Nicole? Go find Nicole. That's a good boy," I said as I headed toward the stairs.

I got only about half way up when Nicole appeared at the top dressed to the nine's.

"Wow, what's the occasion," I asked.

"We're going to dinner and you need to shower, shave and put on a nice outfit," she said as she took my arm and walked me into the bedroom.

I hadn't told her about the stealthy car assassin on the motorcycle and tonight was obviously not the time to alarm her. Plus, I didn't really know enough to sound like I knew what I was talking about. I was thinking if we had company the subject wouldn't come up.

"How about if we invite Merra to join us?"

"Are you saying I'm not enough for you," she said as she turned to face me with her hands on her hips.

"Ah, no, no, ah that's not what I'm saying at all. I just thought since you two were getting along so well. You know what I mean. Beside you and I don't seem to interact with friends in an easy atmosphere much since we moved in together and this pandemic thing and all started." I said as I turned on the shower and closed the bathroom door behind me.

The bathroom door opened just as I got into the shower.

"If I wasn't already dressed, I get in there with you and show you some interacting, but under the circumstances I guess I'll tell you what's happening. We're going to take Merra out for dinner to celebrate her birthday."

In less than 30 minutes, when I stood at the top of the stairs, I saw Nicole and Merra waiting for me in the living room. They were both dressed stunningly which made me feel a little like an old shoe in my sports jacket and slacks.

"Where would you fine ladies like to go," I asked. "And are we sure anything will be open?"

"We're going to the Club, Spider said he would have the chef fix us a meal fit for a Queen and I know how much you've wanted to hear some live blues," Nicole said.

"Yeah, and I hear you were very polite about being bombarded with Beethoven," said Merra. "Besides, I like the blues too. Let's go rattle Spider's cage."

All I could think of was the gods must be smiling on me. "OK, who gets to drive the 230," I said as I took them both by the arm.

Duie wasn't happy when we left him, but I did give him a large bone to gnaw on which usually keeps him busy for several hours.

The chef at the Club put on a great spread of fantastic food and Spider and his small band played some really, really good feeling blues. It's amazing how at home I feel hearing him play his harp and sing. Especially when you consider we both grew up in New York, not the south or L.A.. When he finished a great long version of *Crosscut Saw* he joined us in the booth.

"James is absolutely correct when he tells everyone how great you are," said Merra." I haven't heard Blues that soulful since I was in New Orleans."

"Why thank you and I haven't had a compliment that nice from such a sensational lady in a very long time," replied Spider. "Oh, and happy birthday, it's your 25th right."

Merra gave Spider a big kiss after which he took a swig from his long neck beer and looked right at me with that old home smile. The Chef and all his kitchen aids sitting socially distanced in the rest of the booths gave out with applause and hoots.

"Hey, it was my birthday a couple of days ago buddy and I thought you'd be here. Have you been feeling poorly?" he asked me.

"Damn Spider, I'm sorry. I totally spaced on it. Happy birthday man," I said as I sunk into the seat feeling like a louse.

"To be fair, I took James up into the Santa Monica's for the day and made him hike around with me so we were both really worn-out and spaced by the time we got home," said Nicole. "Besides, I really thought with the Club being closed and all, no one would be here."

"I did get a nice gift from everyone," said Spider as he stood and applauded them. "You'll have to come by tomorrow and let me show it off. You won't believe how much fun it is to fly. I was thinking about taking it into the mountains too. Especially since we'll have to keep the club closed for who knows how long."

"Fly?"

"Yea, it's an unmanned aerial vehicle, you know an aircraft without a human pilot on board, a fricking drone man," he said with a full tooth grin. "It even has a camera. The only thing I don't like about it is the continuous buzz."

"Shit, that's it. A goddamn drone," I said.

"What the hell are you going on about," said Nicole.

"That buzzing sound I heard when the whirly gig fell on me."

"You mean someone filmed the whole thing?" asked Spider. "That dude must have a set of big ones."

"Say, talking about big ones, tell me about how you select the songs you sing," said Merra with a seductive smile and an obvious desire to change the subject. "I mean there's no rap or hip-hop in the set, just straight-ahead deep blues."

Spider took a long look at each of us and came back to Merra with a moan and groan from his harp then said, "The songs I sing explore the psychological state of living as a Black man in the United States. Black men are always in survival mode because this culture is deliberately organized to keep us separated from the general society, oppressed and divided from hope and ourselves," followed by more moan'in from his harp and a big clup of air he continued pontificating. "Having experienced constant judgments based on preconceived falsehoods throughout my entire life, I find freedom only in music." Another harp groan. "My song selection stems from personal experiences I relate to. I'm drawn to lyrics that relate recognizable places, situations and emotions. My goal is to portray my people and their story authentically and with feeling." He stood up and shuffled dance to the bandstand and the entire band joined him in a great Jimmy Reed song.

Merra looked dumb-founded, stupefied and flabbergasted all at once. "I didn't see it coming at all and walked right into it."

"You had to ask," replied Nicole. "If you stay around here for long, you'll discover Spider is much more than he seems at first, second or even third glance. I've heard him give that same speech to others and you're lucky he shortened it tonight probably because it's your birthday."

"This pandemic has brought many of society's ills to light, such as oppression, wage disparities and a long list of injustices while also revealing the true character of each subject. Spider prefers to sing about them rather than march in the street," I said.

Spider stepped off the stage and slid back into the booth while singing *Midnight Special* and playing his harp. When he finished, he said, "Do you really think Luc videoed the falling sculpture using a drone? I mean, I thought all of you art lovers, well, love each other."

"I sure hope he didn't, cause if he did Nell will insist I have him arrested," said Nicole

"Geez as if this pandemic thing isn't scary enough, we have to worry about a deranged soldier," said Merra.

"I'm not buying it. Luc seemed too nice a guy," said Nicole.

"You sure about that?" said Spider. "Lots of folks aren't what they pretend to be and the pot calling the kettle black or white doesn't hold up now-a-days."

CHAPTER 13

"The 19th century French artist Gustave Courbet kept his famously overwrought self-portrait *The Desperate Man* in his studio until his death. He had painted it when he was relatively young. It shows him agitating his disheveled hair while staring wild-eyed at the viewer. One wonders whether he saw himself as the quintessential Romantic artist or as a tortured genius struggling for recognition," I said as I gestured toward Luc Blondin's self-portrait on the easel to my left.

To the right of the easel Luc stood as rigid as if he were still in the Army and I was his commanding officer. I needed to make him feel relaxed so I offered him an elbow bump. He stared at it for longer than one normally does, but finally took a deep breath and we bumped elbows.

"Thank you for allowing the CAsLog crew and myself to visit with you here in your home-based studio," I said. "When did you finish this painting?"

"A few months ago," he replied.

"Was that before or after you made these other portraits?" I asked.

Tilly made sure the way was clear for the cameraman to slowly scan the 4 portraits on the mantel to the side of us and then swing back to Luc.

"Later, much later," Luc said with his eyes cast down giving me an anxious sidewise look.

"These men appear to be about your same age. How did you come to select them as subjects for painting?"

"Subjects, they are not subjects. They were strong, brave men and I owe my life to each one of them," Luc said as he raised his head and stiffened his chin. "I wouldn't be here if it weren't for their sacrifice."

"Yes, I understand. They did not survive a fierce battle you all fought together. So, you painted a portrait of each man in order to honor his memory?"

"This is living art, their life experiences are etched on their faces," he said. "Their fears of the present and hopes for the future can be read in every brushstroke I made."

Tilly's high sign about the not-so-subtle chip on Luc's shoulder caught my eye and I agreed with her … it's time to move on.

"You mentioned earlier you skipped enrolling in any of the college or university art programs around town, so where did you learn about how to make such expressionistic brushstrokes?"

"I participate in the art therapy sessions at the VA here in Sawtelle," Luc said with a degree of pride. "They are taught by Maggie Mayye a wonderful and inspiring friend to all the vets."

"Ms. Mayye does have a captivating approach to bringing forth one's creativity and I understand she brought you to a turning point in your emerging art career. Please tell us about that," I said in hopes of bringing the topic of Luc's art back into the conversation.

"Ah, well, I'm not in a big hurry to reveal too much about myself," said Luc with a bitter smile.

What he said felt true. But he seemed to be an unreal man even when he said true things. We stood with an aura of unreality expanding between us. His hand wrenched and scoured at the lower part of his face as if he was trying to reshape it. His brow knitted, he gave me and the camera an evasive look.

With that somber note I signaled for the cameraman to zoom in on Luc's face so we could take a break. Luc quickly walked off camera and went to the kitchen nook for a glass of water. When he finished, he stood silently staring out the window at his pile of repurposed junk. I asked Tilly to go get him and bring him to the portraits. She did and we started shooting again.

"Self-portraits and portraits of friends or as in this case, portraits of steadfast comrades offer a surprisingly candid look into the personal relationships which have influenced Luc Blondin. In addition, unique to this collection of portraits we will have a highly unusual glimpse into the evolution of how he worked-out the particular artistic ideas he wanted to express. Luc you seem to have a preference for keeping the outer edges of all of your portraits in very dark tertiary tones," I said.

"Bright colors keep your vision at the canvas' edge, whereas dark colors allow your mind to wonder far beyond that limitation. Perhaps into infinity," Luc replied as he himself appeared to zone out again showing his teeth in an unsmiling grin.

"I understand you were assisted in the final development of the portraits and the creation of some label text for each by Miss Maggie Mayye, the art therapist at the Sawtelle Veterans Hospital in West Los Angeles."

"Yes, Maggie ... ah, Miss Mayye runs a great program there and it's available free to any soldier," said Luc. He was back with us again, bright and alert. I was beginning to wonder if he zoned out often or was it only because the filming was stressful for him. Plus, Maggie didn't show up for the shoot as she had promised she would.

"And you also seem to favor thick impasto brushstrokes rather than smooth velvet ones," I said. "Tell us why."

"Being a soldier is not smooth and soft, it's a rough, coarse, jagged life. Plus, thick paint has a real presence on the canvas. It seems alive. Like it has energy within it."

"Like the kinetic sculptures you also create," I said to the surprise of Tilly and the crew. "Let's walk outside and look at some of them."

"No, no, I didn't prepare anything out there for you to film. No," said Luc as he darted to block access to the back door.

"Oh, ok, ok, some other time," I said. "Well, I think we have enough for this segment."

The panic on Luc's face seemed way beyond not wanting to allow anyone to see his scrap heap. He was shaking, sweat began seeping across his forehead and his eyes reflected a single-mindedness.

Tilly and the crew quickly packed up and left while I pretended to be studying the portraits again. Luc had still not abandoned his post in front of the backdoor.

"Hey, you don't happen to have a cold-beer do you?" I asked.

The look on his face was very telling for his whole expression of potential danger was dissolving before my eyes.

His crouched stance gave way and his fists unlocked. "Yes, I sure do and I could use one too."

We moved to the living room and drank while I explained we would list his website address at the end of the segment and also put it on the station's website.

"I guess combat fighting has changed a lot since the army started using robots and drones," I said. "Did you have any experience with them during your tour?

"Nope, you have to complete special op's training in order to use one of those weapons," he said. "Neither I or any of my men had it."

I drove off feeling good about the shoot, disappointed about not being able to nose around in his sculpture work space and to hear he doesn't know how to fly a drone. But I'm still unsure as to whether he has a mental disorder or not.

I didn't drive far before Maggie appeared out from behind a parked car. I stopped and opened the side window. "I would say late is better than never, but in this case you're just way beyond that."

"I planned it that way," she said. "May I get in so we can talk a little more privately rather than in the middle of the street?"

"Certainly, please do."

She got in quickly while keeping her eyes focused on Luc's house and putting on her mask. "Go around the corner and stop," she said as she clasped her hands together in a tight knot.

I did as she asked and managed to find a shade tree to park beneath. "You planned not to attend the shooting. That's not what you promised Luc."

"I know, but he needed to do it on his own. Having solo experiences is important for his therapy. Did he do alright? Did he seem normal?"

"Oh, I see. Therapy. Yes, yes, he did fine. There was just one thing."

"Damn, what?" she replied with a look of complete exasperation.

"Well, he did fine during the segment on the portraits, but when I suggested we film a short bit about the kinetic sculptures he had an anxiety attack and became a bit hostile," I said.

"I was afraid something like that would happen. Luc needs to construct large whirly-gigs in order to paint intimate portraits. Creating monster machines that self-destruct fulfills his need to revenge the death of his friends and I think in a way they also provide a path for his own rebirth as a normal guy."

"Wow, maybe we shouldn't air this shoot," I said as I also felt exasperated. "It should probably be cancelled."

"Oh, please don't. That would send him into a dark hole," she said as she took hold of my hand. "He needs your acknowledgement of his self-worth. It will bolster his confidence and pride. Please. If you cancel, he'll feel like an outsider again. He has worked so hard to fit in with someone other than his fellow damaged soldiers. Please."

Maggie was dressed in her hospital attire and I noticed her name tag didn't include any reference to a job title.

"Your position at the VA is obviously one of a high level of responsibility and I assume you have at least a B.A. in art. Are you required to be a nurse also? I mean your name tag doesn't include your position."

"I am a fully licensed Art Psychotherapist with a B.A. in art and a Masters in Psychology," she replied. "I don't put that on my name tag because the men have a negative reaction to anything that has 'Psycho' on it."

I responded, "Right, I understand. Well what part of the program do the men have the most positive response to?"

"Ceramics," she said still looking distressed.

"That's surprising, I would have thought painting or drawing would be the most popular," I said.

"Have you ever pushed your hands into wet clay?" she said. "It's physicality and creative potential are immediately appealing to the men. They react like kids playing with mud."

"Yea, I believe it. The therapeutic properties of the material are hard to resist," I said as I flashed back on Luc pushing his face about during the shoot.

"Studies have shown creating ceramics has restorative and meditative benefits plus it improves mood, decision-making, and motivation as well," she said with a high degree of satisfaction. "What sets it apart from other forms of art therapy is clay's distinctive malleability and the physical exertion it requires. It's very much like touching a human body."

"Which definitely appeals to men," I said.

"Learning techniques like kneading, pinching, and bonding two smooth, wet forms together helps each man utilize various neurological functions, sensory motor processes, plus visual and high levels of cognitive functions," she said.

The expression in her eyes made turning her down not an option, but I was not ready to let go of believing Luc had deliberately pushed or exploded the whirly-gig right at me. In fact, I was beginning to think he may also be responsible for the Beemer crash. "Was the whirly-gig set to explode at a particular time or did he push it over?" I asked.

Maggie crinkled-up her face, looked at a small watch pinned to her blouse and said, "I can't talk any longer right now. I've got to get back to my patients. Thank you for your understanding. You're an angel."

She sprung out of the car and ran down the street as I acutely exhaled. She got into her car and drove away. As I considered her revelation James Cotton's harp howled from my phone and it sounded so-good I just sat there listening until I noticed the call was from Terratan Landchilde.

"Hello Terratan. How are you?" I said still reeling from Maggie's expose that Luc may have deliberately targeted me with his collapsible monster machine. "What, geez are you alright?"

Terratan proceeded to inform me some Ninja motorcyclist tried to force his car off the Santa Monica Freeway near the Normandie Avenue off ramp. He was not hurt. He just wanted to let me know he too had been a victim of erratic traffic.

"So, you phoned to cheer me up?" I said. "That's it?"

"I just thought it would help to remind you, car accidents are the norm in LA," he said. "I don't' know if the guy was really trying to make me crash or he was just burning off some road rage."

If I recall correctly, Terratan drives a Cadillac Escalade which no doubt enabled him to use its size to dissuade the biker from whatever he had in mind. Which was what? Or rather, why would anyone want to harm Terratan?

"What the hell is going on?" I said out loud as I sat in the shade of a beautiful tree on a pleasant street in a quiet neighborhood. My brassy voice startled a crow as it hopped across the sidewalk to inspect pieces of sparkling cellophane trash at the curb. He pecked at them and flung them about ostensibly just to watch them float in the air. As they did, he seemed mesmerized by their twists and turns and fully engrossed by the playfulness of it all. Watching him was pleasant and strangely riveting for my own mind seemed filled with bits and pieces of the past few days floating about needing to be stitched together.

I recalled Cisco telling me once he had suffered from post-traumatic stress disorder (PTSD) after watching a friend die in a skateboard accident. He had all the classic symptoms including flashbacks, nightmares and anxiety spells. This odd recollection caused my mind to whiplash a series of quick flashbacks of the fight I was involved in last autumn in which two men died followed first by the whirly-gig tornado of metal shrapnel; then my old car being careened into a culvert by a wayward truck; followed by Nicole crashing our sabotaged roadster onto beach rocks and the Ninja attack on Arash's neon studio, which might have been meant for me, not Arash; oh, plus being followed by a stealthy biker.

I shook my head in hopes of clearing all those troublesome images out of my internal theater of reruns, but it was a short reprieve for a second wave of images began to shove their way into focus. They were all of Merra and her enticing advances which generated an even deeper level of psyche angst in my soul.

"No wonder you're a little jumpy," I said to myself.

"So do I have PTSD or am I just being paranoid as Cisco suggest," I said to the crow who bobbed his head, but didn't answer.

"Where the hell is the connection," I shouted out the car window causing all the birds in the area to suddenly flutter away. Birds of a flock. There is no flock, there is only me. I am the common denominator in this paradoxical puzzle of absurd, illogical events.

That said, the first rule when trying to solve a mystery is to start at the beginning. Incident 1 was Luc's self-destructing sculpture almost falling on my head. So, who knew I'd be at that event? Everyone that received an invitation to the Spring Fling Outdoor Sculpture Garden Tour or saw one of its many advertisements on TV, radio or the web that's who. Ah, but how would anyone know exactly when I would be near that particular sculpture? Only by watching me; by tailing me or by hiding nearby in the garden. Or by filming me via a drone.

As I pondered, the crow flew back across the front of the car and dropped a piece of shiny cellophane which seemed to hover right in front of me. The dancing light sparkling off it and the faint buzz sound it made caused my mind to ricochet and my mouth to blurt out 'drone'. Did Luc hide behind a bush somewhere and watch me through a video camera drone so he'd know when to make the sculpture fall? He denied having had training to fly a drone, but that doesn't mean he couldn't have taught himself.

For Incident 2 only Nicole knew I was planning to drive the old car to the PBS Charity Center, but she didn't know I would end up driving through the canyon instead on the freeway. Again, someone would have to have followed me. However, the LAPD claims the whole thing was just an accident caused by a Vet.

Incident 3 was Nicole and I crashing the Roadster onto a bed of boulders and according to Cisco the car was tampered with while she was buying our picnic lunch. Again, someone had to have followed us which Cisco says was most likely a Ninja motorcyclist.

Incident 4 at Arash's neon studio was also an attack by a Ninja dressed motorcyclist.

Incident 5, a Ninja dressed motorcyclist followed me from Arash's to the Club.

There it is 5 confrontations each of which could have had deadly consequences.

And now we also have another Ninja motorcyclist, but I was not his target, Terratan Landchilde was – on the 10 Freeway somewhere near the Normandie Avenue exit.

"Why there?" I said out loud again. "When you have miles of freeway, why pick that spot?

Normande Avenue runs through the heart of Koreatown. I looked at the crow who was bobbing and dipping his head again.

CHAPTER 14

"Come on Duie, let's go," I said as I stepped off the deck. "It's such a beautiful morning, hey fella? Let's go toward Venice for a change." Duie started on our usual path toward the pier, but when he realized I was going in the opposite direction he quickly turned around and sprinted past me probably because the volley ball courts were this way and I'm sure he was hoping to find Shotala there. Given the potential danger of the fast-spreading pandemic, I was hoping we wouldn't for I just wanted to see how the neighborhood was doing and not have to deal with anyone directly, especially a buxom red head.

The temperate weather of sun filled sky and gentle breeze coming in off the waves made the unusual facial topography of wearing a skimpy mask feel silly, but the parade of skaters and bicyclists who were cautiously sauntering along while practicing social distancing felt strangely inviting. Like me, many of them favor a leisurely cruise watching the procession of barely clothed bodies, while others are intent on fast navigating through the obstacle course of humanity, merrily zipping between everyone in their way. The thought somehow this strange decease was dismantling our chosen communal morning and could bring about the total destruction of all humanity was causing my internal angst meter to gyrate as I tried to let go of worrying about a potential Ninja assassin.

I must admit, now more than ever, I was really grooving on all the quirky characters who are gravitationally attracted to LA even those who seem completely out of place here like the animated, eager looking group mounted on new silent electric bikes on a three-hour docent escorted private tour promising to discover the 'soul of Santa Monica—from Muscle Beach to the historic Marion Davies guesthouse'.

According to the vocal tour guide, they had started their adventure at Will Rogers State Beach in Pacific Palisades and the surf breaks along Santa Monica State Beach, went under the pier and were now on "The Strand, a multiuse recreational path stretching all the way to Torrance, packing in 22 miles of inspiring coastal scenery," said the masculine looking young woman using a small, portable microphone and speaking through an odd-looking plastic face visor.

Duie and I plus a number of other walkers and roller-bladders, in booty shorts, waited for them to leave and then we continued strolling along feeling very much content in the benign, mixed parade. Although the sight of two young women wearing matching masks and bikinis felt almost surrealistic and time warping.

"Hey James my man, how the hell are you?" said Royal. "Haven't seen you on the pier in a while."

"Wow, Royal Knight. Nice to see you off the pier. Are you singing on the Strand now?"

"No man, I hit the jackpot at the pier. Space 14 is all mine now," Royal said as he raised his hands to heaven and bowed. "We had a 10,000 head count day last spring break."

"Fantastic and your cords stayed strong all day?"

"Absolutely man. Come on by and bring that beautiful lady of yours with you. I always hit the high notes with a looker like her in the crowd. Besides you said you would film me for your log gig."

"Yes, I did and I will, soon I promise. And I will bring Nicole. That's a good idea."

"Make sure she wears that great bikini I saw her in the other day."

"Right. When was that?"

"I don't remember man, she was with a stunning red head in a tangerine number."

"Oh yea, I know her," I said. "I seem to remember Space 14 is at the end of the pier, right?"

"Yep, it probably sees less traffic than spaces closer to the entrance, but I have the ocean as a backdrop and face two sets of stairs where people can sit. It creates a perfect amphitheater. A great location for me. I love it."

Royal has been performing love songs on the pier for as long as I've been in Santa Monica. He came here from New Orleans and I have no idea what his real name is.

We bumped elbows as he headed toward the pier. I settled into a comfortable pace with the crowd as a young girl skated up alongside me. She had short black hair, naturally brownish skin with deep sienna eyes. She wore a modest outfit of Bermuda shorts and buttoned blouse with a pink floppy pussy hat. We looked at each other and nodded politely. She appeared to be around 20 years old, but I seem to have lost the ability to determine a woman's age some time ago, so I concentrated on her eye expressions which were of caution or concern, but before I could decide which she skated passed me. Maybe it was concern about the pandemic I saw reflected in her eyes. Whatever it was it made me aware of my tiredness, which I felt rising like a wave up through my body to my head.

"Duie, stay with me," I said as he started to follow the girl. "Come on boy, lets head over to the drinking fountain. Would you like some water?" Duie wagged his tail and ran to the fountain where upon he was picked up by a surfer dude. I quickly darted through the crowd to reach him.

"I thought I recognized Duie. How'a do'in Mr. Terra?" said Hurley.

"Geez, Hurley it's good to see you man," I said. "You been sheltering in or on a gig?

Hurely Fann is a surfer of international note and he looks it with his muscular yet lanky, sun bronzed body, wavy blonde hair and sky-struck blue eyes.

"It's good to see you out and about too," he said. "Spider told me you'd been in a couple of car accidents and one of them was up at Blocker Beach."

"Yea, that's right, but I'm OK," I said. "It's good to see you too man. Have you seen any exciting boards lately?"

"No, but there's an exchange happening later this week and I'll keep an eye out for a great one for your collection," he said with a full smile as he petted Duie and put him down. "What about the chickie-doodle in the floppy hat. Who is she?" he said with a flashed smirky leer.

"What? Where?" I said. "Is she behind me on something?"

"Well, I noticed her following you and Duie. That's why I called to him when he approached the fountain," he said. "I hope you didn't give up Nicole cause if you did man, you're fucking crazy."

"No, no I wouldn't do that. I may have gotten knocked about a bit lately, but I didn't lose all my marbles," I said dying to turn around. "I'm going to walk on. Let me know if the hat babe follows. OK?"

"Right, will do," he said.

"Good to see you Hurley," I said as Duie and I mixed into the crowd and continued walking.

We went only a short distance when I heard a squeal, turned and saw Hurley holding the floppy hat girl up by her waist about 2' off the ground.

"Let me down. Now!" she yelled.

"Ok Hurley put her down," I said as I walked in front of her. "No one is going to hurt you, young lady, but I do think you need to explain why you've been following me."

She turned and pushed Hurley back. He raised his hands in surrender and backed away with a wave to me before heading to his friends at the fountain.

"Well, what do you have to say for yourself," I asked.

"I just want to talk to you that's all," she said with a meek smile while looking up through the tops of her eyes. "I owe you an apology Mr. Terra."

"What are you talking about? Are you an artist?" I asked fully prepared to give my standard speech about not accepting studio invitations without having seen their work in an exhibit somewhere.

"Ah, no. I'm Arash's girlfriend and I'm sorry for what happened when you were filming him," she said with tears filling her eyes.

She was wearing a pink tinted translucent mask so it took a minute or more for me to process her statement, but she certainly got my full attention as a small crowd started to gather around us.

"Let's go sit under those palms over there," I said as I took her arm and led her toward a bench. "OK folks, there's no show going on. It's a personal matter that's all."

The crowd gave out with a group whine and moved on. Floppy hat and I sat in silence for a few moments just watching everyone flow by.

"You were somehow responsible for what happened. How?"

"Yes, I am, but you have to promise to never tell Arash. Please," she said lacing her fingers in a tight grip. "He would leave me."

"Well, I can't make that kind of promise without knowing what I'm agreeing with. Now, can I?"

"Yes, of course," she said. "I'm Persian and my family are very traditional."

She squeezed her fingers together so tight they turned a white-ish pale lavender. I put my hand on top of them. "Relax, I'm not going to tell your family anything no matter what it is."

"They and Arash think I'm a virgin," she said while throwing her head back in a gesture of defiance.

That was not what I was expecting to hear. So much so, that I wasn't sure I had heard her correctly. "OK, that's nice, I guess and so? Oh, I get it. The Ninja attacker is an old boyfriend. Right?"

"Sort of, but not exactly," she said while looking around to make sure no one was listening. "It was my girlfriend."

"Your girlfriend. Not a man, but a woman? I said while looking up to see a young woman in a very skimpy bikini skate by.

"Yes, you've got it now. I'm bi-sexual. But, Arash doesn't know and he will never marry me if he finds out."

"In this day and age, especially here in L.A. don't you think you might be cutting him a little short. I mean he seemed pretty enlightened to me."

"Yes, maybe, but our community culture isn't. At least, not in public anyway. If I come out publicly my family will never talk to me again. Hell, I'll be bombarded with insults, abused by everyone and lose most of my friends. I could even end-up in the hospital or dead."

"Well, I know your traditional penal code includes the death penalty for gay sex and 100 lashes for lesbianism, but do you really think that would happen here?" I said while watching two twins skating by wearing bunny rabbit ears and skin-colored bikinis with cotton balls covering their nipples and pubic area. What an incredible time we live in. I looked at floppy hat and she was full on crying and said something in Farsi, but I couldn't tell if it was a positive or negative comment.

"What was that? I asked.

"Dojensgara, it means bisexual in Farsi, a language spoken by about 110 million people most of whom will hate me. Like most American-born Iranians, I will probably never walk the streets of Tehran or stroll alongside the Darband River like my parents and uncles did. But the intensity of that culture is forever ingrained in me—my connection to its roots has been cultivated by the close-knit community in my Los Angeles hometown," she said with downcast eyes.

"Are you wearing bright pink in acknowledgment of the Persian Spring New Year?"

"Yes, I am and I'm surprised you know about it."

"Oh, I know a couple of wife's, of major L.A. based contemporary Iranian art collectors," I replied. "What is your name?"

"Tahmineh," she said. "But, most of my friends call me Mineh."

"So, I'm thinking your girlfriend is the one that behaves more like a man in the relationship," I said timidly.

"Yes, and that's why she attacked Arash and totally messed-up your CAsLog shoot. What can I say? I'm so sorry for you, for Arash and for her.

"She must be very physically fit to have picked up Arash and throw him," I said.

"She works out daily and is on the wrestling team," she said with a shrug.

"I see, uh, did she also follow me on her motorcycle?"

"What are you talking about?"

"Someone, dressed like your girlfriend followed me on a motorcycle from Arash's studio to Santa Monica. Was it her?"

"I don't know, but I will find out. Damn, this is really getting out of control. I'm not sure I can handle it."

"Are you sure Arash and your parents won't be understanding of who you are?"

"For them a woman's virginity is a non-negotiable prerequisite for marriage. Even among most of the richer classes here who live western lives, partying and drinking, the men happily sleep around but will only marry someone "pure". Virginity is seen as a marker of decency, of a good moral family," she said. "They will not be understanding."

"Well, there must be some give and take going on. I mean you are not wearing a black Hijab or even a headscarf," I said. "And Arash doesn't strike me as the kind of man who is going to stay with a woman he hasn't had sex with."

"You're right, we've had the kind we can get-away with, which doesn't mean he will accept my having had sex with woman," she said as she shook her head while watching the twin skaters dance around in a circle with their hands on each other's waist.

"Ah, I don't mean to pry, but what do you mean by the kind you can get-away with?"

"Oral, anal and thigh," she said with her defiant scowl again.

"Mmm. OK, look I promise I will not mention any of this to anyone. But, I want you to let me know if your girlfriend followed me or not."

"I will and thank you for being so sweet. I wish my father and boyfriend were like you."

"If Arash really loves you, he will be understanding. Give him a chance."

"You can't trust guys," she said, "they act like everything is cool, then after you have sex with them, they turn on you. Or if they think you're a virgin, they just want the thrill of popping your cherry, so they'll feed you a line of shit about wanting to marry you. It's hard to be considered an equal in sex with any man."

We stood up, exchanged contact info and Tahmineh stared into my eyes before cautiously embracing me and being swept away by the flowing crowd along with the hugging rabbit eared twins. I looked around for Duie and spotted him with Hurley and his surfing buddies.

"I understand you don't surf, but do collect boards," said a young man with crew cut hair and tattoos too numerous to count. "What do you do with them?"

"They are a great visual history of the constantly evolving surfing culture of L.A. so I plan to exhibit them," I said as I noticed his hair was cut into some kind of geometric design like a crop circle.

"You mean these artists are going to be famous?"

"It's a possibility. Only time will tell."

I'm not sure how long it took to walk back home, but when I entered Nicole was standing in the center of the living room with her arms crossed and chewing her lower lip.

"Met some friends during your walk, did you?"

"Oh, just Hurley Fann and some of his surfing pals," I said. "Oh, and Royal Knight. You know the guy that sings love songs at the pier."

"No one else ah?" she said as she began moving things around on the kitchen island in a constricted manner. "No girls?"

"Did you follow me?"

"No, I didn't and I wouldn't. Let's just say that a little bird told me you met with a girl."

"Ah ha, was it a red feathered bird?"

"Ok, ok, Merra saw you talking with a young skater and said you looked like very close friends. Who is she?"

"Wow, so many people looking out for me. I don't know whether to be thankful or to be annoyed," I said as I took Nicole's hand and sat down with her on my lap.

I told Nicole all most everything about Tahmineh, except the bit about me having been followed by a motorcyclist. She was intrigued and said she would like to meet her and Arash. I wasn't convinced a positive outcome would result, but before I could respond Nicole's cell made its funny giggle sound. She answered it.

"Good morning, Nellie. How are you?" Nicole walked out onto the deck.

Which I took as a sign she didn't want me to hear what she and Nell were talking about so Duie and I went into the studio where I checked my e-mail. There were several in my In Box, but my eye zeroed in on the one from Liz Weinstein, producer of CAsLog. It said she wanted to meet with me for a luncheon meeting at Fromin's Delicatessen on Wilshire, my favorite place for eating.

This didn't bode well. Liz rarely asked to meet with me for lunch or for any reason and picking my favorite place suggest she has some bad news to tell. I emailed her back: Hi, Liz. Hope all is going well at the station and everyone is staying healthy. What's up?

Her reply was instant and stated: a guest from Australia will be joining you during your production completion of the Money Mirage log. I will bring her to our luncheon.

That was not what I had expected and raised questions I just didn't want to contemplate. So, I forced myself to get back to my main concern and wrote an email to Cisco to tell him about Terratan's encounter with a Ninja motorcyclist. His quick reply related his often stated dis-believe in coincidences.

"Three Ninja motorcyclists all interacting with your life within a week is not a coincidence, it's a planned plot. What have you been sticking your nose into now?"

"What Ninja motorcyclists is he referring to?" said Nicole as she put her hands on my shoulders and leaned over me to get a closer look at the computer screen.

"Oh, finished your morning talk with Nell, honey pot," I said trying to hide my startled expression with a cough. "Is everything fine with her?"

"Don't give me any of that sugar on the bone talk, it doesn't suit you. What is going on?"

It took a few difficult attempts at trying to sound nonchalant, but I finally managed to tell her about each of the incidents I was uneasy about.

Her response was anything but what I expected for her eyes sharpened and her body demeanor became noticeably taut.

"Damn Merra. I'll handle her," she said as she started for the door in a heated huff with Duie right alongside her.

"Hold it right there. What the hell does Merra have to do with any of this?"

"I'll explain later, but right now she's going to get a full measure of my wrath."

"No, she isn't. You're going to stay right here and tell me why you think Merra is involved," I said as I stepped in front of her and held her arms then moved up against her to smother her fury.

It took a couple of minutes before she inhaled deeply and relaxed.

"Ok, you win. I should have told you as soon as she showed up."

"Well, it's not too late. You can tell me now."

"Damn James, you never really like to quarrel do you? Everything has always got to be calm and stable."

"We can discuss my predilections another time. Let's concentrate on Merra for now."

"Right," she said as she reached down and petted Duie. "It's Ok fella. There's no danger now."

"Good, so let's hear it."

She walked to the easel and cocked an eye at the canvas perched on it. "Like most new arrivals here in L.A., Merra has always wanted to have a cool job appropriate to her big dreams."

"Yes, OK, I get it, don't all of us, but what job are you talking about?"

"We, ah, I mean she, she is ah…"

"Come on out with it, Nicole. You know I don't bite, I only savor."

Nicole bowed her head and gazed up at me through the top of her distressed eyes which were rapidly spilling over with a chilling look of trepidation. Even her hands were knotted and her torso seemed scrunched by a deep-rooted pain. I thought I should move in and hold her, but she backed away from me and stared at the canvas again. After a moment or two she turned, swallowed hard and seemed to herald an inner determination as she whispered.

"Merra is an autonomous contracted operative for the FBI."

The stilled room filled with an air of darkened anxiety as her words skidded toward me like the cloud crossing over the skylight shrouding her face revealing only a small light glistening off her tear-soaked eyes. Instinctively I went to her and enveloped her in my arms. This time she didn't try to avoid me.

"Do you understand James? I was one too."

"You were an agent?"

"Ah, no, no we were completely independent free-lancers."

"Mmm OK, and that means what exactly? Did you kill people?"

"No James. We just helped find out things about people the FBI has concerns about."

"Well shit, that still sounds extremely dangerous."

"Yes, you are right. It is."

"Wait a minute. Are you still working for them?"

"No. I quit when I married Patterson."

"I see and is Merra still an operative?

"Yes, but please don't tell anyone. That could make things even more problematic. Especially don't tell Cisco."

"Wow, every day since I've known you, you've managed to surprise me."

"I hope you're not saying that's a bad thing. Are you?"

"No, but this surprise sort of puts a new light on a lot of things."

"Are you talking about us or Terratan or something else?" she said with her eyes radiating real concern.

"Well, my first thought is about our situation. I mean is it safe having Merra live right next door?"

"No one in the game knows she lives here."

"The game? And how could they not know? Isn't her name on the deed or the lease?"

"No, it isn't. I own the house and she stays in it rent free," Nicole said as she looked up at me with even deeper concern.

"I see. Another surprise. Were you planning to tell me about all of this or were you hoping she would just leave on assignment or something and you wouldn't have to explain?"

"Probably, I don't know. With the Spring Fling, falling sculptures and car crashes I haven't really had time to ponder it. I did think maybe I'd mention it during our together day at the Peter Strauss Ranch, but things took another direction."

She moved in close and kissed me. My mind was trying to find a connection between Merra and the mysterious Ninja who seems to pop into and out of everything I do.

"Ok, let's put that aside for now and get back to why you think Merra is connected to the Ninja attacks," I said.

"Well, some of the people, her and I spied on, weren't happy about how we went about finding out how they committed their crimes," she said with a degree of deviance.

"I see and you think they've sent someone to collect some kind of vengeance?"

"Maybe."

"Mmm, I don't think so. That wouldn't account for involving Terratan."

"Yes, I guess that's correct. I suppose I was just looking for any excuse to start a fight with Merra."

"Why?"

"Because I don't trust her with you. That's why," she said through clinched teeth.

"Hey, it takes two to create that kind of action and I promised you I wouldn't do that."

"I know and I do trust you. But that doesn't mean I have to step back and let her try to persuade you. And don't try to tell me she hasn't tried. I can tell by the look in your eyes she has. Right?"

"Yes, she did and I admit I was flattered."

"And you enjoyed it didn't you?"

"Yes, but that was all I did. Look, right now it's more important to put our energy into figuring out what this Ninja thing is all about before someone gets seriously hurt or killed."

CHAPTER 15

It was barely passed 7am when Duie insisted on being let out, so I put on my sandals and swim trunks, went downstairs onto the deck and sat on the lounger to watch him play tag with the gulls. He never wins, but really enjoys the chase as though running is his primary goal.

Thinking of 'the game' brought to mind our FBI neighbor Merra. Visions of her whizzed through my visual cortex again and again until the shriek of a gull yanked me back followed by a pitch of sand.

I expected to see beautiful Nicole when I opened my eyes, but it was Cisco standing between me and the morning sun.

"Buenos días," he said.

"Uh, good morning to you too. What brings you around here at such an early hour?"

"I was hoping for something more attractive to look at that's for sure, but I'm here to discuss your Ninja problem."

Sub-consciously I was convinced Cisco wouldn't pursue the Ninja attack on Terratan because it occurred outside of his legal jurisdiction. However, as the incident occurred at the off ramp to Koreatown and Terratan and I had met with Kirill whose wife is from that neighborhood Cisco had decided to look into it through his connections in the FBI.

What he found was surprising. It seems Maytor Kirill's wife is a former Korean soft porn star and spends a lot of time with the young bank executive who is handling the loan on the Snooktz paintings. Plus, that same executive also approved a loan for her father's dry-cleaning business.

"So, it all seems tied together by the same string," he said. "But, I don't like it. It's too easy."

"Yes, it is odd, but more importantly, it doesn't shed any light on why they might be targeting Terratan or Nicole and I," I said as Cisco moved aside revealing Nicole looking down from the upstairs deck.

"Good morning. I hope we didn't wake you."

"No, you didn't, but do I have to listen to shrieking gulls every morning?" said Nicole as she returned to the bedroom.

"Oops, is there a problem in paradise?" said Cisco.

"Not really, we'll get past it," I replied.

"Doesn't have anything to do with a red-head, does it?"

"No, not at all."

"OK, let's get back on track. Assuming for moment Kirill's wife hired the Ninja to sabotage your car, attack you at the neon studio, follow you to the club, and attack Terratan. What is her motive?" Cisco said as he looked up to see if Nicole had returned.

"I don't really know, perhaps to try and stop me from making a CAsLog about the loan."

"How would that hurt her or anyone else for that matter?" Cisco said.

"Again, I don't know, but I suspect it has more to do with the Snookz Jefferies paintings themselves."

"Why? You said they were authentic and Kirill is the legal owner of all of them."

"True, however, Cornish did find one of the paintings had some damage done to it recently," I said.

"By whom?"

"Most likely by the expert hired by the bank executive who is lovey-dovey with Kirill's wife."

"Now we're getting somewhere," he said. "What kind of damage?"

"Damage is probably too strong a word."

"Will you get to it, what the hell are you talking about?"

"In order to make sure the paintings are original the lab tech has to take a small sample of the paint and test it. On one painting, far more paint was taken from underneath the surface layer than was necessary for a test."

"How can anyone make money from it?" he said.

"I suppose you could thin the paint and put it on top of a forged painting to make it pass a lab test," I said. "But that doesn't seem like a reason to hurt or possibly kill someone."

"How much is one of these Snookzie paintings worth?"

"Between 1.5, possibly 2 mil."

"Two million dollars? That is definitely a reason to want to keep anyone from knowing they are making a fake," Cisco said as he headed toward his car. "I'll ask the Feds to check into this a little deeper. They love solving art scams."

"Hold on, I found out yesterday the attack at the neon studio wasn't aimed at me, but at the artist," I said.

"Good, if you're sure, I'll take it off the list."

"I'm positive."

"Have you had breakfast?" Nicole yelled from the kitchen.

"Come on Duie, we better get our bums inside before the lady of the house has a hissy-fit or worst yet a red head and her Fluff shows up," I said walking inside.

Nicole was setting out everything I enjoy eating in the morning: grape-nut flakes, walnut chips, sliced almonds, dried cranberries, blue berries and non-fat, unflavored yogurt.

"Great, now shall I mix it all together in a small bowl with a spoon as usual or we could have a merry diversion and find fun things for me to lick it off of. What would you prefer?" I said grinning from ear to ear.

"James, please be serious. I didn't sleep at all last night. We've got to resolve this whole thing about Merra, the FBI and me," she said with a dismal, glum expression.

"Hey, look we both brought our own personal histories to this relationship and the key word here is 'history'," I said. "We cannot change it, but we can learn from it and maybe even use it to move forward. Not in a brazen or reticent way, but in a forthright, upfront manner using our skills to strengthen our love and devotion to one another."

"Oh, I am so right about you. I knew the first time I heard you talk there is a good man inside that cheeky, mischievous and naughty exterior façade you parade around in," she said as she snugged up to me and gave me a deep-rooted kiss.

"Thank you, I like you too. Now let's see if we can take each one of your nightmare concerns and work some magic with them."

"Really and what witchcraft did you have in mind for Merra?"

"You know, I'd rather start with you first. OK?"

"Me, what about me?"

"I was wondering if you had to take any special training to be an FBI operative," I said as I studied her eyes.

"Wow, you know how to get right to the heart of the matter don't you," she said as she turned from me and began pacing. "Yes, Merra and I took a ten-week course together."

"What did it entail?"

"Everything from physical skirmishing and use of light arms to spying, undercover infiltration and general intelligence gathering."

"And after all that you were not full-fledged agents, just operatives," I said.

"Yes, it gave us much more freedom and we could pick and choose which assignments we preferred."

"I get it, you wanted your independence. Good for you," I said. "OK, let's start today."

"Start? What do you mean?" she said.

"I have a CAsLog shoot scheduled for today at the Pier. So, if you join me, you could be helpful in assessing a potential problem."

"Does it have anything to do with this Ninja guy?'

"Ah, no, but it could slow me down in trying to find him," I said. "Cisco has no hesitation in approaching the FBI for help, but I can't just tell Liz I'm setting everything aside in order to pursue something that probably has nothing to do with CAsLog."

"You want me to help with a CAsLog problem, not with finding the Ninja?" she said.

"It would be a big help and requires a feminine touch."

"Who will you be interviewing. I don't recall ever seeing any artists on the pier," she said.

"You're right. I'm interviewing Royal Knight. You remember him, don't you?"

"Yes, the singer, Merra and I talked briefly to him a couple of days ago. You want me to find out something about him?"

"No, Liz has invited somebody from Australia to watch the filming and I want to know why."

"Do you know anything about this person?"

"I was to meet her and Liz for lunch, but the meeting was cancelled," I said. "Tilly told me she will be bringing the woman to the Pier shoot instead.

"Oh, so this mystery guest is a woman who wants to meet you. Am in, when do we leave?"

Before I could answer a Fleetwood Mac's blues riff sailed out of my cell so a listened until I noticed the caller was Cisco. I hesitantly spoke into the phone.

"What's up amigo?"

"Didn't you tell me this Pasquale Ravanello guy is an authenticity expert?"

"Yes, that's right. Kirill's bank recommended him. Why?"

"You mean Kirill's wife's friend, the executive at the bank, recommended him."

"Ok and so what?"

"Well, the guy is not an expert, unless you're talking about his own paintings. He's an artist," Cisco said in a quick retort.

"He is, well I've never heard of him. How did you find out?"

"My friend at the FBI told me they've been looking at him for a couple of other art scams."

"I see, where's his studio? Did you get an address?"

"You can't go there. You are a known entity. He'll get spooked and probably bolt on us," said Cisco with an even sharper snap. "And my FBI friends will never give me another tip."

"You're right, but this really is a bolt out of the blue and we've got to find a way to check this guy out," I said. "I won't go to his studio, but if you tell me where it is located, I can probably find someone else in the area willing to help us."

"It's a little complicated so I'll text you the directions," he said. "Hey have you seen any more of the red head in the poke-a-dot number?"

"Get her out of your head man. She's probably more trouble than she's worth," I said.

Cisco replied "Oye, soy lo suficientemente grande como para manejar a cualquier bebe" and clicked off.

As I stood there thinking about Merra, the texted directions to Ravanello's studio showed up. It stated the studio was on a street I'd never heard of off the 110 in San Pedro which seemed rather bizarre because it's near the docks at the L.A. Harbor. The quirky note said to park near the alley and walk about 30 yards to a brick building between two old warehouses.

'The studio is on the second floor with metal staircase leading up to it. Rusty entrance door is usually unlocked; no moniker or name placard of any kind nor a buzzer, but there is a motion detector in the hall just inside the door.'

The directions set an unappealing tone, but the real teaser was the footnote about a guerilla style gallery squatting in the same building for over a year and the adjoining storage warehouse filled with "chronically" homeless men.

With ever lingering health concerns being bantered about on the evening news, when you're homeless, finding a place to safely rest one's head isn't easy in L.A.. Perhaps more importantly for my current concerns could that be the reason I haven't heard any whispers in private circles about this gallery.

The entire story seemed shrouded in a veil of mystery, but before I could shed light on its murky content's I needed to get to the pier for the CAsLog shoot.

"Are you ready," Nicole asked as she stuck her head in the studio door.

"Yes, let's go," I said as I crabbed my note pad and mask. "Did you give Duie a bone?"

"He's all taken care of. I'll drive," she said.

The drive was short, if fact, it took longer to find a parking space than it did to get there. By the time we walked to the coveted space Knight was on his que spot 10' from my chair and Tilly plus the crew were all set up and ready to go. As we approached a young woman with her back to us was talking to Tilly in an animated manner which accentuated her tight fitting, short skirt.

Nicole and I looked at each other and nodded in amused agreement.

"James this is Ms. Dolce Jeongeup, from VicFlicks Melbourne, Australia. Dolce this James Terra and Nicole Volkov."

After all greetings were completed, Nicole began chatting up Ms. Jeongeup and I spoke briefly with Royal Knight.

"I understand my crew have already shot film of you singing," I said. "I'm going to ask you a few questions about your life in New Orleans and then we'll concentrate on why you decided to make Santa Monica your home. Does that sound good to you?"

"How personal are the questions going to be," he said as he studied Nicole and Dolce.

"Not much, but I would like to know why you chose the name Royal Night."

"Oh, that's an old reference to Nate King Cole," he replied. "You know he was a very noticeably dark black man as am I. In fact, I really expected you to bring a make-up artist with you just to make me look lighter on camera."

"That's an interesting place for us to start. I'll have the crew start filming and you tell the full story. I really love the connection to Nate and the general history of blacks in film," I said.

Night grinned while putting his arm around me and said, "When we're all done, you are going to introduce me to Nicole's friend aren't you? She's cute and the accent is charming. Is she a nurse? I mean that looks like a special medical mask she has on."

It was my turn to grin as I gave Tilly the signal to start filming. I always know when the shot went well because the time just fly's by and everyone feels like we could just go on and on.

After Tilly called the shoot a rap Royal and I walked over to the ice cream cart where Nicole and Dolce were enjoying a cone each. Dolce was talking in complete sentences, but each one sounded as though it ended with a question mark. A style of conversation Aussies seem to cultivate.

"Victoria is home to a dynamic screen industry and our company leads the way in content and technology. One could say we develop and produce a range of screen formats, couldn't one?

Nicole raised her eye-brows at me and then rolled her eyes in a gesture implying we should be going. Dolce barely stopped to breathe as she continued on.

"VicFlicks engages screen industry experts to assess funding and production and makes recommendations for distribution to national channels and other platforms. A bit ambitious, isn't it?"

I decided it was time to intercede.

"That's great. So why did you want to watch us make a CAsLog?

"One of our interns watches your online posts and blogs, she suggested this format might work well in Melbourne so I was sent over to check it out as you Yanks say. Cheeky what?"

"Wonderful. Good luck with it," I said as I took hold of Nicole's hand. "Unfortunately, Nicole and I have another engagement and have to run. I'm sure Tilly can answer any questions you have and Royal here would be happy to show you around town. Wouldn't you Royal?"

"Hello Dolce," said Royal. "What part of Australia are you from?"

"I was born in Brisbane, wasn't I?" she answered.

Nicole and I headed for the car. We had barely got beyond ear shot before Nicole blurted out. "This is what you felt I needed to help you with?

"I wasn't sure is all. Did she tell you anything beyond her scripted sales patter stuff?"

"Only she'd like to convince you to go to Melbourne with her and film a few logs there for VicFlicks. I'm sure she'll be contacting you soon."

"What makes you say it in a huff?"

"She's enamored with you James. That's why."

"Can't be. We just met," I protested.

"I'll bet she'll convince Tilly to let her present the idea to your producer Liz."

"Damn, I don't need this right now and besides the new travel restrictions are crazy. There's something much more important I need to figure out," I said.

"What? Something to do with the Ninja guy?

"Maybe. That's what I, ah, we have to determine."

During our drive back home, I explained all about Pasquale Ravanello and the gorilla gallery. Nicole seemed keenly intrigued.

"All right, Cisco doesn't want you to go there because seeing you might alert Pasquale or the Ninja guy, but what if I go? I can put on a disguise and masquerade as an airhead socialite," she said with a shrewd grin.

"Mmm, that implies you've done this kind of thing before?"

"Maybe once or twice. Or a few times maybe," she said while avoiding any direct eye contact.

Her disclosure caused everything in my head to shift into protracted slow motion and far off in the dark caverns of my mind I sensed danger. A feeling I didn't like causing me to laboriously say "will you wear a wire?"

"Do you really think it's necessary?"

I was smiling, but my teeth were clinched. "Yes, I need to know you are safe and hearing what's going on will help."

"Ok, I can make that happened," she said with a noticeable level of pride.

I felt mentally locked down and unable to move, but I managed to intone, "Geez Nicole are you really this person?"

"I suppose I was for many years and it does feel somewhat alien to me now, but once I'm in the action everything will click into place and I'll be fine."

My need to dawdle was growing stronger. I really didn't want Nicole to dash off on her own, but before I could voice my objections an easy rollin' lick from Lightnin Hopkin's *Trouble In Mind* glided out of my cell. It seemed overly fortuitous which only added to my apprehensions. The call was from Royal Knight. I took a deep breath before answering and shifted into host mode voice.

"Hey Royal, have you and Dolce fallen off the pier yet?"

"No man, you know I don't leave my stage station when I've got a gig gathering even if it's only a handful. I just wanted to give you a heads up she's headed your way."

"What? Dolce is coming? Now?"

"That's what she said man. You know with a name like Jeongeup she's probably part aboriginal and can track you anywhere."

"Aboriginal? Really?"

"I don't know, man, the name just sounds like she is to me. Got-ta-go. Looking forward to seeing the log man."

He hung up and I still felt lethargic. "Have you ever noticed how time doesn't move minute to minute or even hour to hour on the beach? It seems to be more about how the tides and currents affect the mood of the moment."

"Ok, the mood current right now is telling us to find out about this Pasquale Ravanello dude," she said. "Let's stop by home first so I can put on my airhead disguise."

"Ugh, Royal says the Aussie is on her way there now."

"To our house?"

I shook my head and stopped the car expecting Nicole to suggest some other destination.

"Ok, we can work with that. Let's take her with us. She'll definitely make it seem normal you showed up at the gallery," she said. "You know, she's from Australia TV and you're showing her around town."

"Maybe, but I really want to meet Ravanello. Talk to him and look him in the eye to see if he's shifty."

"Right, so we'll go to his studio first and claim we're looking for the gallery," she said with a smile. "Trust me, I do a very convincing dingbat nitwit and having Ms. Jeongeup along will add to the chaos and confusion."

Mmm, dingbat nitwit. That would make for an interesting title for a painting, I mused.

"*Son of a Blues Man*" by Lucky Peterson let loose from my cell and I let it play for a long time before feeling up to telling Cisco about the plan of visiting Ravanello. To my surprise he agreed taking Nicole and the Aussie with me was a good idea. I left out the bit about Nicole going as a dingbat nitwit. Maybe it would be better as a song title, but before I could study the idea, Nicole nudged my arm.

"So, what did Cisco say about our plan?

"He likes it," I said as we approached our garage. "Hey, I don't see our Aussie friend."

"She's probably on the deck or on the beach," said Nicole as she started taking off her jewelry. "You find her while I change. Was that all Cisco had to say? The look on your face tells me it wasn't."

"Oh, it's just the Feds think Mrs. Kirill is sexually involved with the bank executive in order to guarantee he will give her husband the loan for the renovation of their house and I was just wondering if Maytor knows about what she is doing."

"I don't see how that would have anything to do with the Ninja guy sabotaging our car."

"Neither do I, but I doubt the Feds care much about that."

I drove into the garage and parked. Nicole ran into the house and I walked around to the deck. Ms. Jeongeup wasn't there. Nicole let Duie out and he quickly circled me then took off toward the surf which meant only one thing—Merra and Shotala were there. At that moment I noticed a dress laying on one of our deck chairs. I was hoping it wasn't Merra's. There weren't many people about so it was easy to spot Merra and Shotala. The dogs began romping in the surf. Merra, in a very tiny skin colored bikini, was talking to a woman in a black two-piece bathing suit. They both turned and waved to me. I waved back and started walking toward them when I realized the other woman was Dolce. She was willowy and sweet faced with wavy black hair, small breasted, and kind-of short legged. None of which seemed Aboriginal to me, but more surprisingly, when I approached, I could see she wasn't wearing a swimming suit, but rather her panties and bra.

"Gd-day mate," I said. "I see you're into the swing of things."

"Hello James, I did offer to loan Dolce one of my suits, but obviously none of them would be a good fit for her charming figure," said Merra.

"Well, I'm glad to see you are not wet," I said. "Nicole and I would like you to join us on a little adventure. Are you up for one?"

"As long as it isn't in the bush or back of beyond," Dolce replied as she noticed me scrutinizing her a bit more.

"You will have to put your dress and shoes back on, but it's just a short drive down to the harbor area to locate a gorilla gallery," I said with a grin and twinkle

"That's a new one. What exactly is it?"

"Yeah, I'd like to know that too," said Merra as she ran a finger along the inside rim of her bikini pants.

"It's an illegal gallery squatting in an unoccupied building and doesn't have a business license. Sort of clandestine."

"Oh, it's very hush hush," said Dulce. "Righty-o, no need to put the acid on and its ok if I'm not laired up," she replied as her mouth stretched wide and the flesh around her cheeks crinkled.

Merra and I starred at one another and laughed out loud simultaneously.

"Can I come too?" said Merra. "Sounds like a fun time."

"Sure, but I think you would feel a little more comfortable with some additional pieces to your outfit," I said with another twinkle as we all started walking toward the studio.

"Yes sir, will do," said Merra. "Come on Shotala we need to get you settled upstairs and I need to do a quick change."

Merra winked at me, smiled, quickly removed her bikini top and jiggled before starting up the stairs to her condo. I couldn't take my eyes off of her. I loved every bounce and wiggle.

"Here I was thinking I looked like a bit of a blowin bagswinger, but she is XyZ"

I shrugged and gestured toward Dolce's dress and headed into the studio.

"Right-o, yes sir we're on a bondi tram," said Dolce as she began dressing.

As I entered the studio, Nicole was coming down the stairs and had I not known it was her, I would never have recognized her. She was now a blond with oversized earrings, full, bright red lips, long, long eye lashes, a sheer see though blouse with no bra and a short, short skirt. My mind was whirling with images, all exciting and puzzling.

"Say, something James. Do you think this will work," said Nicole as she did a twirl. "I didn't over-do it, did I?"

"Ah, ah, no I'm sure it will be fine. Uhm, Merra is coming too."

She came to a complete stop and planted her hands firmly on her hips. "Was that your idea or hers?"

"Believe me it was hers."

The drive to San Pedro took a little longer than anticipated, probably because of the implausible, cockamamie story Nicole made up to explain her disguise and Dolce's colloquial Australian slang. Thankfully, the directions Cisco acquired from his FBI pal were spot on which was a good thing because when we exited the car my ribs were actually hurting from laughing so much at the feminine chatter. I would never have been able to find the place without them though.

At the building, we walked up the outside stairs, entered a hall and immediately noticed a hand lettered sign stating Studio Pasquale

Ravanello. Nicole took the lead, opened the door without knocking and we all followed her in. It was a typical artist's studio with several work tables filled with paint containers and brushes, but there was only one small easel and it held a rough sketch on raw canvas. All the finished paintings were much larger and attached to the shabby walls or leaning in piles against new looking shipping crates. Nicole immediately began speaking loudly probably in hopes of making Pasquale appear.

"We are obviously in the wrong place. This is not a gallery." There was a slight edge to her voice. I wondered if she was self-conscious about having told me so much about her former profession.

"Hold on, let's have a look around some of these paintings look interesting," said Merra with a wink.

"Thank you le signore, but my humble work pales in comparison to your outstanding beauty," said a scruffy looking fellow with chestnut unruly hair, dark eyes, a natural tan, soiled cloths and an impertinent unshaven smirk that lined and segmented his face like a puzzle.

"Oh, hello, we were told there is a gallery in this building, but this couldn't be it. Could it?" said Nicole in a little girl-like voice I was amazed came from her. "You don't seem like a gallery director person."

"No piccolo ragazza, I am not little one," said Pasquale. "I am the one and only Pasquale Ravanello painter extraordinaire," he said as he turned to face me.

"Is there something I can do for you Mr. Terra?"

"We really are looking for the gallery that's supposed to be in this building. Ms. Jeongeup here is from Australian TV and she would very much like to see a gorilla gallery," I replied as I pretended to look at one of his paintings.

"I see, well the gallery is at the opposite end of the hall, but there may not be anyone there now. They don't keep regular hours, but the door is usually left unlocked."

"Aren't they worried someone may tickle the peter," said Dolce with a quizzical look.

Everyone laughed except our invaded host. He remained focused on me and what I was doing. I could actually see his frown peeking out from the outer limits of his mask.

"I'm not familiar with your work," I said. "Are you represented by a gallery?"

"Not currently, but I'm too busy to spend any more time with sightseers and tourists so please." He held out his arms in a gesture meant to shoo us out.

"Well can you tell me where you studied or any exhibits your work has been in?

"Not now, no," he said as he held the door open and watched us leave.

"That was a bit of a barney," said Dolce.

Everyone shuffled off toward the opposite end of the drab, dingy hall. "From the looks of this floor I doubt anyone has visited here in some time," I said. "Lots of dust, but no shoe prints."

The double door was ajar. Nicole pushed it open. "It's a gallery of sorts, I guess. Come on in."

"Hello. Anyone here," yelled Merra as she went directly to a desk near the only window and begun rummaging through several papers and file folders. "Nothing here is dated after February 23."

"Not a good sign," I said. "That's when the international health committee visited China and announced the pandemic."

"You think whoever was running this place dropped everything and left because of it?"

"Could be. None of this art is worth looking at, let's leave," suggested Nicole as she stared at me with concern. "I need to make a call and my cell is only getting a weak signal in here."

Merra moved next to her and looked at the cell. "What's the rush?"

"Oh, Patterson went to China on a business trip in January and I'd like to know if he's back yet or not. You know, just to be sure he's ok."

"Right you are," I said as I ushered everyone out the door. "You ladies head to the car. I want to ask Mr. Ravanello a couple of quick questions. I'll catch up with you."

Nicole winked at me and led the group to the outdoor stairwell. I went back to Pasquale's studio and found the door still unlocked, but he wasn't there so I looked around. I was searching for anything looking out of place or odd. The canvases, brushes and paint all seemed normal except one small bottle of blue paint.

The paint itself looked ordinary, but the label got my attention. The plain white label was inscribed 'For SJNTF Prints'. I took a photo of it then opened it and used a small brush to smear some of the paint onto a blank label I found nearby. It smelled like oil paint. I folded it and put it in my pocket as I turned one of the crates around to check the shipping label.

"What are you doing," said a sibilant echoed voice.

I turned around fully expecting trouble, but it was Nicole disguising her voice again. I was relieved. "This label shows the crate came from the Sao Paulo Art Storage. That's a tax-free zone and it will be returned there tomorrow. Mmm, there was a fire there recently."

"Just take a photo of it and let's get out of here now. This place gives me the creeps."

We left the building and found Merra and Dulce waiting for us at the car.

"I sure wouldn't want to be stuck in that place if we all end up having to self-quarantine," said Merra. "It's claustrophobic, dark and smelly. Who would go to such a gallery?"

"Good question," said Dulce. "Looks like a front to me. Ah, I mean a bagman's gazette."

"All right, that's it. Who or should I say, what are you," replied Merra through her clinched teeth. "You are definitely not a TV executive."

"Oh shit, Merra, not now and not here," whispered Nicole. "Everyone please get-in the car. Now!"

I quickly hit the key fob and we all got in without speaking, however, I noticed a sharp eye gesture exchange between Nicole and Merra followed by them both looking at me as I drove away searching for the nearest freeway on-ramp.

"Ok ladies, here's what we all are going to do. First everyone is going to calm down and be polite. Then I'm going to explain the situation from my point of view and you will speak only when I ask you a question. Got it?"

They all nodded and looked frustrated. I couldn't find an on-ramp so I parked where we could look out over the harbor.

"First Merra, Nicole has explained everything to me about your friendship and past history of working together."

"Everything? Are you sure about that," Merra replied in a harsh manner.

"Yes. We'll go into it in detail later," I said in a deliberately jarring fashion. "Now Dolce, none of us believe you are who you pretend to be, so who are you really?"

"How very boorish and disrespectful of you … of all of you. I have nothing further to say. Let me out at the nearest Taxi."

I hit the master door lock button and turned to face her. "No, I'll take you back to Santa Monica, directly to my buddy Detective Rivas' office. I'm sure he'll determine who you are real fast or he may just lock you in a cell for a couple of days."

A sullen chill shuddered through everyone as an enormous cargo ship entered the port casting an even larger shadow over ever thing, instantly rendering us and our erupting drama trifling.

"Or maybe we should just slip some cash to a few of these longshoremen to stow you away on a slow boat to China. How would you like that?"

Nicole scowled at me with disappointment filling her eyes.

"Ok, look there is no need for this to get out of control. I'm sure none of us want to cause any harm," Dulce said with a detached smile.

"Bull shit, let's take her back to that empty warehouse and lock her up in the basement," I said as I started the car.

"Ok, ok, I'm a P.I. and was instructed to determine if you are involved with what's going on with the Kirill bank loan."

"What the hell is a kirill?" said Merra. "Sounds like some kind of fish."

"I know what she's talking about," I said. "So, what's with your name? Jeongeup? It sounds Aboriginal, but nothing else about you seems to be."

She laughed and shook her head. "You Yanks are all alike. Jeongeup is not aboriginal its Korean. My mother is Australian and my father is Korean. She and I are related to the bank President."

"I see, so he hired you to find out what's happening between Kirill's wife and the bank's Loan Officer."

"Yes, that's correct and he just wanted to make sure you and the Landchilde chap are not involved."

"Do you know anything about the Ninja motorcyclist?

"The what?" said Dolce.

"Geez, James what the hell are you and Nicole into?" said Merra as she sharpened her focus on Nicole. "And I thought you were out of the game."

"I am, it's just that James has a knack for getting caught in the middle of things."

"The middle? It sounds more like you're both up to your necks in whatever this is."

"Ok Dolce, all I care about is that my CAsLog video gets finished. Anything about Mrs. Kirill and the bank has nothing to do with it or me."

"Hold on. I want to know what's going on between them," said Nicole.

"Me too," chimed in Merra.

"Well, as near as I can tell, the two of them have been lovers for a while. Probably because Kirill is asking for a loan amount that exceeds the value of the house … so ownership of the Snootz Jefferies paintings is an important part of the deal," said Dolce.

"I see. Does Maytor know how far his wife has gone to insure getting the loan?" I asked.

"We don't know and it isn't important to the bank."

"But how valuable the paintings are is?"

"Plus, ownership is being questioned."

"What makes you think Maytor isn't the legitimate owner?"

"His wife may have used them for collateral for another loan they've already received."

"Wow, she has been a busy beaver," said Merra. "Did she sleep with someone to get that loan too?"

"We don't know. The loan officer has disappeared. Hey, why did you park here? Those massive tanks look like they store enough butane to flatten this entire area for miles if they were to explode. It would make the devastation in Beirut look like a camp fire."

"You are right. In fact, the San Pedro Artists Against Hacienda Holdings has been trying for years to get officials to relocate them off shore," I said.

"How do you know about this?" asked Merra.

"The company's government affairs director contacted me when they heard I was considering during an interview here with one of the protesting artist."

"So what happened?"

"We were denied a filming permit so the shoot was done entirely inside the artist's studio."

"These tanks hold about 13 million gallons of liquid gas and there are homes, a preschool and soccer fields within less than a quarter-mile from here. It's the largest facility of its kind in the state."

"Maybe that's why those industrial buildings are empty," said Nicole.

"Yea, this stuff can vaporize rapidly and is highly flammable and explosive. Several of the local artists told me one professional assessment stated a blast could reach as far as 7 miles away."

"Geez, here we are concerned about what a rogue artists is trying to do, when terrorists would have no difficulty destroying this ticking time bomb."

"Well, supposedly refrigerating the butane keeps it safe," I said, "But there is no accounting for a domino effect and I seem to recall there is an earthquake fault running underneath the entire harbor to boot."

Everyone became quiet, but I felt the need to get back on track. "Are you sure you don't know anything about a Ninja motorcyclist?" I said.

"No, I don't, but I'll ask my associates and let you know."

"James, let's go home," said Nicole as she put her hand on my knee. "Please."

"Righty oh. That's where I'm heading as soon as you get me back to my car," said Dolce.

"You mean, you're going back to Aus?"

"Yes, I have a feeling this pandemic thing is going to bring about a lot of severe travel restrictions and I don't want to be stuck here," said Dolce as she watched the big ship squeeze through the narrow port. "I'd rather be with my family and friends. Ah, no offense."

A sullen stillness surrounded us all as I put my hand on Nicole's. "Ladies we are returning to Santa Monica," I said as a buzz murmured.

"Hello," said Nicole as she took her phone from some unseen location of her clothing and turned toward the side window.

I started the car and headed onto the freeway, but the intense expression on Nicole's face and in her general demeanor as she listened to the caller caused all time to elapse for we arrived home much quicker than I thought we would. She hung up and sat starring at the garage wall.

"What's happened honey?" said Merra. "Is there a problem we can help with?"

"Patterson has disappeared in the quarantine region of China ... he may be dead."

CHAPTER 16

Duie was sitting at the sliding glass door when I managed to lift my eyelids up enough to scan the living room. He wagged his tail and pranced about in a manner indicating he urgently needed out. I staggered to the door and opened it. He headed straight to the nearest Palm.

Nicole was snuggled up on the couch still sleeping. I picked-up the glasses and empty wine bottles quietly and took them to the sink. As I gently sat them down, Nicole's cell buzzed. She rolled onto the floor and reached across the coffee table to crab it.

"This is Nicole Volkov … yes … I see … when … what does that mean?" She sat starring out at the deserted beach. "And then what? … Really, are you sure? … Thank you, I will and I appreciate being kept informed."

She placed the phone down gently and continued concentrating on the surf. I hesitantly stepped in front of her and offered a hand up. She looked directly into my eyes as hers filled with tears. I pulled her up into my arms. "Have they located Patterson?"

"Yes and no. The Chinese turned over his Passport, but have not found his body. He may have been put into a mass grave. We may never find him."

"Who told you this?"

"Patterson's company lawyer Nathan Zevenaar. He has kept in touch with the U.S. Embassy in China."

"So, there is nothing we can do but wait?"

"Apparently, Patterson didn't have time to change his will before leaving," she said as we watched Duie chase the gulls off the deck.

"And?"

"And if he isn't found I may have to meet with the company lawyers to discuss how my shares and the company as a whole could be affected."

"I see, but couldn't all of this also be affected by the pandemic," I said.

"I suppose so. I just don't want to think about it right now."

"What do you want to do?"

"Your work on the new paintings seems to be going very well and I received a text message from Luc Blondin asking me to contact him. Do you have any idea what he wants?"

"Well, you did ask him to let you know whenever he completes any small-scale sculptures. Perhaps he has something to show you."

"You're right I did. Do you mind contacting him to see if that's what he wants?"

"OK, sure."

As I started to write a text message to Luc, a faint familiar voice echoed in the far reaches of my mind causing me to pause. I stood still and listened. It was Maggie Mayye talking about being concerned over Luc panicking when pressured so I kept the text to "What's up?"

Less than 5 minutes later Luc responded with "I was wondering if Mrs. Volkov would have time to meet with me to discuss a traveling exhibit idea I have. It wouldn't take much of her time just a few minutes."

Nicole was in the kitchen fixing breakfast. I handed my phone to her. She read the note and quickly thumb typed in a response and resumed preparing food.

"You know, I was thinking we should let Maggie know about this before responding to Luc. I assume it's too late now."

"Oh, I just told him to put the idea in writing and send it to me, ah, I mean to you. That way we can figure out a nice way to respond."

"That'll work."

We finished breakfast without talking then relaxed on the couch to listen to some easy sax blues when Delbert MaClinton's gravelly voice wailed from my phone.

It was another text message from Luc, one that detailed his exhibit idea. It read as follows:

Title: Totalled / Damaged Art Worth Keeping

Overview: Each year dozens of works of art are broken or damaged due to accidents and/or mishandling. After months of examining them and assessing the damage, insurance company's usually determine it would cost more to repair them than they are worth. So, they pay the owners the insurance premium, declaring the works a total loss and transport them to a large warehouse where they are stacked with hundreds of other artworks now demoted to objects of no merit, significance or monetary value.

This exhibition surveys how to define the intrinsic core value of those artworks.

"Wow do you really think Luc wrote this or that it's even his idea?" said Nicole.

"It is surprising and seems beyond the scope of what Maggie would encourage him to pursue. However, I do believe it merits serious thought and a sensitive answer."

"Yes, but will he be upset if I ask him if the idea is his alone?"

"I'm not sure. I'd just like to know if Maggie contributed to it."

"You know, when you consider it's pretty much how he approaches his sculptures. He takes old broken machines and gives them new purpose as works of art. It's not too far a stretch to see how he'd be interested in taking damaged art and giving it new life," I said.

"Yea, but is it still art? Does it still have any true aesthetic value?" said Nicole with a mystified gaze out the window at the still empty beach.

"Mmm, it certainly would have some educational value on several levels and it would make a great CAsLog," I said. "It really opens up lots of avenues of discussion. I seem to remember Jon Doh talking about it when his studio was destroyed in the last big quake. He even suggested he wanted to exhibit all of the broken works, but most likely his gallery dealer didn't go for the idea."

"Luc is turning out to be a deeper fellow than either of us thought."

"That is for sure," I said as I filled our glasses with more Pomegranate juice.

"You, said that with a rather serious tone. Did something happen I don't know about?"

"I'm not sure. Cisco and I were considering perhaps Luc used a drone to explode his sculpture just at the moment I got near it."

"You're kidding? What makes you think so?"

"I definitely heard a buzzing sound after the sculpture stopped moving and there were a great many small pieces of metal everywhere which doesn't correspond to it just being pushed over."

"Geez, I need to be careful with what I say about his exhibit idea and I'll certainly talk to Maggie first."

"Maybe he blew it up thinking it would be put into a traveling exhibit," I said.

"Here is another empty juice bottle and I'm feeling drained too, let's take a shower," said Nicole as she headed toward the stairs.

I let Duie back in and he followed her up the stairs.

"The beach just doesn't look right being empty on such a beautiful day. What the hell is the world coming to?"

Nicole turned and sat on the stairs. "Love will keep us alive because everyone will adjust their own mental focus zooming in and out on the details. Maybe even shifting now and then to a wider focus to make their personal problems seem small."

"Yes, tinkering with the variables always leads to different outcomes," I said as I watched a lone gull land on our deck table. "And a grateful heart remedies the confusion and distortions. So where does this leave us Miss secret agent woman?"

"One of the things that continues to attract me to you James is how you don't hesitate to act on your intuitive impulses and the results always turn out so right, but please don't refer to me as an agent of any kind."

"Right, I only meant it as a term of endearment." She smiled, but didn't turn to look at me.

"I doubt most people appreciate just how bad things may become with this global pandemic. The performing arts are already dead in the water. The enablers, support crews, venues everyone, everything is trapped … I mean, we all are in the middle of a catastrophe and yet somebody is actively stalking us. It's crazy."

"Why don't you sit out on the deck and relax for a while, maybe in an hour or so everything will feel a little less problematic and a solution will present itself."

"Good idea, come on Duie lets catch a few rays," I said as I walked outside and sat in the deck lounger to close my eyes and relax. The warmth of the sun was instantly comforting.

***

"Mr. Terra sir, can we talk?"

For what felt like an elongated moment I thought I might be dreaming, but my eyes immediately corrected me. Luc and Maggie were indeed standing right before me. "Why yes, of course, please sit. If it's about the CAsLog shoot, no decisions have been made and I'm sure Nicole has yet to complete her review of your traveling exhibit idea. You know the pandemic has put everything on hold. And say, those are very unique masks you both are wearing. Did you make them yourself?" I said as I put on my standard white hospital one.

"Luc made them from old welding shields," said Maggie with a half grin.

"No, it's not about those things, sir. I would like to apologize for causing my sculpture to fall on you."

Time stopped. I couldn't hear the waves crashing or the gulls squawking and my foggy brain cells made the empty beach look like a red haze somewhere on Mars.

"James, James are you alright?" said Nicole as she shook my shoulder and turned to Luc. "What did you say to him?"

"Tell, her Luc. She has a right to know too," said Maggie.

"I designed my sculpture as a Dada performance piece. You know, like a Jean Tinguely. It was supposed to slowly self-destruct. I was trying to make a statement about the human condition. I'm deeply sorry you were hurt Mr. Terra."

A tidal wave of relief rolled over me as the haze dissipated. "Did you deliberately wait until I got near it?"

"No, no, I was watching on the drone screen waiting for the docent led group to walk past. I didn't even know you were there. I was hoping all those big collectors and you Mrs. Volkov would watch it slowly fall apart, but I lost control of the drone and it flew into the sculpture hitting the battery panel which caused the whole thing to explode and go crazy."

The smile on my face was so expansive it caused my face mask to fall down. "Just promise me next time you have an opportunity to show-off a performance piece you'll let everyone know in advance about what to expect."

"See I told you he would understand," said Maggie.

"I hate to put a damper on these good vibes, but I hope you realize Nellie and I will have to put out a news-release explaining how we weren't aware of what you had planned to do … especially since the police are still investigating."

"Do you want me to turn myself in to them?" said Luc sporting a stiff upper lip.

"No, Nellie and I will take care of everything. Maybe we can just post a statement on our website and in social media."

"Understood and I'll be upfront about everything from now on," said Luc. "And will post my apology on my website," said Luc as Maggie nudged him. "and social media also."

"So, are you working on another self-destructing piece" I asked.

"I'd like to make one that falls apart real slow like Urs Fischer's candle portraits. I really admire his work," said Luc as he stared into Maggie's eyes and took her hand.

"You know Luc that sounds as though it would make for a meaningful addition to your CAsLOG segment," I said. "Would one of the guys in your class Maggie be interested in shooting video of Luc working on it once or twice a week until it's finished?"

"I believe so," replied Maggie with a smile and wink.

"And I need a little more clarification about the drone," I said as Luc seemed to stand to attention again. "Were you hiding in the bushes when the crash occurred?"

"Yes, sir and when everyone went inside, I picked up the motor and several of the main pieces."

"And no one saw you?"

"I was a special ops commando sir."

"Right and obviously good at it."

"Uhm, I have one other question," said Nicole. "Do you ever dress up like a Ninja and ride a motorcycle?"

"Ah, no."

"How about any of your fellow commando buddies?" said Nicole with a sweet smile.

"Not that I know of. Why?"

"Oh, just curious," said Nicole as she turned to me. "We've had a couple of unpleasant encounters that's all."

"Hey, if there's some guy giving you two trouble, just give me the word and I'll take him out," said Luc as he stood rod stiff.

"I'm sure that won't be necessary, will it Mrs. Volkov?" said Maggie as she took Luc's arm and started walking him toward the cul-de-sac.

"Hey, I meant to ask you Luc, are there any portraiture artists that you admire?"

"Many Sir, but I'm not interested in emulating them. In fact, just the opposite."

"What do you mean?"

"Take Hans Holbein for example, he was great at rendering the physical appearance of his sitters and really ingenious conveying their values and ideals by surrounding them with jewelry, pets, letters, books, all kinds of stuff. I don't do that. I want to force the viewer to search for those markers in the way the light and shadows swaths the hills and valleys of each face and glistens from their eyes.

"Well said and thank you Luc for your report on the sculpture accident. I look forward to seeing the video of your new piece," I said as they walked away. Maggie looked especially relieved.

"Well, that takes another mystery off the list," said Nicole. "What do we have left?"

"You know what's really starting to bug me," I said. "What is your, maiden name?"

"That's not a mystery. Why do you want to know?"

"Because I don't like hearing you referred to as Mrs. Volkov."

"It's Ms. Nicolette Trenet," with a silent "t".

"Nicole is the French version of the Greek Nike and means victory of the people. Trenet means near water. Does that make you feel better?"

"Yes, it does. Is it alright if I introduce you as Ms. Nicole Trenet?" I said? "Terra and Trenet, I like the sound of that."

"Well don't be in too much of a rush to throw out my Mrs. Volkov title just yet," said Nicole. "While you were hearing Luc's confession, I was on the phone again with Zevenaar. You know Patterson's lawyer."

"Did something happen?"

"No, they haven't found him, but they did discover something else missing," said Nicole in an awkward and apprehensive manner.

"What?"

"Besides not making a new will, apparently Patterson never got around to marrying his girlfriend Hanna either."

There was a long stretch of silence as we both pondered the revelation.

"Holly-cow you realize this means if he's dead you inherent everything?"

"Yes, and this is why Zevenaar and everyone at the company headquarters is anxious to meet with me."

We stood together looking at the deserted beach again and at each other. Our union felt as though time had bolted our feet to the ground and then whizzed us forward while screaming silently.

"What do you want to do?" said Nicole in a soft whisper.

"This raises another possibility concerning the Ninja attacks," I said. "Someone may be targeting you. Who benefits the most if you are not around?"

"Damn, James you could be right, maybe this whole thing doesn't have any connection to Maytor Kirill, his wife nor Snookz Jefferies or Pasquale Ravanello. It just might be a corporate takeover attempt by getting me out of the way."

We stood quietly in each other's arms for a while longer. I got two glasses and opened a bottle of our favorite fruit juice mix. "Let's drink a toast to the future," I said.

"To the future of humanity and our love," said Nicole. "May they survive and thrive forever."

"I love looking at your face," I said softly. "The curve of your cheeks, the glow of your skin, the way you lower your lashes before looking at me with your vibrant eyes and the shape of your mouth as your breath exhilarates when we are close like this. I can't get enough of you."

As we relaxed our embrace, Merra walked off the beach and right to our sliding glass door. Duie jumped against it and started wiggling about. Nicole waved her to come in and as she moved her metallic blue thong-bikini crackled with static electricity. The effect fit the moment perfectly.

"Can I have a glass of whatever that is?" she said as she bent down sparkling to petted Duie. "Yes, I know you're a very good boy." She looked up through the top of her eyes directly at me.

I handed her a full glass of juice. "How are things in the neighborhood?"

"Very quiet. In fact, it feels abandoned. What are you two celebrating? Did they find Patterson?"

Nicole and I looked at each other and smiled. "Go ahead," I said. "Tell her the whole story."

Nicole spared no detail filling Merra in on Luc's declaration of guilt and our joint speculations about corporate clandestine scheming. I couldn't help but notice how attentive and riveted Merra was through the entire presentation.

"All of this is fascinating and makes it easier for me to tell what I found out on my own," said Merra with a wonderful lithe jiggle to her bosom.

"Wait a minute. You've been investigating us?" I said with probably too much volume. "Nicole did you know about this?"

"No, but I want to hear every detail just the same."

Merra stared at Nicole and smiled then began telling how she had contacted a friend, Andre Troussier, at Interpol concerning Ravenello shipping art to tax free storage ports in Europe.

"How is Andre?" asked Nicole. "Is he still involved with Suzette?"

"He is fine and I didn't ask him about any of his girlfriends. We concentrated on Ravenello and his fast shuffling of paintings. He's been making copies of valuable paintings, but nobody seems to know why or what he does with them other than exhibits."

"Do you mean he just copies them then sends the originals back to their owners?" I asked.

"Yes, it's what Interpol claims."

"That's odd. Are they sure he sends the originals back?" asked Nicole.

"Yes, they've all been checked with every shipment."

"I noticed in the gorilla gallery most of the paintings were made by the same artists even though they were signed by several different names. I wouldn't be a bit surprised to find Pasquale made all of them himself," I said.

"None of which sounds like it has anything to do with Kirill," said Nicole.

"Well, I think he's planning to make some Snookz paintings or limited-edition prints on paper. Hell, he may have finished them by now," I said.

"What makes you think so?"

"He has a bottle of blue paint labeled SJXNFTin his studio."

"And that stands for Snookz Jefferies Extra NFT?" said Nicole.

"That would be my guess and I'll bet when Cornish finishes testing the sample dab I took it will match with the paintings owned by Kirill."

"But does that connect to trying to kill you or Nicole?" said Merra. "And what's and NFT?"

"It shouldn't, but the world seems to be getting crazier every day," I said. "Which reminds me, why did Patterson go the China right when all of this pandemic crap started?"

"Uhg, I asked Zevenaar the very same question," replied Nicole. "It seems Patterson made a big investment in a company called Flying Eye which makes low altitude drones."

"So why did he need to visit them now?" said Merra.

"Apparently the U.S. Army Special Operations Command has put the company on a blacklist of Chinese firms subject to restrictions on national security grounds."

"Because?"

"The drones are used by the Interior Department, the U.S. Forest service, Homeland Security, local police departments and a lot of things related to our critical infrastructure which means they can be used for spying and even get access via the internet. Plus, other foreign agents can pull data off of them. So, Patterson was trying to have a kill switch put on them that would prevent data transmission or some such thing."

"That sounds like closing the gate after the horse has bolted," said Merra. "What good can going to China do now? I mean what does Patterson think his going to accomplish?"

"Knowing him, he probably believes he can solve the problem by making a money deal," said Nicole.

"So, you're saying when the Army Corp of Engineers uses one of these Flying Eye drones over a dam, say the Bonneville Dam on the

Columbia River in Washington it not only gets really good photos it can use their wifi system to steal operating codes for the dam and the electrical grid of the entire west coast?"

"That's exactly what the Army Command told Zevenaar," said Nicole.

"Is there any more wine," asked Merra. "I think we may need to open a bottle of something stronger than this juice."

"Hey, I don't mean to change the subject, but where is Shotala?"

"She's in isolation … remember?"

"Yea, that's something we're all going to be in for a while."

"That could be to our advantage," I said. "So, let's review for a moment. We're now down to only two possible assassins. First, is the Kirill loan CAsLog fiasco, which strikes me as a long shot and second is the Patterson corporate takeover debacle with all of its international implications. In the first I would be the likely target and in the second Nicole would be."

"It's odd how all of this, along with self-distancing and isolation, makes one feel in exile longing for home, even though we've all remained in place right here at home," said Merra so deep in thought she didn't hear me.

"Solastalgia," I said.

"Oh, what does that mean?"

"It's a neologism that combines nostalgia, anguish and despair to describe a profound sense of loss and an overwhelming feeling of powerlessness." My face must have changed because she looked at me with alarm.

"OK, if you say so. Well, whatever it is, it makes me feel as though my sense of belonging is eroding. Which is down-right upsetting."

"Homesickness when still at home," said Nicole. "You know psychologists are already saying both climate change and the pandemic may have an acute impact on our mental health. It's important we help each other stay optimistic." Her eyes softened. "Plus, we've also got to keep aware of the third threat … the Covid-19 coronavirus." A shadow of looming loss fell across her face. "You know, all of this has also made me ready for a real bottle of wine too… how about in the hot tub?" she said staring intently at me and speaking in an emotional rush. I didn't interrupt her.

"All three of us?" asked Merra cautiously.

"Sure, why not. We're all friends and we may as well enjoy every bit of life while we can," replied Nicole with a beautiful smile. "We can even sun bath up there, no one can see us on the terrace. Uh, unless they have a drone."

"Right, worse things could happen. There's little future in the present. I'm up for it, are you James," said Merra with a flash of her eyelashes.

"I will be by the time we're up there."

Both ladies moved past me as sensually as possible. Their suggestive movements were intense and deliberately interrupted by glances in my direction as their eyes grew deeper and brighter. My blood pressure surged as I envisioned what was to come.

I woke up reluctantly with a sated smile and a huge hard-on. Nicole and Merra were not in sight, but I could hear them talking on the terrace. I left the bed and moved a little closer, but stayed quiet and out of sight.

"He doesn't talk about his family often," said Nicole. "He was only ten when his father died and apparently the family's status dwindled quickly."

"That's surprising, he always displays the outward demeanor of a life of privilege."

"What do you mean exactly?"

"He exudes confidence and is always slightly aloof," said Merra. "I suppose that could be because he is handsome and svelte with great proportions and a wonderful speaking voice."

"Yes, believe it or not, it was his voice which attracted me to him before I even saw him and he has lots of natural gifts too."

"I noticed those tonight for sure, but I was surprised to see so many scars all over him. Oh, does he always leave the night light on every time you have sex? I mean it's not even sunset yet."

"Usually and with the three of us, he will probably insist on it. He's an artist and wants to see everything and his aloofness comes from being an artist too," said Nicole. "All artists seem that way to me."

"Are you sure he is alright with you and I being so close?"

"Yes, being open minded is also a trait most artists have."

I reran the early evening activities over and over in my mind. I was physically exhausted, but somehow completely mentally rejuvenated. I got up, put my shorts back on and joined them on the terrace.

"Hey ladies, I have one more need for the evening and I hope you'll join me," I said casually.

"Really, there was something we didn't do. What?" said Nicole. "If it something kinky like handcuffs or gags you'll have to find yourself two-other ladies."

"Ugh, no, no I want to go for a midnight sky hike."

"What is a sky hike? Do you mean get high?"

"Nah. We'll drive up to Leo Carrillo State Park and take the star-studded 2-mile hike through giant coast live oaks and sycamores to the top of the canyon. It has fantastic, tranquil views of the night-time Malibu coastline, ocean panoramas of the sunset and an incredible awe-inspiring view of the cosmos. No Ninja's, in fact the only danger is the dense groves of prickly pear cactus and we can rest on the sand when we come back down," I said with my arms open ready to be embraced.

"After the two-hour sex romp we gave you, you still have enough energy to walk up a canyon wall to stare at stars," said Merra. "I'm in just to see how long you last and those cacti better be the only pricks around."

Nicole was shaking her head and putting her top back on. "Ok, James, but I'm bringing the new Torch flashlight, Duie and my gun. If anything jumps out of the brush's I'll shoot it."

CHAPTER 17

"Hello." Nicole came out of the dressing room with the phone to her ear and gesturing the call was from Merra next door. "Yes, I've got it. OK, be sure to wear your mask and take hand sanitizer with you. Mmm, yes, he's finally awake. I will, take care." She clicked off and looked at me. "You look very relaxed. I hope that means you enjoyed our ah everything delight celebration last night."

"It certainly does and I want to make sure we all understand each-others ah … point of view … ah related to the current need to be very mindful of what's happening to society in general."

"Agh, what does that mean?"

"I assume Merra is going somewhere … somewhere where there may be contaminated people, food, surfaces and who knows what else. Then she will be coming back here?"

"You are right, we need to set up some protocols. Which means I need to go to the market and get some cleaners, sanitizers, gloves, toilet paper and food."

"But first you're going to tell me what Merra just told you."

"About us or Ravenello?"

"We can talk about us another time, right now I want to know about Ravenello."

"Right. It seems some ultra-wealthy Russian art collector accepted a shipment of paintings from Ravenello, so there is speculation about the replicas he has of the masterpieces in the guy's collection."

"Where are they?"

"He keeps some in his Georgian residence and others in an art storage locker in London."

"None of that feels related to anyone targeting you or I," I said as I headed toward the shower. "Does Merra really understand what we are focused on? Or is she just caught up in the whole idea of being some kind of secret agent?"

"You're right. She has been considering joining the FBI. I'll talk to her when we all get together tonight. I'm going now, bye."

"Hold on," I said while holding the pillow over my manhood. "Be sure to pay attention to your surroundings and especially for anyone following you. Oh, and park the car where there are lots of people. Come to think of it, why don't I drive you."

"No. We're not going to get all paranoid about Ninja's or this Covid thing. That would drive me crazy. Let's stay calm at least until we know more," she said as she headed down the stairs.

"You mean how you were not paranoid last night every time the breeze rustled the foliage?" She didn't answer and before I could gather my thoughts, *Call Me the Breeze* by JJ Cale eased out of my cell. The caller was Liz Weinstein.

"Hi Liz, I hope all is going well for you and everyone at the station."

"Thanks James. As far as I know we're all still healthy.

"Great, what can I do for you?"

"Some decisions have been made regarding filming for the rest of the season. Do you have enough material to finish editing the Money Mirage segment?"

"Yes, I believe so especially if I do a few voice overs, then there won't be need for anymore filming."

"That's good. What about the segment on the three emerging artists?"

"I haven't looked at what we got before the lights went out in Arash's neon studio... ah, sort-a-speak. I suspect we'll need to shoot more. Or maybe we could put in the Royal Knight log?"

"All right, but try to avoid it. Now for the rest of the season you remember your idea of doing a follow up segment about the artists who have died since the program started? Well now's the time for it. Pull those segments out of archives and see how many new versions you can make from them by re-editing plus using edited out segments and voice overs."

"Right. I got it and it sounds good. I'll also talk to Arash to see what we can do," I said while looking out at the closed pier. "What are we going to do if this thing isn't over with by next season?"

"Let's not dwell on it now. Keep me updated on what you are doing and don't send the crew anywhere without checking with me first. Be careful and stay safe. Ciao."

I disconnected and noticed the deserted beach felt like an omen for teetering on the brink of disaster. The magic that draws people to it seemed to have been set aside. Its welcoming embrace and occasional stormy temper didn't compare to the power of a deadly virus. Plus putting one's fate into a small, pathetic looking mask felt like an odd way to protect oneself and humanity.

I'm not sure how long I sat there musing. Living at the beach tends to do that to one. "We are all in the same boat," I shouted above the waves, but there was no reply of any kind. Just silence.

"Hey, I could use some help bringing in the groceries and everything else from the car," yelled Nicole from the garage.

I jumped to my feet and took the bags from her arms just as they began slipping. "There's lots more. Bring them all in here so we can sort and sanitize everything."

"Do you ever feel really small when looking at the ocean?" I asked. "It sort of puts things in perspective for me. Does it do that for you?"

"I often feel born again when I get out of the surf. Did something happen while I was gone?"

"No, not really. I spoke with Liz about how we we're going to handle doing the show for the rest of the season that's all."

Nicole had started up the stairs, but turned and sat on them. "Love will keep us alive because everyone will play with their own mental focus. Zooming in and out on the details. Shifting now and then to the wide focus to make their problems seem small."

"Are you feeling alright or are you just testing me?" I said.

"What are you talking about? I feel fine and why would I want to test you?"

"Then we've got a problem," I said while putting my arms around her. "You said that same thing to me yesterday word for word then I answered 'Yes, tinkering with the variables always leads to different outcomes.' Don't you remember that conversation?"

She sat watching a lone gull walking back and forth on our deck table. "Oh, yea and you said something about a grateful heart remedies the confusion and distortions then called me Ms. Secret Agent?"

"Right," I said as I too watched the lonely gull.

"Then you went on about people not appreciating just how bad things are and we are in the middle of a catastrophe and it's crazy somebody is stalking us."

"Whew, at least you remember, but what made you repeat yourself?"

"I don't know, exactly, for some reason that particular conversation keeps bouncing around in my mind," she said. "Let's change the subject. I was surprised to see how many people wore masks today. Masks are a new obligatory accessory. I saw white ones, black ones, colorful ones, politically expressive ones, but none of them looked comfortable or attractive. They are simply a necessity. Are you going to create your own or wear one of the commercial ones I purchased?"

"At this point all I care about is they be efficient and protect us," I said as I watched her seem to zone out again.

"I'm sure for some they will become a symbol of self-expression and political identity," she said. "And of course, the fashion world will probably zero in on them as a positive and healthy accessory." She moved with awkward diffidence and reluctant shyness.

"Yeah, which means they'll be expensive," I said as I sat on the step a few below her. She moved down and sat directly behind me embracing my back and snuggling her torso up close. "Do you know why I enjoy live full-blooded blues? Because it's like a strong vitamin with a hot shot of adrenaline as a chaser."

"Hey, which reminds me about the net?" she replied. "Can't Spider, the band and guests perform live online and charge admission or ask for donations like a telethon? They would be able to make a little money and feeling the vibes."

"I suppose so, but the energy emanating from live audiences is what really gets the creative juices flowing in singers and musicians. Staring at a camera isn't going to cut it," I said. "Plus, do you know how many bands are already doing this ... thousands and thousands."

"How about if we pool our email lists and send everyone a link?"

"Your generosity is commendable, but do you really believe the Beverly Hills and Malibu upper echelon art collectors on your list will welcome an invitation from a small blues club in Santa Monica? Oh, and will they be happy knowing you are the one who gave away their email address?"

"Yea, you're right and Nellie wouldn't be happy with me either." Her natural brashness left again replaced by an odd quietness.

We stared at the waves and watched gulls eagerly searching for food in the surf. "You know what, we need to make is a video about Spider or the club that will go viral," she said timidly.

"That's a wonderful idea. Just keep in mind creative entrepreneurship is deadly," I mused as the gulls seemed to have given up and flew away. "Networking and self-promoting leaves one with even less time to build a meaningful oeuvre and now a pandemic is isolating everyone even further."

"Yea, you're right. Plus, Spider may have other ideas. How long can the two of you afford to keep paying the band and the staff?"

"I'm not sure. The biggest bill is the monthly mortgage payment," I said. "Most of the band have day jobs … oops, no I guess those are gone too. You know that implies they should all move in together. That way there would only be one bill due."

"Yeah, and if they all move into the club you and Spider can make that payment."

"Well, that's a thought. I'm not sure how many of them would be comfortable living together," I said. "Let's see. Spider plus 3 band members, the cook, 2 waitresses, 1 cleaner and who knows how many significant others."

"That could easily total 15 people or more," said Nicole. "That would require a lot of beds, and food."

"Maybe Merra should move in with us and Spider could move into her place," suggested Nicole. "Does he have a girl friend at present?"

"Hold on. We're moving too fast," I said. "We're creating a domino effect. No one has lost their job or home yet. Let's slow down and just see how things go for a while."

"Thank you, James. You've renewed my faith in our relationship."

"What do you mean?"

"You didn't insist on asking Merra to move in with us. I thought after last night's ménage à trois you might."

"It was wonderful and you both were very generous, but I feel we should keep that kind of action for special occasions," I said with a twinkle. "Is that ok with you?"

"Yes, James it certainly is and it's a tremendous relief off my mind," said Nicole with a sweet smile. "By-the-way how did you and Spider manage to pull together enough funding to buy the club?"

"Geez Nicole you're really bouncing off the walls in all directions," I said as I held her tight. "Everything will be alright."

"Great. So where did the money come from?"

"Most of it came from my mother's will and life insurance policy," I replied. "I had to pay off my student loan, but everything else went to the club."

"So, what did Spider add?"

"He did all of the work and took no salary at all. He lived there 24/7. Did all the renovations, the daily cleaning and performed every night."

"It must have been hard going for a while," said Nicole. "Is it in the black now?"

"Yes, but if this pandemic goes on too long, it won't be."

"How did you make the jump from discussing our three-some with Merra to asking about how Spider and I funded the club?" I said as casually as I could. "I mean did I miss something?"

"Oh, no I just ..." Nicole's phone jingled. She answered it, looked concerned and walked out onto the deck before speaking. I decided to go into the studio and check my email. There wasn't much needing immediate attention other than a curious message from Snookz.

CHAPTER 18

The dense fog of night had become the syrupy fog of morning and turned my fast walk into a slow cautious stroll as I got close to the marina. I could hear people about, but only caught a glimpse of them as they passed by. We'd give each other a quick once-over as we emerged out of and into the damp ashen veil while checking to make sure we were socially distant and wearing a mask. It was a new experience and made for some intriguing visual images.

The next person to materialize was a young woman wearing bright yellow shorts, a deep violet crop top, silver sneakers and a fluorescent blue mask plus a big awkward looking face shield. She was closely followed by an elderly couple walking arm and arm holding a clear plastic umbrella in front of them and wearing what appeared to be army style gas masks. I was beginning to feel under-dressed. Duie even backed away from some of the more eccentric rigged individuals.

As we stepped onto the concrete promenade to head toward home, I wondered what kind of get-up Nicole may be wearing. Pondering that thought didn't last long for Duie ran ahead and disappeared into a dense pea-soup wall of murkiness. "Duie come here boy, come back," I yelled through my damp mask which caused me to cough.

"He's ok. He's right here. Aren't you boy," said a voice I recognized even though I couldn't see anybody.

"Is that you Merra? Where are you?"

A hand materialized and gently went around my waist. "Good morning lover," said Merra. "Duie is with Shotala."

"Please don't say that in public."

"Oh, sorry, I didn't realize it was a secret," she said with a hint of remorse.

"You never know who could be standing right next to us in this stuff," I whispered as I coughed again. "The station expects me to maintain a high level of decorum in public."

"Right. Understood, but I hope that doesn't mean you weren't pleased with last night's merrymaking."

"Are you kidding? I was thrilled. In fact, I still am," I said as I hacked a couple of more times.

"Great. So, what are we doing today and are you ok?"

"Oh, it's just this mask. This damp fog has made it useless," I suggested. "Ah, Nicole has a meeting with Zevenaar about Patterson and the fate and his company. I'm meeting with artist Snookz Jefferies."

"What does he want?"

"I'm not sure. I suspect he wants to view the CAsLog video before I finalize it."

"Would you like me to go with Nicole? You know, just to keep an eye on her."

"What justification could she give for bringing you along? I mean how would she even explain who you are?"

"Her older sister? A cousin?"

"No, if there is some plot brewing to take over the company the conspirator is bound to have investigated Nicole's family background," I said with probably too much authority. "You come with me. If Snookz asks I'll say you're an old girlfriend."

"Perfect. I like the sounds of that. Can I dress sexy?"

"No. Remember decorum."

"Yes sir."

She was wearing a clear plastic poncho-hoodie, over the smallest thong bikini I'd ever seen. The moisture droplets on the plastic made her look out of focus and all wet.

The mist started lifting a bit and we caught sight of Duie and Shotala playing tag around a stand of palms, it was disconcerting to see so few people about. A stark reminder the world was quickly going into lock down mode. I didn't like it.

As we walked along the dogs investigated anything that caught their fancy. "What did you find boy?" I said looking at a jumbled pile of shells, pebbles and trash half buried in the sand. I couldn't resist sorting through it and precariously stacking items asymmetrically on a small knoll of sand. "Most people will pass this by without even noticing, but artists will find it inspiring."

"Some people have all the luck," said Merra. "Most of us ordinary folk find it difficult to reignite our sense of wonder by looking at a pile of trash."

"Well, it's not just a matter of being attentive to your surroundings," I mused. "You have to be true to yourself. If something moves you, acknowledge it. Use all of your senses to fully take it in."

"Is that what you did last night and do you talk this way to everyone or is the fog, the pandemic or last night's hot tub play making you feel philosophical?"

For some reason I almost felt lachrymose. "Everything does seem to be getting to me. I …"

Before I could finish my thought a strange mechanical hum grew louder as if it were coming right at us. My first thought was of the concrete sidewalk cleaning machine so I looked forward, then behind, but Merra, Duie and Shotala were all looking skyward.

"There it is, over there," said an old beach vagrant I'd never seen in the neighborhood before. "It's one of those drone things and it's coming right at us," he yelped as he lunged under a picnic table. Merra corralled Shotala and Duie in her arms and laid her body over them in the sand.

"James," yelled Merra. "Watch out. It's going to hit you."

It barely missed hitting my head and I could feel my blood beginning to boil. I quickly looked around for something to swat the thing with, but it whizzed up and disappeared into a cloud of swirling mist.

"You're a lucky fella," said the old man as he struggled to stand. "That contraption's got your number. You best be careful out in the open."

Merra still had her arms around both dogs while striving to wipe the clammy sand off her legs. "Damn it sounds like it's coming back. Listen."

I heard it, but the sound was much stronger this time. I grabbed the metal trash can from next to the picnic table. Merra led both dogs to behind the palm trees. "What are you doing James? Get over here, it won't be able to maneuver much here."

I stood in the center of the promenade with the can in hand looking up in every direction as the buzz got louder. I'd had enough of this game.

Suddenly the few strollers behind me hurried off the path in all directions as a formidable looking Ninja motorcyclist charged through them like a rampaging steel bull heading straight for me. I stood my ground. I was in no mood to run, but Duie rushed alongside the creep, jumped on his back and began biting his neck. He pulled at Duie and lost control of the cycle. Duie jumped off and I furiously swung the trash can slamming it hard against the guy's side. He veered onto the sand hitting the picnic table. The impact threw him and the bike high into the air. As he descended his head hit the edge of the table with a loud snaping sound and he fell like a limp rag onto the bench sliding off into a sand cloud in slow motion.

As the dirt and sand settled, I could see he wasn't moving. I cautiously checked his pulse anyway. He had none and wasn't breathing either. Merra rushed to my side. "Is he …". She let it hang "…dead?"

"I think so."

"I'll take Shotala and Duie home. Don't mention my name to the Police. I wasn't here. OK?"

I nodded and watched her take the dogs into the fog and felt happy they had not been harmed. Looking around as I dialed for Cisco on my cell everyone else had left too. Even the old man had vanished. Having no witnesses was not going to please Cisco or his Captain.

***

Ring-billed gulls are common seabirds in Ocean Park and they are opportunistic thieves and food hounds. As I studied the dead Ninja one walked close to tug at a piece of sand-caked kelp from beneath the cycle's front tire. As he freed it, the tire spun causing sand to fly at the bird's head making its protective membrane close over its yellow eyes, but it remained focused and calm for finding food was serious business no matter what the nearby foolish humans were up to.

I resisted the urge to search through the pockets of the dead man or to even remove his helmet. I simply sat on the bench and waited for the fog to rise and Cisco to arrive. As time passed, I found myself hoping this would be the end of the Ninja mystery, but deep within me I knew it wasn't. I felt as though I was undergoing a process of aging.

CHAPTER 19

The early twilight dimly revealed Cisco walking onto the deck wearing a classic red bandana. Duie hesitated, but decided to run to the sliding glass door and jump against it yelping as he did. I slid the door open and he scampered straight to him. Cisco began petting him and gesturing for me and Nicole to join him outside. I shook my head in the negative and he said "It's nice out here. Come out and bring Nicole with you. We need to talk."

Nicole smiled, I shrugged and we both put on our masks as we walked out. "You two are so lucky to live on the beach. It's beautiful."

"Yes, but it can also be lethal," said Nicole. "What did you find out about the dead man?"

"Right to the point. I guess I can understand your desire for answers to all your questions, but unfortunately there isn't much to tell," he said as he looked us hard in the eyes. "We haven't been able to find anything about the guy. His prints and mug shot photo are not on file with any local or national agency and we haven't heard back from Interpol yet. So, we don't have his name, age, address, nothing. Even the motorcycle is a dead end. It was reported stolen yesterday. Our only lead is we now have confirmation someone is really targeting you, James. You need to do some serious soul searching so we can get on top of this matter before there is another attempt on your life. There must be someone you've ticked-off."

"I hear you and believe me I've been thinking about it ever since this whole thing began. If I had even a slight idea, I'd certainly tell you."

Nicole wrapped her arm around mine and snuggled up close. "Let's go over everything about the Money Mirage video."

"The what?" asked Cisco. "What money and what mirage?"

"It's just a title I made up for a CAsLog episode I've been developing. What Nicole means is we should look harder at Kirill Maytor, his wife and bank, plus Snookz, Terratan and maybe Cornish Tweed," I said.

"Sounds like a real odd combination of individuals. Surely, they aren't all plotting together. Let's break them into groups and see if we can find one who stands out from the others," suggested Cisco.

"Right. Well, Terratan and Cornish would be one group," said Nicole. "And the Maytor's and their bank would be another."

"You are saying this Snookie guy isn't connected to any of the others and Cornish Tweed has no connection either," said Cisco. "Correcto?"

"Not exactly. Terratan Landchilde knows Maytar, Snookz and Cornish," I said. "But there is no way I could ever believe he would be involved in anything criminal. Plus, Snookz didn't even know Maytor existed before I told him during the video shooting."

"So, we're back to Mrs. Maytor and the bank VP who may be hoping if you are taken out the Money Mirage video will never be televised and therefore whatever it is they are up to, beside sex, will never be discovered. Correcto?" said Cisco now completely exasperated. "It doesn't feel like a reason to commit murder. I mean, let's assume for a moment you finish the video this week and you get murdered next week. How long would it take the station to decide on whether to air the program or not? A week, a month, what?"

"I have no idea, but you have convinced me to finish it this week," I said. "I'll persuade Liz we should air it before any of the other already scheduled episodes. That way the criminals will be forced to make another attempt soon."

"Ok, even though I don't like the idea. It does seem like the best way to get them to show their hand. Send an email to each one of them stating the video has been approved and will air next week," said Cisco through his teeth.

"But, what if it isn't them?" said Nicole. "What if it's somebody else we know nothing about? Oh, and you didn't say anything about the possible accidental homicide charges against James."

"They've been dropped," he said. "A witness came forward and corroborated James' story."

"That's a relief. Who is it?" said Nicole. "We need to thank him or her."

"Well, that's another mystery. It seems a Federal agency provided the statement and they are not going to share the name of the witness."

Nicole and I stared at each other. "Ah, that seems odd," she said. "Doesn't it James?"

"Look, I'm trying to do my best here and I want to believe you both, but I think you know about this whole thing," said Cisco as he took off his mask. "Just keep in mind you are stretching our friendship to its limits." He looked at us with distress. "Every witness has his own way of creeping up on the truth."

We all stood in silence for a moment until Cisco shook his head in disgust, walked to his car and drove off. Nicole and I looked at each other and said "Merra" then walked arm-in-arm back into the house and began quietly making breakfast. As we sat the food on the table Merra gracefully strode across the deck and joined us.

"Did Cisco have anything valuable to tell us about the Ninja?

"Not really, but he is getting fed-up with us not telling him everything.

"Speaking of which, I received a long email from Andre last night," said Merra. "He says Ravenello's paintings are on the move."

"How, why and where are they moving to?" I replied.

"They were loaded onto a truck at the Russian collector's house in the Caucasus region of Georgia."

"That's at the intersection of Eastern Europe and Western Asia near the coast of the Black Sea which means they could be heading almost anywhere."

"Yes, but apparently Andre's Interpol contacts at their headquarters in Lyon, France is confident the truck is going to Paris," she said smiling broadly. "I love Paris."

"Why would they do that now, at the start of a pandemic lockdown?" asked Nicole. "Surely all of the galleries and museums are going to close."

"Well Interpol is the world's largest international police organization, with seven regional bureaus worldwide and a National Central Bureau in all 190+ member states so I'd say they must know something we don't."

"I asked Andre about that very same thing and he replied their contacts have confirmed Ravenello has had several solo exhibitions in Europe and received terrible reviews by most critics for always showing bad copies of works by famous artists."

"Hold on, if those exhibits were in top tier galleries and reviewed by leading critics we've been looking at this all wrong," I said with surprise even to myself. "If he is constantly getting bad reviews and hasn't changed what he is doing, but instead doubles down by showing even-more bad copies during a pandemic then that is his objective."

"What the hell are you talking about?" said Merra. "I don't get it."

"He is a legitimate, serious artist," said Nicole. "And he is probably thrilled he has access to paintings in private collections even if it the owners aren't aware of it."

"And the Russian mafia dude probably gets a big cut of the profits every time someone buys one of the copies."

"But does anyone actually buy them. I mean especially if all of the critics are saying the stuff is crap."

"It's what Snookz's talks about in the video," I said. "The avant-garde think it's cool to make knock-off's of originals, especially those owned by the 1%."

"I still don't see how anyone other than Ravenello benefit," said Merra. "And isn't it risky for him to be associated with no-necks?"

"All he has to do is convince a few legitimate galleries he is serious, which he obviously has done, get them to represent him, then leave the rest to the Russian … who will tell those who owe him money to buy one of the copy paintings. The money goes to the gallery, then into their bank, then a foreign exchange service plus maybe a wire transfer to move it across borders to send Ravenello his cut. He then pays crating and shipping companies which the Russian probably secretly owns. It's a classic money laundering scheme. It's often called smurfing."

"I see. So why is he based here in L.A.?" asked Merra. "Wouldn't it be easier if he were in Europe?"

"That's a good question, but I doubt it has anything to do with Maytor, the Korean bank executives, Terratan, Cornish or Snookz," I said. "However, he did have that small bottle of paint sample from Snookz's painting in his studio."

"OK, so maybe there is a connection to Maytor's wife and her lover," said Nicole. "But murder seems far-fetched for whatever they are planning. However, a corporate takeover of Patterson's holdings could garner millions for whomever is the last man standing after this pandemic wave crashes."

"The inevitability and futility of violence in search of power and wealth," I said as I put my arms around my two lovely ladies. "The question is do we sit here and wait for the villains to attack our peaceful home or do we take the battle to them?"

We looked at each other and said in unison "it's another hot tub session."

"That sounds wonderful, however, Nicole I have something to say to you first," I said as I put my arms around her. "Merra would you check the temperature in the tub please and make sure it's not too hot. I don't want to boil my ah, the family ah."

"Right, I got you," replied Merra with a wink.

"We'll be up in a few minutes," I said smiling and feeling a bit hesitant.

"I certainly will and you two take all the time you need," said Merra as she took the stairs with grace and a whisp of stylish charisma.

"Nicole please don't speak, just listen. I've given this a great deal of thought and need to say it now," I said with all the sincerity I could summon. An expression of deep apprehension filled her eyes. "This pandemic threat and Ninja nonsense has given me cause to examine my feelings for you and our future together. You bring an inspiring sense of curiosity to everything we do together and always lead with an open mind. You are always inquisitive, always wanting to know more. You never make decisions out of the blue that are absolute directives. You seek collaboration and spend lots of time listening when anyone speaks to you. You even endure and tolerate my quirks, eccentricities and shortcomings. Because of this and so very much more I love you deeply."

We became lost in a kiss I could feel within every fiber of my being and when we opened our eye's she looked at me with sheer glee and said "I have only one concern. Did you select this moment to convey this declaration because we are about to join Merra in another joie de vivre celebration?"

"In a way, yes. This horrifying pandemic and violent attack on our lives has made me cherish every moment we have together even those we share with others and especially those with Merra because it is obvious you two have a loving bond and commitment to one another. I'm honored you allow me to be a part of it."

"Oh James, I tremble with love for you whenever we are together. Do you not feel my love in every word I say to you?"

"I do and I've been waiting quite a while for the perfect moment to express, in a spirit as serious, as trusting and as loving as possible my complete devotion to you. But this bizarre uncertain present and fragile, tenuous future has over-whelmed and restrained me," I said as we gently embraced one-another. "My art has always been my truest explanation of my state of mind and heart. In it, I put my life force and spirit. You, Miss Nicole Trenet, understand this better and fuller than anyone ever has. And I clearly understand the love it has evoked and accepted by both of us with joy. With that thought in mind, we must live every minute, every hour, every day to its fullest."

"Yes James, however, I don't want you to take anymore crazy chances like standing in front of a charging motorcycle or even standing up to Cisco without a mask on. OK? Promise?

"I do."

CHAPTER 20

The mid-day light was bright, the sky clear blue and the pristine white sand completely devoid of beachcombers. The gulls weren't around and even Duie hesitated to venture over to the trees. I sat quietly reading the Times when Nicole came out just as Merra walked over from next door carrying a tray of glasses and a pitcher of iced Lemonade.

"According to Zevenaar many of the top international corporations have a registered letter-box company in Hong Kong," said Nicole. "They use it for the sole purpose of buying and selling products and services without having to pay taxes on transactions. They have no offices or employees there other than maybe one secretary. All of the acquisition, maintenance, and sale of whatever is being sold is actually done here or in Europe, but the legal exchange of paperwork is completed in Hong Kong where the company's income is non-taxable. Then they transfer the funds to another tax-sheltered haven like Samoa."

"So what?" said Merra as she filled the glasses. "How does any of that connect to whomever the bad guy is here in L.A.?"

"Well, it seems Patterson sold the drones to a corporation owned by a Petrus Leihtt based in Samoa."

"Ok and?" I said.

"He's the one who sold them here in the U.S. and also has the service contract on them."

"So, he's in an ideal position to gather and transfer any sensitive data garnered from them and then sell it to the Chinese," I said. "But your eyes are telling me there is an even deeper connection. What is it?"

Nicole snuggled up against me and gave me a quickie-kiss. "I'm so very happy you understand me."

"Well let's just say I'm making a concerted effort to pay attention to your, tells," I said with a grin. "You know, those little changes in your demeanor. I'm just not sure yet if they are deliberate or unconscious."

She smiled and looked out at the vacant beach. "Leihtt is the one who gave Patterson's passport to the Chinese and told them he died of COVID-19."

"Mmm, but there is more. Isn't there?" said Merra.

"He also holds several promissory loan notes on Patterson's corporation, which if not paid on time will give him 50% of the company."

"Who will own the other half?" asked Merra.

"I will," replied Nicole.

"So, if you're out of the way he gets the whole enchilada."

"Over my dead body," Nicole replied with her hands on her hips.

"Don't think like that. What exactly is a promissory note anyway?" asked Merra.

"It's more commonly referred to as a note payable in which one party promises in writing to pay a determinate sum of money to the other, at a fixed future time or on demand of the payee under extraordinary circumstances," replied Nicole. "Patterson's death could be considered as just such a circumstance. A circumstance which makes it impractical or impossible for the company to comply with the provisions of the agreement."

"But the lack of a body could be enough to get a judge to delay any final decision. Right? I asked.

"Probably, but the Board of Directors will still have to select a temporary President and I sure don't have the qualification," said Nicole. "So, Nathan would be the most logical choice."

"And who is he?" I asked.

"Oh, ah Nathan Zevenaar. Patterson's V.P. and lawyer."

"And what do we know about him?" said Merra.

"The only thing I know is Patterson always seemed to trust him," said Nicole.

"Is he married, have a family, where did he come from?" I asked.

"I don't know," said Nicole. "The more important question is can he pull together enough cash to pay off the promissory notes if a judge were to rule in Leihtt's favor."

"James, you have a troubled look again," said Merra. "What is bothering you now?"

"Well, we don't really know anything about either Zevenaar or Leihtt," I said. "I mean are you sure they aren't working together?"

"It's time for me to introduce myself to Leihtt," said Merra. "Is he here or in Samoa?"

"Hold on, why him and not Zevenaar?" I asked.

"Nicole already has a strong connection to Zevenaar, ah Nathan. She can work on him," said Merra with a wink. "I'll find a way to ferret-out Leihtt."

"Mmm, I don't like it, but I suppose it could be the quick way to determine if either of them is master of the endless chain of Ninja's."

"I just remembered, Nathan said something about Leihtt owning a building in San Pedro where he stores shiploads of new drones," said Nicole. "I wonder if it could be the same one Ravanello's studio is in?"

"Cisco isn't going to like the sounds of that. He doesn't believe in coincidences," I said shaking my head. "You are right, we have to find out more about both of these men."

"Are you suggesting there is a connection between Ravanello, Maytor's wife, the bank and Leihtt?" said Nicole. "That sounds highly improbable."

"At the very least we need to know more about Zevenaar and Leihtt," said Merra. "They are the big hitters in this game. I'll check with the Bureau to see if they have a file on Leihtt and Nicole you need to get closer to Nathan."

Nicole looked at me. "One thing I know already is he doesn't wear a wedding ring, but I promise I won't go over the top to find out more."

"I'll check with you later," said Merra as she headed across the deck toward her house.

Nicole, staring out at the empty beach, spoke in a soft remote manner and hugged herself. "I didn't realize how much I enjoy watching people strolling by."

"It's a way of sharing, of empathizing with those we don't know," I replied.

"And may never know," she said as she turned and snuggled into my arms. "Please tell me something I don't know about you James. Maybe an event you experienced on this beach that has stayed with you, one you feel you'll always remember."

A slight gust sprayed a wave into the air causing a veil of buttercup light to sparkle. "Mmm, well you know the painting I've been working on?"

"Yes, the one with the yellow scalene."

"That's right. Well in many ways it was inspired by an incident that happened on a dreary and drizzly morning here in Ocean Park. The beach was deserted like it is now and looked forlorn, the palms limp and the gulls were hiding. Even the waves appeared shapeless. Plus, the painting I had spent the night working on had developed a mind of its own, which I disagreed with and editing my latest CAsLog video for PBS didn't seem a necessity. I felt the blues coming-on," I said as we walked inside and sat down on the couch still wrapped in each other's arms.

"As the sky darkened, erratic wind gusts sprayed a mixture of murky water and sand against the windows and the sliding glass door of my old studio. Duie barked half-heartedly then curled up facing in the opposite direction. He hadn't been outside since 2 a.m. and showed no interest in going out in those conditions. I couldn't blame him.

I filled my favorite cup with boiling water, put in a bag of Earl Grey and waited with my eyes closed for its enchanting aroma to inundate my paint fume saturated olfactory receptors with flavorsome Bergamot.

As I stood there musing the irritating wind gradually sailed out to sea replaced by a calm hush. I was relieved. The tranquil moment lingered. I picked up the tea cup, inhaled deeply and took a long swallow. My body welcomed the flavor and warmth of the smooth liquid. Duie and I were alone. With cup in hand, I moseyed up the stairs to my bedroom loft thinking the view from the terrace may present a more welcoming morning. Duie begrudgingly followed me.

At the top landing I turned toward the large plate glass windows and was shocked to see a bright yellow scalene flying haphazardly in a squall-like violent gust of rain and sand. It skidded sideways and obliquely over the slippery beach then turned so quickly my tired eyes couldn't focus on whatever the hell it was.

I shook my head and stood there mesmerized as the glistening form doubled back and looked increasingly lethal, like a racing dart as it swooped over my terrace railing then hit the glass door with a breathtaking wham causing everything inside to rattle and the glass door to splinter in all directions. Duie began growling and snarling in a dogged attempt to scare the thing away. He undoubtedly thought it was alive. I wasn't sure.

I told Duie, it was OK, that it was just an umbrella or so I thought."

"That's it? That's what inspired the painting?" she said as she shook her head.

"Ah, no, that was just the beginning," I said with a duplicitous smile. "The yellow canvas was embedded in the fractured glass, but untethered sections kept flapping and thumbing furiously as though it was made of something far more substantial. Then a shrill voice yelled 'HELP, HELP.

Get me out of this damn thing'. I was astonished and carefully slid the damaged door open a few inches. Instantly a small, thin boned hand grabbed the metal frame and the screaming voice rang out again. 'Hey, is there someone there?'

"Of course I said yes and asked if it might hurt her if I slide the door open a little further? She shouted 'I don't know. Just do it.' I slid the door open a smidge more and by taking a deep breath I was able to squeeze out the narrow opening only to discover a young woman pinned face down against the badly cracked glass. Her clothes were snagged in several places along with the yellow canvas scalene and a perfusion of bits and pieces of what look like machine parts and computer innards or some-such thing. I asked if she was hurt? If anything felt broken or cut and she said she couldn't tell. She just wanted to be detached from the glass.

I told her I'd try to make the lower spots let go first so maybe her feet would be able to touch the terrace. I pulled insistently on the fabric, but it didn't let go. Everything was snagged. I told her I would have to cut her clothes."

"Was she OK with that?"

"Yep, I rushed into the bathroom, found the scissors, returned in seconds and began cutting off large swatches of her outfit. She shifted slightly causing her left foot to drop enough to touch the terrace. That made it a little better, but I needed to cut even more to get her upper body free. I remember asking her if she was okay with that and she just said 'Don't talk about it. Do it.'

"I carefully cut away larger sections around her elbows, shoulders and hips and asked her what she was doing out in the extreme weather?"

"What did she say?"

"I'll always remember she said 'Oh, I don't know. I just wanted to dance with the wind.'

"Uhg, the Santa Anna devil wind, you must be kidding me," said Nicole with a snap.

"Well, before I could make another cut, she squirmed and wrenched about causing the fabric to rip, and tear plus more mechanical debris dislodged including a small propeller. Then with a resolute grunt she heaved and fell into my arms."

"Of course, she did," said Nicole as she elbowed me in the ribs. "And she was probably adorable too."

"Well, our eyes met as we scanned each other discretely, but she was disorientated and totally exhausted. It was then I realize I was dressed in only my pajama bottoms and sandals so I stood her up carefully and stepped back to make sure my manhood wasn't liberated and she wasn't too uncovered."

"So, what did she say?"

"She stood there in a daze rubbing a big, deep purple bump on her forehead with one hand while trying to cup her exposed breast with her other hand. Then she whispered 'I smell Earl Greee' as her eyes fluttered and she began to sway awkwardly. I quickly caught her on my shoulder, laid her on my bed and got a wet washcloth for her ever-swelling bruise. The foul looking thing made me realize I should check her to make sure there weren't other nasty abrasions or punctures needing attention. She passed out as I began."

"Sounds terrible," said Nicole.

"Yeah, the process of looking and feeling my way over torn canvas, skin, and bits of some kind of wetsuit generated an odd mixture of curiosity and self-reproach. Even rolling her over didn't improve the onus duty. As I covered her with a blanket, I noticed part of a logo on what was left of her get-up. It read 'Mer__Pop__inb__ella'. I decided to let her rest, but a gust of wind shook the broken door again And I sure don't need another blast showering the room with shards of glass."

"So, what did you do?"

"I ran down to the studio, took everything off of my portable table, folded its legs and a grabbed a roll of duct tape then scurried back up the stairs, slipping only twice. The perplexed expression on Duie's mug was priceless as he wisely stayed out of my way," I said as I readjusted my position on the couch. "I managed to get the glass door closed. In fact, the embedded yellow scalene helped to keep the remaining glass in place. I then taped the table directly to the metal door frame using the entire roll in the process. Duie finished the job by barking at it incessantly. His gruffness caused my visitor to shake her head and reach for the washcloth as it slithered down her cheek to her breast."

"Naturally," said Nicole with a snigger. "Go on."

"Well, her eyes opened and I helped her sit up and I thought it might make her feel better if I said 'that was a hell of a dance you put on. How do you feel?' Her reply was simply 'I'll live. Where am I and who are you?'

"I gave my name and told her she had flown into my glass door on some kind of magic carpet and asked where she came from? She said she had come from the pier."

"That's a little hard to believe. She flew all the way from the pier to your studio by just holding onto an umbrella?"

"I said the same thing and that's when she explained it was actually a parasol drone. Which made me think maybe her head wound had had a deeper effect than I realized."

"A parasol-drone? I've never heard of such a thing," said Nicole.

"I never think of it that way. To this day, I still think of it as the yellow scalene," I said with a shrug. "Especially since she wanted to return it to the company who owned it before anyone missed it."

"She didn't own it? She stole it?"

"Well borrowed might be a little more accurate.

"So did she put it back on and fly away?"

"No, I'm afraid its flying days were over. There were only a few pieces of it left intact, but not enough to reassemble."

"I see, so you drove her home?"

"No, she was visibly destressed until she suddenly recognized me and came up with what she thought was a brilliant plan."

"Say, what is this woman's name?"

"Ophelia Fiske. Why do you ask?"

"Oh, just curious. You know in case I ever encounter this wonder woman," said Nicole as she walked around the room a bit before returning to the sofa. "Ok, go on tell me more about Ms. Fiske."

"Uhm, my phone went off, but I wasn't sure where it was. Duie found it and when I looked at the name on the screen I decided not to answer."

"I assume it was Stephanie, right?" asked Nicole with a guffaw.

"Yes. So I told Ophelia to get a shirt and pants from my closet so she wouldn't be walking around half undressed."

"That means you expected Stephanie to show up."

"Yep, so I gathered up my cloths and headed down the stairs and told Ophelia to join me when she got dressed. She said she understood and asked for a cup of Earl Grey Tea? I quickly slipped into my clothes, put a pot of water into the micro, set out two cups and washed my face in the sink. As I mopped my unshaven mug with the dish towel, Duie ran to the front door and the buzzer sounded. I opened the door.

Stephanie entered and instantly wanted to know what I was doing when the phone had rang and then she spied the two cups I'd sat out and said 'Is she upstairs in your bed?' I tried to explain the whole thing about the crash on the terrace, but she thought I meant Ophelia was high or drunk so she charged up the stairs. Even when I told her about the big bump on Ophelia's head and she might need to go to the hospital she didn't believe me."

"Well, you have to admit any story about someone flying off the pier with a parasol drone strapped to their back is a little hard to swallow. So, what happened next?"

"Both of them came down the stairs arm-in-arm."

"You went to the hospital?" Nicole asked.

"No Ophelia was feeling better and just wanted an ice pack for the lump. I rummaged through the freezer and found a bag of frozen blueberries which both of them laughed about. We sat down and enjoyed Earl Grey and Ophelia explained how the drone worked and about the company owners who referred to it as the Merry Poppinbrella and I should feature it in a CALog segment."

"Hold on, didn't you say she had taken it without permission?"

"Yeah, but she felt if she told the company I wanted to make a video about it, maybe they wouldn't sack her."

Stephanie stressed to her my CAsLogs concentrate on art and music, not recreational drones. Plus the project would obviously be a huge insurance risk."

"But, just imagine the headlines 'CAsLog Flies With Merry Poppinbrella'," said Nicole with an a big smile. "That would get you colossal ratings." She giggled.

"The network would never have green lighted it and besides it was totaled, remember?" I said.

"And all of that inspired you to make this marvelous yellow scalene painting. You were lucky the drone wasn't chartreuse. By-the-way, is Ophelia still in the area? I would like to meet her, she sounds like someone I should know."

"I'm not sure. The last time I saw her she was talking about returning home."

"And where is that?"

"Bristol."

"You are right this place is a crossroads of the world. Have you ever considered writing these mini encounters down?" she said with an expression of deep satisfaction.

"No, I haven't, but I've often thought I might write a creation myth for each painting I finish," I responded.

"I wonder how everyone in London is doing right now?"

"You know what I miss most since this lockdown thing started is hilarity," she said twirling a ringlet of her hair. "It was infectious. Especially when it comes from strangers when you flash them a knowing glance. I relish it. It can be so infectious. Just plain, loud, unabashed laughter makes me feel good all over. I miss it."

"Yea, our whole social scenario has been stifled and feels repressed. Plus, all these crazy people who question scientists, I'm tired of them making everything into a political conflict?"

"Their inability to understand the difference between those who offer explanations based on legitimate value judgements from those who thrive on disinformation and screwy conspiracy theories is sickening."

"Mmm, and is there a moral to this story?"

"What do you mean?"

"I've noticed, whenever anyone asked you something personal, your tone and demeanor change significantly plus you always manage to put your answer into a bigger, more universal context which gets further and further away from being personal."

"Nicole, what are you driving at?"

"Since we've been together, you've had a near miss with a motorcycle, been beat up, shot twice, survived two car crashes and another motorcycle encounter, but you've never once told me anything deeply personal about how you face the world every day or how you deal with life's threatening challenges. Even now, here we are facing a world-wide pandemic while somebody is obviously stalking us and what do you do, you zone out on making a tableau out of trash you found in the sand and tell me a story about a young woman who had a near death experience with a parasol drone while you're still preoccupied on the yellow scalene she left smashed into your window," said Nicole with an exasperated frown.

"To me, first impressions aren't very important. The last impression I get from someone is the one that stays etched on my visual cortex; the one I want to fully comprehend. Fights, crashes and near misses do not feed my inner being, my soul. They leave only muscle memory of intuitive actions without conscious thought. I get the most value from objects and events when I find connections between them and different aspects of culture. Anything that connects those dots to the bigger picture moves me the most."

"I'm not sure I understand and I'm sorry I brought the whole thing up," she murmured.

"My priorities are friends and family — and yes, those have been altered to a degree by Covid, but creating art is its own inviolable thing. It is a drive, a way to be, to feel and live. Nothing will ever alter that unless we're all running for our lives. The unexpected is what keeps me sharp while painting, interviewing an artist or making love. We can't let fear cause us to just sit here and think you're living our best life. If we do that something profound will go missing, we need the rush and viscosity of a populated world."

"When you say family, who specifically are you referring to?"

"You, Spider, Cisco and Duie are at the top of the list. Except for a few distant cousins, whom I haven't seen in decades, all of my blood relatives are gone, as far as I know."

"I see. So, what are you going to work on today?"

"I'm considering adding a short voice over about mental health to the Money Mirage video. With the pandemic changing everyone's mindset about the beliefs they hold about themselves and how they interpret and interact with everyone around them it seems appropriate to address it. What do you think?"

"It's true, our belief systems not only impact our behavior, they also influence our ability to solve simple challenges like what to wear in public."

"Well, I was thinking of how we conceive of mental health and categorize patients has evolved drastically now more than ever. The definition of sanity and normalcy are shifting along with diagnostics and treatments. Just look at all the homeless people living on the streets around here. Most of them look and sound normal to me. They've just lost their job and home so they're scared and nervous, but they are not crazy."

"Be careful, you don't want to come across as playing armchair psychiatrist. You know pathologizing the artist or are you talking about mingling mainstream and outsider art?"

"You have to admit listening to Luc talk about his art touches on romanticism and everyone's desire for sincerity which often feels missing from the business side of art."

"You mean compared to how Snookz discusses his art."

"Yeah, I guess I do and in his case there is a very distinct cultural divide as well."

"Mmm, Luc is from a small mid-west farm and Snookz is Stanford ivy league. I would say the boundaries between those two types of artmaking may be dissolving here in L.A., but there are still firm prejudices tied to both artistic heritages and the contemporary art market."

"That's why I think it will be healthy to at least mention it before Luc is locked into any particular profile. Because later he will find it hard to change it."

"Hey, why are you so dressed up? Where are you going?"

"I'm meeting with Zevenaar to discuss what to do about running the company? She said as she headed for the garage. "I'll phone after the meeting. Bye. Oh, thanks for the charming yellow scalene Fiske story, I loved it."

As I started to finish the voice over, the text message light on the computer flashed revealing another note from Snookz Jefferies. It read 'imperative we meet ... will be at Paradise Cove bluff at noon'. I didn't like the implied tone and I wasn't in the mood to listen to any of his whining about the CAsLog video, but I always enjoy the cove. There was just enough time to get there without breaking too many laws. I put Duie in the front seat of the 550s and took off up PCH. Traffic was lite and it was a wonderful spring day. I opened all the windows and tuned in my favorite blues station.

The Malibu coastline rivals the French Riviera. It has lush, green hillsides of sage and blooming Yucca descending into secluded crescent-shaped shorelines tucked under tall cliffs and dotted with stunning rock formations. Paradise Cove is just such a place plus it has a restaurant where one can easily happen upon a fellow artist or even a celebrity.

As I turned into the bluff parking lot an electric bike group was just setting off for a tour of local vineyards. I turned around so the 550s was facing the driveway entrance and left all the windows down. Duie was leaning on the passenger side window sill and the moment I turned off the engine he began barking toward the far end of the bluff. I stepped out and could see a man standing at the edge of the cliff holding something in his hands while looking out to sea. He was wearing a mask and sun glasses. Duie suddenly turned his attention skyward and I could hear buzzing. My first response was to reach for the door handle until I realized the man was flying a drone out over the waves and then diving it low along the beach.

"It's okay Duie." Duie stopped barking, but continued to watch the man and the drone. No doubt he had strong memories of our last encounter with an annoying noise maker. "Maybe he's looking for the private nude beach?" I said, but Duie didn't react. I leaned on the back of the car and watched a beautiful sailboat glide gracefully northward. All three of its sails were full and it was moving at a quick clip. It looked as though there were several people aboard, two of which raised their arms and waved. Drone man and I, both waved back and then saluted each other. I felt relieved by the gesture.

In fact, everything in Malibu seemed normal until I heard and saw a Ninja style motorcyclist paused in the left-hand turn lane about to enter the parking lot. Duie immediately jumped out of the car and charged at the rider who raised the bike up on its back wheel and drove right toward me. I moved to behind the car and yelled, "Duie no!" The Ninja lowered the front of the bike, came to a stop in a cloud of dust, put his feet on the ground and took off his helmet. It was Snookz still wearing his beard. I wondered if he wore it as a mask.

"What's with the tire iron James? I was only foolin' around."

I put the tire iron back into the trunk. "Sorry, I had a run end with another Ninja recently that didn't turnout so well. Duie stop barking, it's Snookz."

"Yea, well. Hey, you want a cold one? I've got a six pack in the saddle bag."

"Sure, sounds good. Why did you choose to meet up here instead of at the restaurant?"

"Oh, lots of clean air and wide-open views. Everyone can easily see what's going on."

"So what is going on? If this is about the CAsLog video, the editing is all done, no further changes can be made."

"No, no it's not about that. I mean, I heard about how your run-in with another guy on a bike ended in the fog so I thought we could have a friendly talk here in the sun."

"Friendly talk, okay about what?"

"Let's sit over on those rocks by the bluff. How's the beer?"

"It's fine, but I'm not going toward the cliff unless you tell me what this is about."

"Look, you know Pasquale Ravanello don't you?"

That was not what I was expecting. "Yes, we met once, but I wouldn't say I know him well, why?"

"He and I are working on a project together and I'd rather you hear about it from me rather than from any of your friends. You know what I mean."

"No I don't. What friends are you referring to?"

"The kind with badges and international connections."

Again, I was caught completely by surprise.

"I see, so what kind of project are we talking about?"

"Let's just say it involves some aspects about the Kirill collection."

"Aspects, that's a curious word. Does it include taking a generous paint sample from one of those paintings?"

"I knew you'd find out about it. Look you remember me mentioning I was thinking about making some prints?"

"Yes and?"

"I decided to make some NFT's and the paint sample will be used in their development."

"Is this coming from you, your dealer, or your Family Foundation?"

"Does it really matter? Look all I'm asking for is there be no investigation into the taking of the paint sample."

"What if Kirill files a law suit against Ravanello?" I asked.

"He won't." His face became congested by dark blood even in the bright sunlight.

"What makes you so sure?"

"I'm going to give him or his wife a free NFT," he said as his eyes crossed slightly.

"If NFT's and the whole cryptocurrency thing is anything other than a scam I will be amazed. Plus, you know Cornish Tweed and Terratan Landschilde are also aware of the paint sample fiasco?"

"I figured they are and I'm prepared to give them each an NFT too. Given your feelings about them I won't offer you one, but perhaps you'd be interested in being the first to tell the art community about my minting and when I plan to drop them."

"I'll say this much, I love the idiotic, silly, exploitative terminology of NFTs, but it feels more like money laundering than mined, blockchain-based value transfer and you wanting to meet here, out in the open where everyone can see what's happening, tells me you are afraid of something more than a digital commodity exchange."

"That's rich coming from you. Damn right I'm scared, you've all-ready killed one guy this week."

"Was he sent by you?" I queried as I stepped toward him.

"No, no, I didn't have anything to do with whatever that's about. Look, I don't know what I'm trying to say. All I know is, last year three artists you knew were murdered; you and your buddy Cisco killed two men and now you knock off a third one which Cisco doesn't arrest you for or even file charges against you, he just lets you go. Plus, Pasquale tells me Interpol has been snooping around his studio right after you were there with three suspicious women. So, stealing or re-claiming a little paint from one of my old paintings seems like child's play compared to you. I just want you to know I'm no threat to whatever you and your friends are into," he said as his face flushed deeper and secretion appeared above his eyes.

"All right, but I still have two more questions. First why are you dressed like a Ninja warrior and did you try to run Terrantan off the Santa Monica Freeway dressed this same way?

"I dress this way when I ride because it feels safer and yes, I tried to get Landchilde's attention, but I certainly wasn't trying to run him off the freeway. I was surprised to see him driving in the lane next to me and wanted to talk to him about my project, that's all."

"You wanted to talk to him about the NFT's? Why?"

"I heard he has bought a couple of them from other artists and thought he might be interested in getting first crack at my drop."

"That's surprising. I had no idea he owns NFT's."

"You better move on it yourself or you'll be the last one out of the gate."

"I'm not ready to make that kind of leap just yet."

"Okay, well, are we clear now?" he said as he finished off his beer and collected my empty bottle.

"I have no idea whether Kirill will press charges about the damage to his painting or even if he knows about it and I have nothing to do with Interpol investigating Ravanello. But, if you hear about anybody asking about me or Nicole I would appreciate being told. As for announcing your NFT project on CAsLOG, I'll see if I can add it to the voice over text."

"Great. I'm going to head back to the studio. You take care and stay healthy."

We bumped elbows and he drove away like a bat out of hell as Duie barked at his heels. I phoned Cisco and told him to take the Terratan's Ninja incident off our list. "So, we're down to only two possibilities: Mrs. Kirill and the Korean bank V.P. or the possible takeover of Nicole's corporation by Petrus Leihtt," I said. "And after my meeting with Snookz it's obvious we shouldn't surrender to the mindset that the Ninja attack had anything to do with either one of them."

"My bet is on Leihtt," said Cisco. "But there's no evidence to connect him to anything illegal which means all we can do is wait for whatever happens next. Unless, you've got a plan I know nothing about."

"What do you mean?"

"Oh come on James. You get attacked by a totally anonymous Ninja who you kill and another anonymous person steps forward via the Feds and backs up your story, but you have no idea about what's going on. I told you and your lady to not lie to me cause I'll step back from the whole thing and leave you floundering."

CHAPTER 21

It felt strange to be the only person on the broad-walk, even though it was early morning. Duie looked about as if to ask what's going on. When we approached the pier there were a few masked people social distancing, but all of the rides and concession were closed. I headed up Colorado Blvd. and was amazed to see it completely devoid of vagrants, panhandlers and tourists.

The Indigo Club was dark and the closed sign included a hand written note stating 'take care & stay safe'. I used my key and walked in to find Spider sitting at our favorite booth nursing a beer in almost complete darkness. Duie approached him cautiously.

"Kind-a early for that," I said as I reached over the bar and snatched a Dr. Pepper.

A weary smile spread across his dog-tired mug. "Time is moving agonizingly slow and yet simultaneously fast," he said before finishing off the bottle in his hand. "I can't shake off this gut-wrenching feeling of anxiety," his voice dwindled to a bodiless whisper. "And the uncertainty of what tomorrow will bring is killing me from the inside out."

"Yeah, I'm right there with you, but I trust your sense of optimism is still intact," I said as I handed him the Dr. Pepper. "You know, my dear old mom used to say that people live in their dreams and that you've got to hold on tight to each and every one of them."

He answered me in a tone of casual indifference. "Well, this has been a very curious and abnormal year which makes me feel unprepared for the next one. I mean, how in hell can we keep everything we've worked so hard for together man?"

"You may never know the value of a moment or an experience until it becomes a memory," I replied. "Do you remember that one? It came from old Professor Faiss. Remember?"

"Yep, but a sweet guy like him would never survive in today's mean-spirited world," he said as he began peeling the label off his bottle. "This has been the most challenging year of my life."

"I'm sure many folks feel the same, but the new normal looks different for each of us," I said as I watched him take a swallow and grimace. "I bet you still love the blues and it can still bring a smile to your droopy jowls."

"Yes, it can, but it would be even better if I could share the feeling with others. The only human interaction I've had has been through my computer and it just ain't the right way to live. My life feels as though it's getting smaller every day," he said with clenched fists beating his flanks. "Has everyone gone crazy?" he yelped at the dark ceiling.

"Mmm, Nicole and I were talking about the same thing," I said as he finished his drink with one long swallow and raised the bottle in a gesture to hurl it. "Have you given any thought to doing an online concert with the band?" He put the bottle down.

"I have, but we'd be short a couple of guys. Jake and Chino have already gone back home to the delta, so it would just be the original trio."

"Well, remember when we first opened it was just you doing a solo night after night. There was no spontaneous interaction. All the energy and good vibes were generated by you alone."

"Yea, you're right buddy. I think a trio will work just fine, but we've got to have a few close friends in the audience. I can drape the stage behind a clear plastic curtain and issue everyone a free mask." A wave of relief spread across his face.

"We'll need a real sharp internet nerd to post it live and record it. Do you know anyone?"

"Sure do. He's a hot-shot that's been bugging me about putting the Club online. I'll get him in here today."

"Great, what's his name? Oh, and how old is he?"

"Joots."

"Is that a name or a condition?" I said with wriggled brow. Even Duie tilted his head as if to say 'what's that'?

"It's a nick name. I don't know his legal handle man or his age."

"What does it mean?"

"Just wait until you see him," said Spider with a heartwarming smile. "You'll figure it out then. You know, he says he can make this place a virtual concert that will look 3D, not like those 2D image grids you see on zoom."

It was wonderful to see him coming back to life. "Great," I said as I finished the last drop of my Dr. Pepper and headed toward the door. "It was great to see you Spider. Start thinking about what the trio will play."

"Hey, maybe you should text or email me instead of walking over here. You know, with wild Ninja's, drones and this crazy flu stuff flying about you shouldn't be out in the open making yourself a target." His words were punctuated by gasping breaths as though he hadn't breathed much lately.

"You're probably right, but being out in plain sight might be the only way to get the bastards to reveal themselves."

"Man, you're not thinking straight. There's a lot of people depending on having you around so don't make it easy for the bastards, if they're going to take you away from us, make them work for it."

The light in his eyes looked as though it had come from a star a thousand years away. I responded with a nod as I opened the door and was hit by a sharp shaft of sunlight which caused me to step out quickly and lock the door behind me while glancing around for any suspicious looking characters. Finding none I headed back toward the pier and my cell rang out with a sweet blues riff from Kingfish Ingram. It was Cisco.

"What's up Cis?"

"You got time to talk?"

"Sure. Did you find something?"

"On a hunch, I had a DNA test done on our drone flying Ninja phantom and you'll never guess where he comes from," he said with a hint of satisfaction in his Latino-tinged voice.

"Hey, that was a brilliant idea, does it help us?"

"He's 98% Icelandic."

Before I could process that tidbit, Cisco moved on. "This means we should probably concentrate on Leihtt. Wouldn't you agree?"

"It's better than sitting around waiting for him or anyone else to make a move and it makes me nervous about someone else too."

"What? Who are you talking about? Do your mean Nicole?"

"No, I mean Merra."

"Ah, is that the name of the red head?"

"Yes, she is a very close and dear friend of Nicole."

"And what does that have to do with Leihtt?"

"Merra volunteered to find out everything she can about him."

"Damn, James there's already far too many amateurs mixed up in this thing. Reel her in right now."

"That's a lot easier said than done. I'm not even sure where she is at the moment and I don't have her cell number."

"Well get it from Nicole," he said severely.

"Not right now. She's chatting up Nathan Zevenaar. You know Patterson Volkov's V.P."

The silence on the line made the light ocean breeze sound like a rushing squall inside my head. When Cisco finally spoke, I felt like I'd been summoned to the Principles Office.

"Somebody is lying to me James and I think it's you. I'm asking you cercano amigo don't cross that line."

Anytime Cisco has ever spoken to me in Spanish he has always been deeply serious. "Give me a little time. Come over tonight. Nicole, Merra and I will explain ourselves. Just know that everything we've done so far has all been on the right side of the law."

"I'll be there at 9."

He clicked off and I found myself standing at the end of the vacant pier without remembering walking there. Duie was sitting at my feet and a gull perched on a nearby pylon cocked its eye at me causing my mind to drift far back to a conversation I had with Cisco when we were first bonding. He was explaining the concept of Aztlán, the legendary place of origin of the Aztecs and the Chicano movement el Movimiento a term used by Chicano activists to define the lands Mexico lost to the U.S. in 1848 now known as the Southwest and why the positive contributions Chicanos made since then were hardly ever acknowledged.

As I stood there daydreaming I scanned Venice, Santa Monica, the bluffs, the mountains, Malibu to the northwest and the beach in all directions mirrored in the undulating shimmer of the sea. The whole area seemed like a sun-washed noir landscape flailing in anguish and distress or maybe it was just me. I started for home hoping I wouldn't encounter anyone.

As I headed down Appian Way, Old Mac stepped out from behind a parked motorhome looking spent and weary. Someone inside the vehicle slid a side window closed with a loud thud. The sound pushed Mac out of his grief filled, half-waking day dream with what appeared to be tears welling from the hallows of his grey eyes.

"We all have it, or else we'd be dead." His voice was dry with distraught.

"Hello Mac, good to see you out and about," I replied with a surprisingly shaky voice. "Are you referring to wearing a mask?"

"Oh, James. Ah, no I was thinking about hope," he said while lifting his hand to his face and mopping across it almost slower than I could stomach. "We all must have it to stay alive and to have it we must be social and to be social we have to follow laws. It takes courage to have hope."

"You got that right Mac, but what's got you on this tangent?"

"Do you trust me, James?" He turned his head and threw his words away.

"Why yes, I do Mac. Why do you ask?

"Because we have to trust each other or else we can't make a life for ourselves."

"And so?"

"Everyone seems to not trust anyone any more, not even me and I'm no threat to anyone. How can I live, if no one trusts me?" Clutching his old Macinstosh, tears formed in his blurry eyes again and he looked at me anxiously, as though he expected me to miraculously expound the perfect solution to his imaginary dilemma.

"It's never easy to adjust to a new way of living," I said. "Maybe it's time you get-off the street Mac."

"Yeah, those councilor people tried to get me into one of those free motel rooms over in Culver City."

"Why not try it for a month? You never know, you may feel better about things. It's never easy to adjust to new ways of living, but hey, you've handled bigger changes than this in your life. Right? Find a new rhythm."

He smiled, saluted and faced toward Culver City for a brief moment before walking off in the opposite direction toward the pylons under the vacant Pier. I shook my head and thought about calling out to him, but I felt a nagging need of my own to get home.

When I arrived, I headed into the studio to google Petrus Leihtt and Nathan Zevenaar. Most listings for both of them centered-around their business affiliations and past investments plus both appeared to be single and weren't very visible on social media. All though, Leihtt was obviously richer, much more internationally connected and kept a super yacht in Marseille and a slightly smaller one in Newport Beach.

Marseille is the second-largest metropolitan area in France after Paris. It also has small fishing villages on the outskirts of the city and a rugged coastal area interspersed with small fjord-like inlets which I'm sure would appeal to Leihtt given his main business headquarters were in Norway rather than his Iceland homeland.

Nathan Zevenaar immigrated to L.A. with his parents when he was just a child so most of his business interests are based on the west coast. However, none of the articles mentioned where either man lived and gave only their business addresses.

As I finished reading the last listing, Duie began barking at the sliding glass door. I started walking toward it and could see he was excitedly jumping about because Merra was approaching from her deck. She looked sexier than ever in a stunning black business suite and carrying a pair of flaming red high heels over her shoulder.

As I approached the door, I noticed my reflection in the glass and realized I'd forgotten about having taken off my shirt, pants and shoes when I came home, but it was too late to turn around. We met at the door and I welcomed her in. "Please excuse my lack of decorum."

"That's OK lover, I'm just getting home," she replied and then gave me a kiss.

"I'm surprised any place around here was open. Where were you?"

"Out carousing no doubt," said Nicole from the top of the stairs. "Did you get anywhere with Leihtt? Oh, James, please put your pants on."

"You met him? Where? What's sort of man, is he?" I said as I slipped my jeans on and began setting out some snacks. "Who does he think you are?"

"You walked the tight rope last night, didn't you Merra?" said Nicole. "Did you land on your feet or back?"

"I held on just barely," she replied. "The man is challenging. He lives on a super yacht in Newport Beach marina and he thinks I'm a high-class pole dancer."

"He fell for that one. I'm surprised. Did you put on a show for him?" asked Nicole shaking her head with lines of discontent running down from the sides of her chin.

Merra smiled, "There was no other way, but I held on tight to my dream."

"Did you get anything worth-while in return?"

"I had to take a ride out to the desert first and listen to the "William Tell Overture".

"What are you talking about?" I said as I sat out more food tid-bits.

"There's a road out near Lancaster with strategically spaced rumble strips that make tires sing the notes to the theme from "The Lone Ranger", said Nicole with a sly smile.

"Right, replied Merra. "You have to drive exactly at 55 mph for it to work. And of-course to get it right, we had to drive it about a dozen times."

"It was originally done as some kind of marketing stunt for a car company years ago," replied Nicole as she nibbled on a carrot.

"I see and Leihtt, what about him?

"Well, first-off according to everyone at the Golden Waterfall Club, Iceland has earned the reputation of being one of the hippest destinations in Europe and the epicenter of cutting-edge rave culture," replied Merra. "With Leihtt as its brightest light, no pun intended."

"OK, and what kind of business could he possibly be involved with in Iceland other than fish?" said Nicole.

"Apparently, according to Andre and Interpol, he has some way of laundering Russian mob money through Norway. In fact, it might be that he also smuggles drugs from China, packed in freeze-dried fish, to several ports in Europe."

"But how does any of that have to do with Patterson's company," said Nicole. The only product he buys … ah, bought from China was drones."

"They are used to ferry the drugs from fishing boats to luxury yachts to exclusive roof-top clubs and restaurants," said Merra with a dismayed shrug. "If he owns the company he can have special heavy-duty drones designed and built off-record as well as control and secure all of the necessary infrastructure in the cloud while stealing our national security secrets as well."

"And the clients come to the club and buy fish?" asked Nicole as she set out a plate of cheeses and breads.

"No, they order shus-hi which has been prepared on the yachts in the harbor."

"Wow, that has to be very expensive shus-hi," I said nibbling on a piece of cheese. "And of course, in a big city like L.A. there are hundreds of shus-hi bars as well. You actually met Leihtt, looked him in the eye?" I asked. "What kind of man is he?"

"The kind who likes redheads, ram testicles and hard liquor."

"Are you kidding?" asked Nicole as she bit her lower lip. "He didn't make you eat the testicles, did he?"

"It's an old Icelander tradition or superstitions, I'm not sure which. At least you get to wash it down with vodka and the balls are pickled." Her voice was low and hummed like an overloaded electric circuit.

"Where you pickled too?" asked Nicole groping for a fair-minded attitude.

"I was a little looped which helped me give a pretty-convincing pole dance."

"Could you tell if he is a killer?" I said "Is he the one controlling the Ninjas?"

"I do and he does. He almost insisted I bite the balls off one of them." There was an undercurrent in her voice of no-expense account blues.

"How did you get out of that?" asked Nicole in a low purring tone more in keeping with her normal self.

"I swung around the pole and kicked the Ninja guy in the nuts so hard he went overboard." Her wide shouldered coat swung out with the energy of her gait as she flung it onto the couch. "Let's eat. I'm ravenous."

"He must have been madder than hell when they got him back on board. Could he even walk?" said Nicole with a cautious back-glance at me.

"They left him out there. I doubt he made it to shore alive."

"Geez, how did you get off the yacht?"

"I promised to come back and bring a girlfriend," said Merra turning to look deep into Nicole's eyes and then give me a wink.

"No Merra, no. I will not," said Nicole with the most repulsive sneer I've ever seen on her sweet face.

All of us stopped snacking to look at each other. I was relieved to know who our mutual enemy was, but couldn't conceive of Merra and Nicole taking on a super yacht full of thugs.

"What do we do now?" asked Merra. "He's expecting me to be at tonight's rave."

"Nobody is going anywhere. We all stay here and wait for Cisco," I said. "He'll be here tonight."

"I'm still so juiced on adrenaline, I don't know if I can just sit around here until then," replied Merra. "Maybe I should check with the Bureau and see if they have any plans to make a move on the yacht?"

"Is Leihtt doing real raves, you know, laser lights, fog machines, glowsticks and pasties on the girls and all that?" asked Nicole still incensed and talking through her clenched teeth.

"Yes, plus, they have an array of licit and illicit drugs including Ecstasy, Ketamine, LSD, Fentanyl, and the old standbys LSD, angel dust and magic mushrooms. As well as over-the-counter stuff such as menthol inhalants and vaporizing ointments. They even provide baby pacifiers to suck on in order to cope with the drug's jaw-clenching and teeth-grinding side effects."

"Maybe that's the answer, those drugs enhance ravers' sensations and boost their energy so they can dance and cavort all night long," I said. "If we could make sure everyone has free access to as much as they want maybe Leihtt and his cronies would get so wasted it would be easy for your FBI buddies to arrest them."

"No, Leihtt's watchdog Chief of Security, Max Traxl, never touches any of that stuff and he's a mean son-of-a-bitch," replied Merra. "I was damn lucky he didn't turn me over to his elite clique of fiends. I think they gang banged the girls who agreed to go below decks."

"How did you get away?"

"Leihtt was busy with some Century City big wigs who came aboard and I slipped onto the shuttle boat when it left to return to the marina."

"So you've now got another international gangster goon after your ass," hissed Nicole. "I think it's time you change your hair color again."

We all walked away from the food and went outside in hopes of a spectacular sunset. The beach was completely deserted. Not a single person in sight, not even on the pier. "I'm not convinced," I blurted without thought. "I mean how do we really know Leihtt is responsible for any of the attacks on us? What proof do we have?"

"We don't have anything specifically related to us," said Merra pressing my arm with her strong fingers. "All the Bureau has is a long list of suspicions and the way he keeps a dozen or so Ninja types around him all the time doesn't prove he orders them to do anything either."

"Did you see any of them without their helmet or a mask?"

"Yes and the ones that brought the girls onboard were especially hyper. Why?"

"Were they Asian or European?"

"They were European, but I couldn't tell from where exactly? I didn't see anyone who appeared Asian."

"Look," yelped Nicole as she pointed toward a sail boat just beyond the breakers. "That's a nice way to distance yourself from COVID." She waved, but no one returned the gesture. We watched until the boat was out of sight. "Did Leihtt and the VIP's wear masks?" she asked quietly.

"No, they are too macho and none of the party girls or crew did either. Most of the men refer to themselves as Icelandic folk heroes or Victory Vikings. They've even got identical VV tattoos on the right side of their neck."

"Of course they do," I said. "Do they take the VIP's back to the Marina on a regular schedule?"

"No, it's just whenever there's more than one who wants to leave. Plus, Leihtt restricts the upper decks to his VIP friends so the VV's don't mix with them or have access to the high- class escorts either."

"So how did you get invited on board?"

"The Bureau told me which nightclub the Ninja guys usually pick-up party girls from and I convinced one of the club managers to let me do a pole dance when they started arriving," said Merra smiling. "I guess they liked my moves, plus one of them is actually an undercover Bureau man."

The late afternoon sun glaring off the water made it sparkle as an occasional lone biker, skater or jogger would venture by. Each wore a mask and waved or nodded as they passed. At sunset Hurley came from the direction of the volley ball area. He wore something that looked like a wave crashing on his face and included speedo swimming goggles and a snorkel mask with a fancy looking air filter on top.

"Good-da. How's it hangin' Jammin James? Ladies? You all are looking fit and healthy."

"Were there enough for a game?" asked Merra.

"No, I went to the Marina, but no one there wanted to risk bumping up against someone with the scourge. I'm going out on my board and wait for the evening tide," he said as he passed with a rather inquisitive look. "Hey, did you hear about the shoot-out down at Newport?"

"What, a shooting?" yelped Merra. "Who was shooting who?"

"Some bad dudes on a super yacht and the FBI that's all I know. Take care."

Hurley put his goggle get-up back on and walked on. Merra darted into the house straight to the TV. Nicole didn't move.

"Are you feeling all right," I asked.

She pushed herself upright while a slow thought labored across her eyes and a slack, vacant smile took hold of her face. "Maybe, between bullets and COVID they'll all kill each other. Maybe we'll all die." Her voice was armored with a cautious grumble. She clasped her upper arms and hugged herself tight as she rose abruptly and walked inside. I followed her.

"Can I join you?" It was Cisco. I welcomed him with a manly handshake. Merra turned off the TV and quickly walked toward us. "Hello Cisco. I'm Merra, I'm happy to finally meet you. All though I wish it were under better circumstances."

"I assume you know more than what's on the TV about the shooting in Newport," I said. "Did any of it involve Leihtt and his gang of elusive Ninja nemeses?"

"Amigo, my friend, you and your two lovelies are truly blessed … bendecido… muy afortunado. While neither I or any of the FBI team know all details about the fight, the bottom line is everyone on the yacht was either shot, has the virus or both."

"Wow, Nicole you called it."

Nicole managed a slight smile as she cleared tears from her eyes and cheeks. Merra moved over next to her and put her arm around her shoulders.

"Apparently, one of the Ninja's went berserk about having been thrown over-board and swim back to the marina causing him to miss most of the party so he drank an entire bottle of vodka which fried his brain causing him to start shooting everyone and they all joined in," Cisco said disdainfully. "And before you ask, yes Leihtt was wounded, but perhaps more ominous he has a very bad case of this China virus. He's in intensive care and not expected to recover."

"You are a bearer of good news. So, we may have a respite for a while. Wonderful," I said as I reached for a wine bottle. "How about drinks all around?"

"There's just one thing that's not clear. The party girls told the Bureau the whole thing started because the pole dancer kicked one of Ninja's in the nuts and he fell overboard, but no one knows what happened to her. She seems to have vanished. The Ninja swam back to yacht got drunk and started shooting everyone."

"Cisco, you and I should talk. Let's go for a sunset walk," said Merra as she wrapped her arm around his. "So, tell me about yourself. I've heard so many good things about you. Are you married?" He suddenly looked stunned as though he was experiencing severe dry-mouth and had to force himself to swallow as she walked him off the deck toward the surf. I didn't want them to leave. Nicole took my hand and we sat still on the couch and watched the two of them walk arm-in-arm toward the water's edge. Their voices grew faint in the fading twilight, their shadows stretched across the sand and the seagulls rose off the dark water as nightfall enveloped us all. It was hard to envision a new day, a new time, maybe even a new era, but we all knew it was coming.

EPILOGUE

"Don't tell Cisco about my pole dancing. Isn't that what you said," asked Nicole. "I'll bet there was a lot more you didn't tell him about. Wasn't there?"

"Yes, but there was one question he asked, ah, it needles me every time I close my eyes. I can't let go of it."

"Well you know what they say … just spit it out," I suggested. "You are among friends and we don't bite, ugh unless it's called for or ah desired."

My two ladies smiled knowingly and gave me their woman stare, which I took as a signal I should get back on track. "So, tell us, we're here for you."

With a deep-rooted intake of salty sea air Merra smiled and said "Cisco suggested I should go legit. Not as an FBI agent, but as an independent. You know with an office and a framed license on the wall. He even believes it would pay better than the Feds. What do you think?"

Nicole and I were struck silent.

"DDA, Dawne Detective Agency, has a nice ring to it."

"More like destressed damsel again," scoffed Nicole. "Or daring damsel or …"

ABOUT THE AUTHOR

U.S. National Endowment for the Arts Fellowship recipient M. Lee Musgrave has had his art exhibited in numerous solo and group exhibitions, lived most of his life in Los Angeles, was born in Australia. As a former professor of art and curator, he organized hundreds of exhibitions at museums and galleries involving artists, collectors, critics, gallerists and an array of related enthusiasts. His writings related to those exhibitions contributed to their success and to his ability to relate that community to others. Those many experiences and his ongoing art activities inform his creative writing about the exciting contemporary art community. He is the author of novels *Brushed Off, The Beautiful One* and many short stories including *Quitessence*.

NOTE FROM THE AUTHOR

Word-of-mouth is crucial for any author to succeed. If you enjoyed *Off Kilter*, please leave a review online—anywhere you are able. Even if it's just a sentence or two. It would make all the difference and would be very much appreciated.

Thanks!
M. Lee Musgrave

We hope you enjoyed reading this title from:

www.blackrosewriting.com

Subscribe to our mailing list – *The Rosevine* – and receive **FREE** books, daily deals, and stay current with news about upcoming releases and our hottest authors.
Scan the QR code below to sign up.

Already a subscriber? Please accept a sincere thank you for being a fan of Black Rose Writing authors.

View other Black Rose Writing titles at
www.blackrosewriting.com/books and use promo code
PRINT to receive a **20% discount** when purchasing.

www.ingramcontent.com/pod-product-compliance
Lightning Source LLC
Chambersburg PA
CBHW050157120726
47903CB00002B/655